I FAIL at the AFTERLIFE

THE AFTERLIFE TRILOGY

BOOK 1

ANNI SEZATE

Chicken Taco Publishing
Phoenix, AZ

ISBN: 979-8-9870656-0-0

Library of Congress Control Number: 2022912774

Any references to historical events, real people, or real places are used fictitiously. Names, characters, and places are products of the author's imagination.

Printed in the United States of America.

First printing edition 2023.

Chicken Taco Publishing

www.annisezate.com

Publisher's Cataloging-in-Publication Data

Names: Sezate, Anni, author.

Title: I fail at the afterlife / Anni Sezate.

Description: Phoenix, AZ : Chicken Taco Publishing, [2022] | Series: The afterlife trilogy ; book 1. | Audience: Young adult.

Identifiers: ISBN: 979-8-9870656-2-4 (hardback) | 979-8-9870656-0-0 (paperback) | 979-8-9870656-1-7 (e-book) | 978-0-9995379-9-2 (audiobook) | LCCN: 2022912774

Subjects: LCSH: Dead--Fiction. | Future life--Fiction. | Young adults--Psychological aspects. | Demonology--Fiction. | Good and evil--Fiction. | Teenage superheroes--Fiction. | Young adult fiction. | LCGFT: Paranormal fiction. | Bildungsromans. | Young adult fiction. | BISAC: YOUNG ADULT FICTION / Paranormal, Occult & Supernatural. | YOUNG ADULT FICTION / Diversity & Multicultural. | YOUNG ADULT FICTION / Religious / General.

Classification: LCC: PS3619.E998 I14 2022 | DDC: 813/.6--dc23

*To all the twenty-somethings
going through their quarter-life crisis.*

Also by Anni Sezate

THE AURELLA TRILOGY

Aurella the Witch

Aurella the Sorceress

Aurella the Demon

THE AFTERLIFE TRILOGY

I Fail at the Afterlife

Greetings from Rock Bottom

Untitled Book 3

chapter 1
THE SNEEZE

If I had known I was going to die at age seventeen, I wouldn't have been so obsessed with my ACT scores. Then again, if I hadn't been so obsessed with my ACT scores, I probably wouldn't have died.

Yes, you read that right. I'm very dead.

Go ahead. Fill yourself with sympathy for my untimely death. You should feel sympathy. Not because I'm dead, but because of how it happened. I wish I could say I died a hero, jumping in front of a bullet to save a beloved public figure. Or a skydiving accident. Or even something normal like a disease. But no. In true David fashion, my death was embarrassingly lame and totally avoidable.

It all started with a sneeze . . .

"David! Lunch break's over, *mijo*. Come down from that platform."

"Just a sec, *tio*."

I barely glanced down at Uncle Richard. I worked two jobs back in high school to save up for college and one of them was working construction with my uncle. Not a super glamorous job, but if my second attempt at the ACT wasn't higher than my previous score, I was out of my scholarship, which meant no money for college. Dad paying for me was out of the question, since my big brother was nearing the end of his undergraduate at an ivy league that we really struggled to afford. I didn't resent him for it, but it was very *Sam* of him to take up all my college money.

"Come on, Baby Blues!" Uncle Richard called again. That's what he liked to call me because he thought it was *so* funny that his half-Mexican nephew had blue eyes.

I shook my head and blew the sawdust off my ACT prep book. That was a dumb move because the cloud of sawdust blew back into my face and I sneezed. My black, thick-rimmed glasses flew off my face and tumbled to the ground twenty feet below, shattering on impact.

"*Híjole*," I muttered with a wince. Mom was gonna kill me.

I decided that was my cue to climb down from the metal platform my feet were dangling from. I'd found that the scaffolding platforms were ideal for studying because the higher up you are, the farther you are from the noise of hammers and saws and the radio blaring. I shook the sawdust from my hair and stood up, leaning against the guardrail. It creaked ominously. With a nervous grimace, I lifted my hands and shuffled back.

Unfortunately, I wasn't done sneezing yet, and as my body lurched forward with another one, I slipped on a nail left lying around and my feet rolled out from under me. I quickly grabbed hold of the creaky guardrail as my body slid through the gap between the bar and the platform. My legs scissored back and forth as I dangled twenty feet from the ground. I was momentarily grateful I wasn't wearing my glasses and couldn't see the details of whatever construction equipment lay below me on the ground.

"Holy crap . . ." I started hyperventilating as I dangled back and forth. My heart felt like it was going to hammer out of my chest. I tried to pull my legs up high enough to climb back onto the platform, but it was too high and I cursed my lack of flexibility.

"Help!" My voice barely squeaked out.

"DAVID!" Uncle Richard spotted me and sprinted to the bottom of the platform. "*No te muevas! Ya voy, David!*"

Of course my body chose that opportune moment to sneeze again. I managed to cling to the rail I was hanging from, but I guess the Big Man really wanted me to fall to my death, because then the rusty bolts holding the guardrail to the scaffolding snapped on one side. With a creak, the guardrail swung from horizontal to vertical in less than a second. The jolt loosened my sweaty hands from their death grip and slipped off the end. I was airborne long enough for a three second scream and my body joined my shattered glasses on the ground.

I remember the *crunch* sound the most.

Did it hurt? Um, yeah. A lot.

But only for a minute. Before I knew what was happening I was floating over my body in a panic and Nana Maria was squeezing the life out of me. She had died about a year prior. After calming me down, she guided me to The Resting Place all the while lamenting about how skinny I was and how I should have eaten more tamales. My dad's mom, Grandma Gertie, was there too and the first thing she said to me was, "I know just the girl for you! She's really cute, and she died just last week, isn't that wonderful?"

Yeah, I was dead all but three seconds, and already I was getting crap from my grandmas. I was happy to see them, though. Death is freaky, but it's not so terrible if you know people on the other side.

So that's how I died. But that happened a long time ago and that's really not what this story is about. This story is about how I screwed up my entire afterlife with one stupid mistake.

chapter 2
DIVINE PRANK-FLUENCE

"All right, now tie the rubber band around the sprayer faucet so it holds down the little lever," I whispered.

My five-year-old niece, Ginger, teetered on the stool in front of the kitchen sink as she followed my directions. She couldn't see me, but that didn't mean I couldn't put ideas in her head. Being dead did often have its perks.

"Wrap it around one more time."

"What are you doing?"

Ginny and I froze, then looked around slowly. My sister, Elena, had my three-year-old nephew on her hip and a dirty pull-up in her hand.

"Quick, tell her to turn on the sink."

Ginny hopped off the stool and smiled innocently. "I was trying to wash my hands, but the sink won't turn on."

I whistled at her quick lie. Elena frowned and set down the toddler and the pull-up. She looked closely at the faucet as she turned the handle. The results were dramatic and instantaneous. Water sprayed in all directions, drenching her face and shirt. Screaming, she tried to find the faucet through her own personal waterfall. Her children and I snickered.

When she finally shut off the waterfall, Elena spun around, trying to hide amusement behind annoyance as water dripped down her chin. "Your uncle David used to do that. It was annoying then and it's annoying now."

I took an elaborate bow.

DAVID, WHAT ARE YOU DOING?

I bit my lip. Caught by Hermes. He's the head angel, and he's like telepathic Santa Claus. He always knows where we are and what we're up to. Hermes isn't his real name, by the way, that's just what everyone calls him.

ARE YOU UTILIZING YOUR DIVINE INFLUENCE AS A GUARDIAN ANGEL TO TEACH YOUR NIECE AND NEPHEW HOW TO PULL A PRANK?

Maybe . . .

DO YOU REMEMBER THE CONTRACT YOU SIGNED WHEN YOU APPLIED TO BE A GUARDIAN ANGEL TO YOUR FAMILY? YOU PROMISED TO USE YOUR GIFTS TO INSPIRE, PROTECT, AND DEFEND.

I know, but they liked it. Look, they're laughing.

WE'LL DISCUSS THIS LATER. YOU'RE NEEDED BACK AT HEADQUARTERS. YOU'RE ON FRONT DESK DUTY.

All right, beam me up, Scotty.

I could almost feel him rolling his eyes.

Fine, I'm on my way.

I apparated over to The Resting Place. You may be more familiar with the word "teleport" but I like "apparate." Because Harry Potter.

The Resting Place is where angels hang out. It's not up in the clouds like mortals tend to think. Condensed water doesn't make for a very solid foundation. Also, it would be really annoying to be interrupted by planes blowing through us in the middle of our meetings. The Resting Place is actually on Earth, but the location is a secret, so no, I won't tell you where it is.

I could tell when I passed the borders because the sounds of traffic and nature muffled until I couldn't hear them at all. Other than a few trees, benches, and fountains, the main feature of The Resting Place is headquarters. That's where angels work when we're not going around helping people. It's basically a fancy office, with a huge open lobby and a bunch of conference rooms down the hallways.

I floated through the glass doors of headquarters under the famous crystal chandelier. I stopped to file a report at the front desk before joining my Nana Maria behind it. Guardian angel reports are where we write down all the stuff we see our assigned mortals do — good and bad. Mind you, we also have to report everything we do, so I often tattle on myself.

Nana Maria passed me a blank report and I grabbed a pen.

Let's see . . .

GUARDIAN ANGEL REPORT

Name of Guardian Angel: *David Garcia*

Family Members Visited/Relation to Angel: *Maria Elena Davis (sister), Ginger Davis (niece), Rocco Davis (nephew)*

What did you observe during your visit? *Ginger and Rocco played dino barbies with each other while their mom was on the phone with a friend from work who is going through a difficult divorce. Ginger and Rocco got into a fight, because Rocco's dinosaur "ate" the princess barbie who was supposed to get married to the stegosaurus.*

Elena walked in and took Rocco out to change his pull-up. Ginger decided to pull a prank on their mother by tying a rubber band around a faucet sprayer so that it would spray Elena the next time she used the sink.

What did you do during your visit? *I may have put her up to the prank . . .*

Reasoning for your actions: *It was funny and they liked it.*

Signature: *David Garcia*

I passed my report to Nana who glanced at it and gave me a shrewd look.

"That's confidential," I said.

She tutted and shook her head as she filed it away. "Come help me with these papers, *mijo*. You can tell me all about what trouble my great-grandbabies have gotten into this time."

I pasted on a fake smile, trying to hide my inward sigh. Paperwork was boring and I was getting tired of it. All I ever did anymore was visit my family and file reports. Some angels got messenger jobs. Some were warriors against evil demons. My job? File papers. Oh what joy and excitement it brought to my afterlife.

I should have been content with the boredom considering what was about to happen right there in the lobby.

chapter 3
ENTER THE BAD GUY

Grandma Gertrude took Nana Maria's place after an hour. She typically signs up to work the front desk when I'm doing it. She calls it family time. I don't always like "family time," because all Grandma does is call me out on how blaringly single I am and always have been and probably will be until I die.

Wait . . .

"David, you're such a nice young man. Why haven't you settled down yet?"

I sighed. "Because I'm dead?"

"That does not mean you can't still find yourself a companion. There are plenty of young girls here to choose from. Not as many as there were back when girls were always dying in childbirth, but age doesn't really matter here does it?"

I shrugged and continued filing, ignoring the fact that my grandmother was talking about young girls dying like it was a good thing. "Believe it or not, I don't think anyone's interested, and I'm fine with that." I supposed I hadn't put forth much of an effort; it just didn't seem all that important. Also, I had a crippling fear of rejection, so dating sounded like a literal nightmare.

"You have to make eyes with the girls."

I snorted and turned around. "What does that even mean?"

"You stare at them with your beautiful blue eyes." She grinned and fluttered her lashes.

I laughed. "Grandma, you look like you're having a seizure."

She froze and her jaw dropped, her eyes widening in fear. A chilling scream flew from her mouth.

"What the—"

A darkness fell over the room, so quickly and so solidly that it went from day to night in an instant. My not-real blood ran cold and I found myself cowering behind the counter. I couldn't see a thing. A deep laugh echoed around the room so you couldn't pinpoint where it was coming from. I could feel a presence drawing nearer. I squeezed my eyes shut and held my breath.

"I was in a hurry," the Darkness whispered in a breathy croak. "But your fear is *so* delicious."

Something slithered toward me like a snake, then the sound of boots, then the click of claws against the tile. Either there were multiple creatures in the building, or this thing was shapeshifting. A wet snout sniffed my hair. "No abnormal trauma in your past. That's disappointing. It's the scarred ones that have the most delicious fear. We'll just have to create our own little traumatic experience…"

Soft, creeping hands encircled my throat, and instead of struggling, I froze. I couldn't move. Couldn't breathe. The Darkness clawed itself inside me, incapacitating me with fear and hopelessness and the worst memories of my existence. It was like a dementor. I kept seeing my mom screaming as she approached my dead, broken body. That feeling of being yanked away. That pure confusion as people I knew to be dead were suddenly smiling and hugging me while my family mourned me below. Attending my funeral where people kept crying over the things I would never get to do because I died young: grow up, get married, have a family. How I would never make something of myself because I died before I had the chance. My life had been utterly useless and my death was completely avoidable. I ruined my family with my own stupidity. Of course I deserved to die.

Then the memories morphed into things so horrible, I'd never even considered fearing them. Things I knew would *never* happen, but seemed so real in the moment. A man broke into Elena's house, shrouded in Darkness— definitely possessed. He took out a gun and shot Ginny and Rocco, then beat Elena and took advantage of her. Sam became so depressed he jumped off a building. Mom and Dad became so inconsolable at the loss of their children they lost the will to live. They deteriorated until there was nothing left of them but two wrinkled bodies staring out into nothing, unable to recognize anyone or anything. And it was all my fault! I wasn't there to save them!

I'm not sure how long I was trapped in the loop of sorrows and fears, things I'd actually experienced mixed with nightmares so dark I'd never known to be afraid of. I couldn't move. I couldn't see. I couldn't hear anything but those torturous thoughts tearing me apart from the inside.

The most terrifying thing about it was that as an angel, you don't usually feel negative emotions. We're too busy helping people to think about ourselves. I hadn't allowed myself to feel a truly negative emotion since I'd died, and the sudden blast of horror was all the more terrifying because of it.

Light flickered to my left. Grandma Gertie was trying to scare it off, but the *thing* swallowed up her Light, leaving us in darkness once again.

I couldn't help but think that we were going to die there.

Then I remembered we were already dead.

"DON'T MOVE!"

The voice echoed with a power that shook me to my core and a blinding light pierced the darkness. Hermes in all his glory slashed a golden whip of Light through the air. Before it could wind itself around the demon, he disappeared.

He'd gotten away, and I had done nothing to stop him.

I'm pretty sure I would have fainted if I were capable of it. I fell back against the counter and Grandma Gertie squeezed my guts out.

"What was *that?*" I asked in a shaky voice.

Pretty soon the room swarmed with angels flying this way and that, like a beehive a dumb kid threw a rock at.

"David?" Hermes said from behind me.

Grandma and I turned around and he put his hands on my shoulders. "Are you all right?"

I shrugged and nodded, too shaken to really say anything.

"It's going to be all right," he said. "I promise."

For a minute, I believed him. I felt total confidence and was completely reassured that everything would work out. I even smiled, which felt weird because my dead heart was still racing. Hermes can do that to ya. I'm not sure how he does it, but it's like he carries around a bag of warm fuzzies and just tosses them out like candy to whoever needs them. He left to go calm down the other angels who were freaking out. They were way more worked up than me and Grandma, which annoyed me, because they weren't even in the room when that *thing* came by. I was the one it attacked. I was the one that just let it go.

It had to have been a demon, but it was like no demon I'd ever met. Normal demons are pretty easy to get rid of, actually. You just throw some Light at them and they scatter. This was a demon of a completely different caliber. Also, how did it get in? Demons can't get into The Resting Place. You have to be "worthy" in order to find it.

It took about an hour for Hermes to round everyone up to the empty stadium he found. The Resting Place doesn't really have space big enough for all of the angels to gather at once, so we often use sports stadiums. Angels use mortals' space all the time. While you're sleeping, there could be some angels having a meeting around your coffee table. Or sitting in on your classes at school. Or even chilling behind your couch while you're watching *Stranger Things*. I have definitely never done that.

The annoying thing about this stadium was it had the kind of seats that folded up, so you had to sit on them to keep them down. Angels don't really have weight though. If we focus, we can move stuff mentally, but in the state we were in, none of us could really focus. Seats kept popping up with angels still in them and I had to hide a laugh with a cough. Eventually everyone just chose to stand. In this case, acting like mortals wasn't worth the trouble.

My moment of humor didn't last long. I could not shake from the feeling of being in that demon's clutches. That feeling of hopelessness and uselessness. What *was* that? How did he get into headquarters? I'd never felt that frightened in my life, not even when I died, because that was an accident and no one was trying to hurt me. This was pure evil. He literally had his hands around my throat! Not that it really hurt; I mean, I don't technically need to breathe, but as far as putting your hands on someone, that's one of the more threatening moves. It tends to imply that, you know, you want to kill them. As a dead guy, I wasn't exactly sure what that meant for me.

And what had I done when he'd attacked? Nothing. Absolutely nothing. I just cowered and froze, unlike my grandma who at least tried something.

"I understand you are frightened," Hermes said from the center of the stadium. Hermes tends to speak in a calm, quiet voice, but he projected it loudly for all of us to hear. "I also understand that you have many questions. I will answer to the best of my ability."

He started telling us about how that thing was a very old and powerful demon they called Malum. According to Hermes, Malum was so bad, the Big Man ordered the angels to keep him under constant guard, because he was tempting people above what they were able to resist and hurting people beyond what they could endure. The last time he was captured, it took fifty angels working together. Hermes didn't elaborate on how they did it, but it sounded like it took immense effort.

"That is why we are creating a new demon hunting task force," he said. "These individuals will help capture The Son of Evil and put him back in his prison. If you are interested, you may pick up an application at the front desk. If you choose not to apply, I ask that you leave this stadium and put this matter from your mind. Continue to fulfill your duties and all will be well. You may now return to your regularly scheduled activities."

Everyone began speaking at once, creating that annoying white noise of a frazzled crowd. Order dissolved into chaos as angels flew from person to person, speculating and worrying before flying off to the next friend. They looked like bees pollinating flowers.

"Hey, you were on front desk duty weren't you?" a random dude asked me. "Did you see him? What was he like? What did you do?"

A crowd began to form as people started shooting questions at me faster than I could respond. I was overwhelmed and confused and embarrassed because the answer to "What did you do?" was nothing. Absolutely nothing. I froze and curled up like a rollie pollie and left my *grandma* to attack the evil demon by herself.

"Hey look, it's . . . a thing!" I said, pointing toward the stage.

Yeah, I couldn't come up with something specific on

the spot, but it still worked. Anytime someone shouts "hey look" people do it.

Once everyone's back was turned I disappeared.

chapter 4
NO SOY LUCHADOR

I wandered around The Resting Place lost in my thoughts. Eventually I sat on a bench and stared at my feet while all the worries in my head swirled around and around until I felt like I couldn't breathe.

I came to a decision just as someone sat next to me, startling me so much I floated up off the bench and yelled, "*Híjole!*"

"Hey mate, I heard what happened. You okay?"

It was Jake, my best friend. We have an interesting connection: We died on the same day at the same age. Except his death was a tad more dignified. He was killed in a rugby incident, whereas I was killed by a sneeze.

Jake's one of the best people I know. Sort of a jock, but an *aware* jock, if that makes sense. I could never see him picking on someone or even allowing that to happen. He was the cool kid that took a girl with Down's Syndrome to the school dance, or stuck up for the nerd whose head was about to get flushed down a toilet.

He died during a huge high school rugby tournament. (Or, do they call it "secondary school" in Australia?) He never told me the details of it—I mean, no one really likes talking about how they died—but it was some kind of head injury. And it wasn't a quick death like mine was. I think he was suffering for a while, poor guy.

"I'm fine," I said, floating back down to the bench.

"You sure?" Jake asked, raising an eyebrow. "You look real devo."

I shrugged, trying to pretend I understood his "Straya" slang. "I'm more embarrassed than anything else. I just stood there."

"How could you have done anything? The maniac had his hands around your throat."

I looked at him sideways. "You would have done something. I doubt you would have frozen."

Jake shrugged, neither confirming nor denying what I'd said. Whether or not he would have stood a chance against Malum, we both knew he would have at least tried to defend himself. You see, while I have the stimulating job of front desk worker, Jake is what we call a defender. All angels are trained in scaring off demons in order to protect our families, but defenders are on a completely different level. They're like our army. They're the ones you call when a demon situation gets out of hand.

"I think I'm going to apply as a demon hunter," I

blurted before I could lose my nerve.

Jake snorted. Then he looked at my completely serious face and started laughing. "Oh, you're serious?"

I gave him a dry smile. "Thanks for the vote of confidence."

He gave me a condescending smile and put a hand on my shoulder. "David, you're many things, but you're not a demon hunter."

"I could be," I said. "If I was trained. If someone trusted me with a job that involved something slightly more dangerous than a paper cut."

"Look, you don't need to feel bad about what happened. There's nothing you could've done." He was talking to me like a little boy who was crying over a toy soldier that just got flushed down the toilet. (That may have happened to me once when I was five. It was traumatic, okay? Bartholomew was my best soldier!)

I sighed. "I bet you're applying."

"Defo."

"Definitely? Do you have to shorten every word over two syllables?"

"Yeah."

I didn't say anything so he just patted my back, running out of condoling statements.

I decided to ask a second opinion, because Jake didn't know everything.

I should go to someone older with more experience.

I followed Nana Maria when she went to visit Tata Ramon, her husband. Tata was eating an omelet with beans and a tortilla at his kitchen table while reading the newspaper. The sun was just barely coming up, sending twinkling rays of light through the curtains. A couple of birds twittered through a crack in the window. It was pretty peaceful, actually.

"Something on your mind, *mijo*?" Nana asked me as she watched Tata eat his breakfast.

"I think I might apply to be a demon hunter."

Nana gave me that same condescending smile that Jake had.

"*Mijo*, leave that to the defenders. They're trained to fight those *demonios*."

"But I can help. I want to help."

She shook her head as she floated around the kitchen. She leaned down toward Tata. "What do you think, Ramon? Your *nieto* wants to fight demons."

Tata didn't answer her, obviously, but she turned back to me and smiled. "He says, '*Ay caramba! David no es luchador!*'"

I raised an eyebrow. "Very funny."

I apparated back to The Resting Place, admittedly moping about how badly that had gone. Why couldn't anyone just tell me what I wanted to hear?

"You're amazing, David! Of course you should sign up for the

demon hunters. You'll probably save the entire world. Also, you're super handsome. I know a ton of girls that are literally dying to go out with you."

I shook my head and decided it didn't matter what other people said. I knew what I had to do. I snatched that application off the counter and began filling it out. I had so little experience, I included things from when I was alive to try and beef it up a bit.

Name: *David Garcia*

Years spent in The Resting Place: *10*

Work Experience:

Front desk duty at headquarters (10 years)

Construction (1 year)

Camp counselor (1 summer)

Hot dog on a stick (1 summer)

Demon Combat Experience:

Casting out demons tempting family members (10 years worth of demons)

Fighting Malum, the son of evil, single-handedly

Awards and Achievements:

Filing two hundred reports in one day (current record)

Would have been top 10% in my graduating class

Ultimate frisbee champ

Additional Qualifications:

I once met the llama from Napoleon Dynamite.

Okay, that last one wasn't true, but I didn't have a lot of strengths, so I was hoping humor would soften them up. This was probably the worst application anyone had ever filled out, but it was all I had. My main hope was that they would be so desperate for people to join the task force they'd be forced to take people like me who were completely unqualified.

I felt someone next to me and looked over to see Jake raising his eyebrows at the application in my hands. I thought he'd make another condescending comment, but he just smiled and held up his application.

"You want me to turn yours in too?"

I handed it to him. "Yeah. Thanks."

He gave me this look that seemed to say, I think you're crazy, but I've got your back, mate.

I appreciated that more than I cared to admit.

chapter 5
STAY AWAY FROM MY MOTHER

I decided to go visit my mom while I waited for the demon hunter people to review my application. I apparated to the front office of my old high school and found my mom answering non-stop phone calls and dealing with confused parents of high school kids. It was the first day of school, so naturally the front office ladies were getting yelled at because it was their fault certain students didn't get signed up for the right classes and didn't know where to go. I didn't know how Mom had the patience for her job.

As I was trying to figure out what I could do to make her day less hectic, a couple of visitors floated in the door, holding hands and crying.

"Oh, no. Out," I said, pointing back where they came from. "The office doesn't have time to deal with your shenanigans."

Do I sound enough like a crotchety old man?

The two tortured spirits gave me their best puppy dog faces, but I knew their tricks. See, not all dead people are angels. Some become demons, if they're super bad, but others are just aimless wanderers. They refuse to move on, so they just float around moaning about their tragic death and haunting mortals in their spare time.

The two that just entered the front office were notorious for haunting the school. Thirty years ago they died in a car crash on their way to class, so now they thought they owned the place. They were a pain in my butt. I had tried to help them and show them how to get to The Resting Place, but they refused to listen. Dang teenagers.

I wasn't a teenager anymore, was I? I could never figure out how old I was. Was I supposed to keep counting after death? Was I seventeen forever, or was I twenty-seven? I felt somewhere in between.

I groaned as I saw them scheming about what crap they could pull. "Yo, Moaning Myrtle. Go away. You too, Malcolm Crowe."

They didn't like my nicknames.

Malcolm got ready to blow all the papers off my mom's desk while Myrtle giggled behind his back.

I got ready to blast them with Light. I closed my eyes and thought of where Light comes from, then my hands started to glow and shake. Once I was holding as much Light as I could stand, I shot it out of the palms of my hands.

The creepy dead teens cringed away. It wasn't quite as powerful on them because they weren't demons, but they still didn't like it. Eventually they both blew me raspberries like mature adults and flew through the ceiling.

None of the billions of people in the office had any idea there was a dead person battle going on. Which was fine. I mean, I didn't need recognition for what I had done, but some acknowledgement would have been nice once in a while.

Mom looked really tired and she hadn't had a break yet, so I traveled to the guidance counselor's office and whispered in her ear.

"Hey, you should do that really nice thing where you take over for one of the receptionists so she can eat her lunch in peace."

Betty looked through her office window and saw Mom and Yvonne swamped with phone calls and parents. Like the nice old lady she was, she did exactly as I suggested. I love it when people listen to me.

She recruited the other guidance counselor to come with her so both the front office ladies could chill in the back for a minute. I followed them, partially to provide help if necessary, but also because eavesdropping is fun.

"Welcome to day one," Yvonne said as she unwrapped her sandwich.

"It'll calm down in a week or so," Mom said. "It always does." As she opened a text on her phone, she lifted her glasses dangling from her old lady chain to read it. "Oops, wrong ones."

I shook my head. My mom wore necklace chains for two pairs of glasses. One pair was her actual reading glasses. The other pair was my old glasses that she'd had repaired after I died. She wore them all the time. It was kind of weird, but I guess it made her feel like I was close by or something.

"I'm worried about my sister's girl," Mom said as she pulled her chorizo burro from the microwave. "It's her first day of high school and she is so anxious about it. She's been begging Rosa to let her stay at her old school, but Rosa wants her to learn how to stick it out. You know that whole push for inclusion and such. It was quite the debate between her and her husband, Daniel. I wish Daniella had some kind of buddy to watch out for her. She's just so fragile right now."

I smiled and shook my head. Sometimes I wondered if my mom knew I was there. She had the same tone she used to use back when she was trying to subtly hint for me to do my chores. "*I wish someone would do the dishes . . .*"

"All right, I can take a hint."

I knew she couldn't hear me, and she didn't really know I was there, but it felt good to pretend. Because as much as I loved my job, it really sucked sometimes that no one could see me.

chapter 6
WHO, ME?

After floating around for a while, I found Daniella's class. Freshman World History. She was sitting in the very back of the room, her head resting in her hand as though trying to appear as small as possible. I knew why she was embarrassed, but she didn't need to be.

The teacher cleared her throat. "All right, settle down. Everyone get to your seats and put your phones away. Now, please!"

Daniella's ASL interpreter went to the front of the room and began translating everything the teacher said into sign language.

When I got a good look at the teacher, I froze. Tight black curls, brown eyes, and dark skin that somehow maintained a subtle spattering of freckles across her nose and cheeks. I knew her. Her name was Sandra Johnson, my old lab partner from chemistry. It took my mind a minute to readjust to the fact that people my age were old enough to have real jobs, while I still felt like I belonged in high school. I'd have continued reminiscing on times gone by, but Daniella was noticing the looks people were giving her as they realized the interpreter was there for her. She kept sinking lower and lower into her chair.

I patted her back and said, *"It's gonna be fine, Dani. I'm here. I got your back. Not because I'm patting your back. I meant that figuratively."*

"Excuse me, young man? Yes, I'm talking to you. Find a seat, please."

For a minute I swore Sandra was looking at me. I looked behind me, but there was nothing but wall there. When I turned back to Sandra, she had this weary look on her face like someone just told her she'd have a meeting during her lunch break. Weird.

She began lecturing the students on her expectations of respect and responsibility. Her lecture lasted the entire class period and it was so boring that I wished I had the ability to fall asleep.

When the bell rang to leave, Daniella threw her notebook and pencil in her bag as quickly as possible and booked it to the door, forcing her interpreter to race after her.

"You did great, Dani!" I yelled after her. "One class down, five billion more to go."

"David."

I froze. Then I realized there were probably like fifty

Davids in this school and there was no way someone could be talking to me.

"I'm talking to you, David Garcia."

What the freak?

I slowly turned around and Sandra was looking directly at me. I almost had a heart attack, which is quite difficult when your heart's no longer beating.

"What are you doing here?" she asked.

Then I noticed the phone to her ear. She wasn't talking to me. She was on the phone with some other dude named David Garcia.

I got ready to apparate over to wherever Daniella went, but then Sandra said, "Don't you disappear on me. I hate it when you guys do that. I just want to talk."

Okay, maybe she really is talking to me, I thought. *But what's with the . . . Oh. Smart. She's putting her phone to her ear so it doesn't look like she's talking to herself.*

What was I supposed to do? It was against my contract to reveal myself to mortals, but this one just saw me. Was there a protocol for that? The whole situation was very uncomfortable. Like someone walked in on me naked. I nervously turned back and stopped in front of her. She nodded her head to the classroom and I followed her back in. Once the door was closed she put the phone away and said, "Why are you here?"

Feeling like I was breaking all the rules, I said, "I'm just seeing my cousin off on her first day of high school. She came from an all-deaf school and she's really nervous and embarrassed that an interpreter has to follow her around everywhere. Can you really see me?"

She nodded tiredly as though she's gotten this question before, many times.

"Can you see all of us?"

"All the ones around me."

"How long have you been able to do that?"

"Forever."

I frowned. "You never told me about that."

"You were just my lab partner. We weren't that close."

True. I don't think our conversations ever got past what we ate for lunch, which, believe it or not, was a more interesting topic than you'd think, because I'm not sure any of the cafeteria food was actually edible.

After an awkward pause she said, "Hey, I'm sorry about your death. I know it was really hard on your family."

"Oh, um, it's fine. It's not a big deal. How long have you been teaching?" I asked to change the subject.

"It's my fifth year. I thought you were one of my students at first."

"Do I still look like a teenager?"

She studied me. "Kind of. It's hard to say."

Jake chose that moment to come barreling through the ceiling and slap me on the back. "D-man! The demon hunters need you back at HQ."

I grimaced. You could always count on Jake to just come barreling in unannounced.

He looked back and forth between me and Sandra. "She's fair dinkum looking at you, mate. Did you reveal yourself to her? You know that's not allowed, right?"

"I didn't reveal myself. She just sort of saw me. She can see you too."

Sandra waved at him and his jaw dropped. "I've never met a medium before! We could use someone like you. If we tell Hermes—"

Sandra held her hands up. "I'm not looking to get involved. I have enough of you wandering spirits begging me to intervene in some way."

Jake jumped onto his high horse. "Hey, we aren't just wandering spirits. We're angels. We have important jobs and missions. Missions to help mortals like you."

"Dude, chill," I said, trying to wrap my mind around the weirdest interaction I'd ever had. "What were you saying about the demon hunters?"

"They're interviewing applicants," he said.

I blinked. "They're actually going to give me an interview?"

He shrugged. "I think they're interviewing everyone. They're pretty desperate for people."

I gave him a dry look.

"I mean, out of all the applicants, they saw something really special in you. I think it was the summer at Hot Dog on a Stick that really tipped the balance."

I shoved his shoulder, trying to hide my smile. "Shut up."

Sandra looked back and forth between us, her mouth pulled tight.

"Yeah, we're being really rude," I said, shoving Jake away. "Sorry, we're not used to mortals being able to hear us. Excuse us, S-Sandra. Maybe I'll see you around."

I took Jake's arm and performed side-along apparition. (That's nerd-speak for we went "poof.")

chapter 7
THE INTERVIEW

"So—David, is it? —why did you apply to become a demon hunter?"

I drummed my fingers on my thighs. It was just me and a panel of interviewers. This was a legit interview. I'd never really done one of these before. Hot Dog on a Stick basically begged me to take the job. And the camp counselor thing was a volunteer position.

The interviewer on the right leaned forward, waiting for my answer. He had a long, curved nose that looked like a beak.

"I want to help," I said. "I don't like the idea of that thing loose on the Earth, especially with my family out there."

He nodded and wrote something down. The other interviewers did the same, though one just kept staring at me.

After a too-long pause, Beak Nose said, "And what do

you think qualifies you for this position?"

Well, crap. Here was the question I had no real answer to.

Before I could say anything, he asked, "You've been dead ten years? That's not a very long time. We have applicants who have up to eighty years of angel experience. Some even more. You were young when you died and you're young for an angel. Why should we consider someone so inexperienced?"

His question wasn't accusatory. I could tell he wanted me to give him a good answer. He was testing me. So I really thought about it. In school, I was pretty good at BS-ing essays. Adding fluff when I ran out of actual content was kind of a specialty of mine. All I had to do was apply that concept to this interview. Try to spin it to make my weaknesses look like strengths.

"I know I'm young and inexperienced, but that isn't a problem."

"How so?"

"First of all, I'll be trained. As far as I know, when a person is trained in a job, they receive the same training as someone who has more experience than them. Everyone starts from scratch, so it doesn't really matter what my background is." Okay, that was stretching it a bit, and I could tell I was losing some of them, so I tried switching gears. "Also," I added quickly, "my inexperience could be an asset. I wasn't around for the first round of demon hunters and I was never trained as a defender, so I won't be bogged down with how things used to be, or how things are supposed to go. I could come up with fresh new ideas, which is something people with lots of experience often struggle with. There's a reason kids do better at learning languages than adults. Adults have had more time to rely on and latch on to their primary language, while kids' minds are still open and malleable. I think the same concept applies to me. Not only will I learn fast how things used to be, but I'll provide new ideas on how things could be."

Dang, Garcia. That wasn't half bad.

The panel was silent and they stared at me a moment before adding to their notes. I had no idea if I'd made any sense to them. For all I knew they were writing, *"This kid thinks he's smarter than us old fogies, but he don't know squat!"* They wouldn't have been wrong. About the last part, not the first part. I definitely did not think I was smarter than any of them.

"One more thing," Beak Nose said. "You are not wrong, you will be trained, but we need to make sure you are adequate in at least the very basics of defending against demons. Please create a ball of Light in your hand."

I stood and closed my eyes. I thought of where Light comes from, and as I felt the power wash through me, channeled it onto the palm of my hand until I held a glowing yellow orb.

The interviewers nodded, then, out of nowhere, one of the dudes on the panel threw a ball of Light at me. I quickly shaped mine into a shield and the projectile of Light was absorbed into it.

There was more nodding and note-taking.

"Thank you for your time," Beak Nose said. "We'll be in touch. You should know within the hour whether you will be invited to the next round of interviews."

"There's another round?" I asked.

"A test, really," Beak Nose said. "Do you have any questions for us?"

Yeah, um, what is this test and how do I pass it without knowing anything about what I'm doing?

"Yes," I lied. In my life skills class they said you should always ask questions in interviews. I racked my brain for something from the list. "I know the purpose of a demon hunter is to track down Malum and capture him. But what does the average day look like? Obviously, it's going to take some time tracking him down, so what do they do in the meantime? I guess what I'm asking is, what are the duties of a demon hunter?"

Beak Nose folded his hands and leaned back in his chair. "Demon hunters are in the business of information, really. Think of them as our intelligence force. Demon hunters will be sent on missions to extract information from other demons by blending in as demons themselves."

"So, like, undercover?" I asked.

He nodded. "Once enough information is gathered, we will work with the defenders to create a plan to capture Malum and make sure his prison is secure. Do you have any other questions?"

I shook my head. "No, thanks for your consideration."

They sent a messenger to tell me I would be invited to the next round of interviews and that it was happening right now. I must have been one of the last people they interviewed.

One of the panelists met me in an empty conference room and explained the test. They were going to send me to an unknown location where there was a demon waiting for me. My job was just to get the demon's name. That was it.

It seemed simple, but to be honest, I'd never really spoken with a demon, and the idea kind of creeped me out. Fighting demons, not a huge deal. With the exception of Malum, they all scatter once they see Light. But talking to one of them? How did one actually do that?

"Any questions?" the panelist asked.

I had about a million, but I just shook my head.

"You have about five minutes to plan out your tactics. You will wait in the hall with the other applicants. When it is your turn, I will touch your arm and send you to the location of your test."

I wondered how they would know how I did if they weren't coming with me. Maybe an angel would be invisible somewhere, watching what I did.

The lady sent me out into the hallway, and I leaned against a wall next to a giant of a man who could scare someone just by saying "boo." By the look of the other applicants, most of them were defenders. They had that look in their eyes like they weren't afraid of anything. As I looked around at the men and women around me, I thought of what I'd said about my inexperience being an asset, and a plan began to form in my mind. It was probably stupid, but it could work if I spun it right.

Just as I was finalizing my ideas, the lady came back, tapped my arm, and I popped into existence in an alley I'd never seen before.

chapter 8
TRYOUTS

Act human, I kept telling myself. *Act human.*

I resisted floating and forced myself to sink to the ground. This was my tactic. It could work, or it could blow up in my face. I saw other contestants in the hallway practicing disguising their aura of Light with Darkness. I saw them switching out their white angel robes and smiles for leather jackets and sneers. My tactic? Act mortal. A really good demon is good at blending in. That's how they deceive the poor souls they torment.

I put all my focus into walking across the ground. It's harder than it sounds when you don't have weight. We're kind of like balloons. Old balloons filled with stale helium that hover just above the ground. Not only is walking unnecessary, but it's also really difficult to do convincingly, to make it look like gravity is pulling us down as though we are a physical being. Lucky for me, Jake and I used to practice walking when we got bored. I hoped that was enough experience to do it convincingly now.

Down the alley was the demon I needed to get information out of. If I could get his name, I would pass the final test. I took a deep breath and walked down the alley, wearing the clothes I died in. Sounds morbid, I know, but I wanted to look as human as possible, and even though I croaked ten years ago, the first outfit I could think of is the last one I wore—blue t-shirt, paint splattered jeans (genuine paint, not jeans you spend $200 on for *looking* distressed), and black Vans. I even created myself a fake backpack.

I sensed the demon right away, but didn't look him in the eye. Instead I sighed and sat with my back against the wall. I let my fake backpack plop onto the ground and hung my head.

"What's a school kid like you doing in a place like this?" the demon asked.

I looked up at him and repressed a shudder. The guy just radiated power. "Just taking the long way home. I'm not in any hurry to get there and tell my mom how bad I did on my third retake of the ACT."

Of course I had to bring up the ACT. Freaking test killed me.

"Well, I suggest you get out of here before someone mugs you, or worse."

I stood and frowned, looking around at the sketchy

alley. The walls around us were mostly blackened brick and the asphalt beneath us had more potholes than flat ground. A homeless dude slept in a box down the way and some lady to my left was talking to the wall. In the distance you could hear a man and a woman screaming at each other. "You're probably right."

The demon nodded in dismissal.

I started to walk away, then stopped. "Wait, what are you doing out here if it's so dangerous?"

He shrugged. "Maybe I'm up to no good. Maybe I'm the kind of person I was just warning you about."

I frowned. "Why would you warn me to leave if you meant me harm?"

"I'm meeting someone here. I don't have to hurt you, but I will if you don't get the hell out of here, kid."

I hesitated. "Are you doing something illegal?"

The guy pulled a gun on me. The odd thing was that the sight didn't scare me. If he was a demon, it wasn't a real gun. Even if it was real, it couldn't hurt me. I was trying to pass as a living teenager though, so I stumbled back and held my backpack in front of me.

"I'll call the cops!" I said.

He cocked the gun. "Not if I shoot you first."

This was certainly not going according to plan. I wasn't any closer to getting the information I needed than I was before. The thing was, the demon couldn't actually shoot his fake gun. It was just made of Darkness and smoke. A real gun would just slip through his fingers. But if I didn't run away, I'd blow my cover. A real teenage kid would run. What was more important? My disguise as a living kid, or getting information out of the guy? I mentally sighed and cut my losses.

With a laugh, I tossed my fake backpack aside and let it disappear. "Lose the gun," I said with mock swagger. "We both know you can't shoot it."

The demon raised an eyebrow, then laughed. He tossed his fake gun away and it disappeared like my fake backpack. "You almost had me there." He held his hand out for me to shake. "This is my alley though. You're gonna need to find your own."

"What's so great about this alley?" I asked.

"Mind your own business." Darkness gathered around his hands like smoke billowing toward me.

I repressed a growl. How was I going to get the name out of this guy? He was going to attack me and the only way I knew how to fight demons was with Light.

I studied his face. He had all the characteristics of your typical demon—an aura of Darkness, an expression of anger and hopelessness, the carelessness of one who had nothing left to lose. Yet, there was something off about him. Almost like . . . he was *trying* to appear demonic. A closer look had me laughing. Because this guy was good. Really good. But I could see by the twinkle in his eyes that he was not what he said he was. Also, he looked familiar, and I thought I knew where I'd seen him.

He scowled at me, Darkness now pooling around his feet. "I mean it, kid. This is my alley. Find some other poor soul to torment."

I did the weirdest thing ever. Something that would make me look really stupid if I was wrong and this all blew up in my face. I held my hand up and said, "Nice disguise, brother."

For a moment I feared I was wrong, but then he laughed and slapped my hand. His disguise melted away until I saw a glorious angel before me, white robe and everything.

I pumped my fist, unable to help myself. "Nailed it!"

"You're good, kid." He grinned. "But I'm a little miffed you saw through the disguise. That's worked on everyone else. Now I don't even get to see how you would have interrogated me."

"You mean no one else has seen through it?" Wow, was I actually cool?

"I was in the panel of interviewers for every applicant and you're the first one to have recognized me so far."

I grinned from ear to ear, then coughed and tried to appear somewhat dignified. "Well, I've always had a bit of an extra sense. I can tell when people are lying. It's probably why I have such low self-esteem because I can tell when people are lying to me to make me feel better."

I closed my eyes and smacked myself in the forehead.

What was that?

He smiled and raised an eyebrow. "You're weird, kid. But we're gonna use that. Welcome to the demon hunters.

chapter 9
THE CONTRACT

Rajesh was my evaluator's name. He was very smiley, even by angel standards, and yet I had no doubt he could take down multiple demons at once. He had a certain assurance about him which made him intimidating. I wondered how long he'd been dead. He may have even been around the last time Malum escaped.

Rajesh and I returned to headquarters and he said I was dismissed and that he'd call me back when it was time for our first meeting. I just stood there in front of headquarters staring at nothing for who knew how long. I'd done it. I had actually made it into the demon hunters. I'm not sure what I expected to happen—the evaluators laughing in my face, completely failing the test, getting kicked out of angel-dom—but it certainly wasn't this. Was this a mistake? I hadn't actually thought about what it would mean for me to get in because I didn't think it would happen. I was really excited to replace Hot Dog on a Stick with demon hunter on my resume.

DAVID, IF YOU'RE FINISHED WITH YOUR INTERVIEWS, YOU'RE NEEDED AT THE FRONT DESK.

I shook myself from my excited and nervous thoughts. *On it,* I said, floating through the doors of headquarters. The lobby was packed and I felt really bad I'd just been standing outside staring at nothing while I could have been helping in here. I hopped over the counter. A man named Kamsiyochukwu was currently working the counter by himself. (I still can't pronounce his really cool Nigerian name so I usually just call him Kam.)

"Hey, Kam," I said. "Busy day?"

I tried to convey my meaning telepathically, because he only spoke Nigerian, and I only spoke English. As angels, we don't just magically learn all languages, but we can communicate mentally by conveying images and feelings.

"*Kedu*, David!" He grinned and waved at me. Then he sent me an image of himself literally drowning under a mountain of paperwork. I laughed. Yep, busy day.

I did what I could to help shrink the piles of reports and get them filed under the correct names. There were also all kinds of applications and messages we had to sort into different mailboxes to get to the correct angels. In addition to that, we had to keep track of who was doing what in which conference room so angels could rent out rooms for meetings. The lobby was so busy there was a line all the way to the door.

After an hour or so, a messenger angel popped into existence right in front of me. "You're needed in conference room nine. Demon hunter business." Then he disappeared.

I felt a leap of excitement. This was it! I'd actually made it. I wanted to leave right then, but then I looked around at all the unfiled papers and the line of angels waiting to turn in reports. I couldn't just leave Kam here by himself.

Hermes, can you please send someone to take over for me and Kam? I gotta go, and Kam's been here a while.

CAMILLE AND RICARDO ARE ON THEIR WAY.

Thanks.

I did what I could to at least get the mess organized before our replacements arrived, then I booked it down the hall to conference room nine.

"Sorry, I was on front desk duty," I said as I barged into the room.

"You're late." A woman with a strict ponytail raised an eyebrow at me. I wanted to ask if she'd actually heard me because I had just explained why I was late . . . but she kind of scared me, so I decided against it. She gestured toward the group of chairs positioned in a circle, like they were about to spring an intervention on me. There were nine other angels there, including Jake. We grinned and slapped each other's hands as I took the seat next to him. I was so happy we were on the same team, I didn't even feel like rubbing it in his face that I'd made it in when he'd doubted me. Which was good, because he looked "fair dinkum" happy to see me too.

"Is this all of us?" I asked, looking around. "Just ten angels?"

Rajesh floated forward. "Twelve, technically, if you count me and Ying Yue here." He gestured toward the stern teacher-looking lady who already didn't like me. They both took a seat in the circle.

"This is one of many demon hunter task forces," Ying Yue said. "Rajesh and I are the leaders of this task force. Our job is to train you in demon hunting, then send you on missions that will bring us closer to capturing Malum."

"Do we get code names?" Jake asked. "I want to be Van Helsing."

"Van Helsing didn't fight demons, he fought vampires," I said.

"And other monsters. Plus, he's played by an Aussie."

"No code names!" Ying Yue said.

Jake and I closed our mouths and listened like good little angels.

"This isn't a game," Ying Yue said quietly. Something about her tone caused the room to fall still. "I need you all to remember why you signed up for this, because each and every one of you will wish to quit. This job will cost you."

My earlier excitement dissipated.

A man to my right leaned forward. "Cost us what?"

"Happiness. Light. You will be tempted to let go and give up, but you mustn't, for you are a holy angel and you must persevere."

"Could you explain what you mean by that?" I asked, anxiety coloring my tone.

Rajesh stood up. "Look. The demon hunters serve a different purpose than what you might have suspected. Guardian angels protect and defend our loved ones with Light and provide guidance with angel whispers. Defenders fight demons in groups, much like soldiers. The purpose of a demon hunter is to root out Malum's location in order to capture him. To figure out where he's hiding, we will need to spy and gather information from other demons. Doing this requires learning how to blend in with demons and get close to them."

"How does that cost us Light?" a girl asked. I did a double-take. She looked about five years old. I wondered how she died.

"We will show you the demon hunter contract," Ying Yue said. "If you wish to sign after reading it, wonderful. If you wish to leave the demon hunters, you may do so."

I felt a strange apprehension in the pit of my stomach. Something about this seemed dangerous, which was an odd feeling for a being that couldn't be hurt or killed. When Rajesh handed me a copy of the contract I read it through three times.

I _________________ , *commit to take on all the responsibilities of a demon hunter, including, but not limited to: following commands of my task force leaders, spying and retrieving information from demons, and aiding in the capture of the demon called Malum. I understand that as a member of the demon hunters I may find myself in situations in which I must commit "wrongful" acts with the appearance of sin. These wrongful acts may include: lying and deceiving, speaking harmful or unkind words, and even creating real and true Darkness. I acknowledge that using Darkness will cost me happiness and may disturb my ability to use Light.*

In order to keep myself in line and worthy of my title I will follow the directions of my task force leader and will report to my task force leader after each and every mission. I understand that I will not be required to include my acts as a demon hunter in my guardian angel reports. When on a mission, I am answerable first to my task force leader.

While a part of the demon hunters, I understand that I will not be expected to devote all my time to the demon hunters. Missions will be taken in shifts so that I may continue to fulfill my other duties, such as that of a Defender, Messenger, Comforter, Usher, Front Desk Worker, etc. I understand that I am still expected to perform the role of Guardian Angel (if I have living family), and if at any point my demon hunting causes me to neglect other priorities, I may be asked to resign.

By signing below, I commit to the above duties. If at any point I no longer desire to serve as a demon hunter, I will give my task force leader advance notice so as to avoid disturbing plans and missions already set in motion.

Angel Signature: _______________________

Task Force Leader Signature: ________________

*Signature of Head Angel:*__________________

"What is this about using Darkness?" a lady across the circle asked.

Ying Yue seemed to brace herself for a reaction. "Angels have the ability to use Darkness too, just as a demon does. The difference is, we only use it when absolutely necessary. As demon hunters, your duty is less of a warrior and more of a spy. In order to gather the information we need to capture Malum, you will need to go undercover as a demon yourself. Get close to other demons and figure out what you can. Using Darkness is part of your cover. You will need to play your part convincingly."

The room filled with whispers and expressions of confusion. Angels using *Darkness?* People that used Darkness were demons. Wasn't that how we categorized them?

But then I remembered I *had* seen an angel use

Darkness before. During my final test, Rajesh, disguised as a demon, created Darkness. I was so caught up in my own euphoria of catching him in his disguise, I never considered how freaky it was that he made actual Darkness with his hands.

"What's this cost thing it's talking about?" asked the guy to my right.

"Darkness comes from the Evil One," Rajesh explained, "but it is fueled from within. It comes from your fears and sorrows, your secret yearnings. Demons understand this. They use these dark and painful thoughts within themselves and within their victims to fuel their Darkness. As angels, we will not be causing, or obtaining Darkness from mortals. We will rely on our own Darkness."

"But . . . we're angels," Jake said. "We don't have Darkness."

Rajesh took a deep breath. "Just because we're dead, it doesn't mean we're perfect. David, you were there when Malum broke loose, weren't you? Don't you remember that feeling of all your darkest and most painful thoughts imprisoning you in your own fears?"

I nodded, wishing he hadn't brought up that awful memory. Also, how did he know I was there? Did everyone know about that? Did everyone know about how I froze?

"If you were there," Rajesh continued, "you would not

argue that angels, while creatures of Light, cannot have Darkness within."

Well, that was a comforting thought. What was he implying? That all the terrible thoughts and feelings I had came from within myself and Malum just enhanced them?

The man from before got up. "I appreciate what you're doing, but I want no part in this."

Rajesh nodded. "Go in peace, brother."

He disappeared and the rest of us looked at one another, wondering who else would leave. *Should I leave?* This seemed like a very fine line to be dancing around, and I didn't like the idea of using Darkness from the Evil One. Was it okay to do something bad for a good reason? Wasn't that kind of a villain mindset?

"Do we have to sign this right now?" the woman to my left asked. "Can we have some time to think it over?"

Ying Yue looked impatient, but Rajesh put a hand on her arm and said, "Let them consider. This is a serious commitment. We will meet back tomorrow at the same time and you can decide then if you are ready to sign the contract."

The angels dispersed. I wandered through the halls as I contemplated what I might have to do. As an angel, our whole purpose is to help and protect mortals with kindness and Light. We don't believe in fighting fire with fire. Yet the demon hunters were sounding like angels who justified wrongdoings for the greater good. We got to break the rules because we were the good guys and we were doing it for the right reasons. But what if I did something bad for what I thought was a good reason, but was really just me taking things too far? Where was the line between protecting and attacking? And how could I trust myself to know where that line was in a heated moment?

As concerning as these issues were, I knew deep down I had to do it. Even if my part was so small it made no real difference, I would still try. It was the only thing I could do to make up for freezing when Malum got loose. Maybe if I'd done something, I could have held him long enough for Hermes to come and capture him. I couldn't stand the idea of doing nothing again.

I signed my contract before I could lose my nerve and returned it to Ying Yue. It was too late to chicken out now.

chapter 10
DARKNESS

You know that moment when you're so bad at something that your teacher or coach or dad has to pull you out of the group and try and pound the concept into your thick skull one-on-one? That's how it felt when Rajesh pulled me aside in the middle of our training session the next day. I did great at defending myself with Light. He even showed us how to sculpt Light into different shapes and I made this awesome Lightsaber and I felt like a legit jedi. It was the coolest I had ever been. Then the Darkness part of the session came, and I was starting to think I had a learning disability.

"Come on, David, let's have a chat," Rajesh said as he steered me toward the bleachers. We were using a football field as training grounds because no one was using it, and we didn't really have wide open space like this back at headquarters.

"Try again," Rajesh said once we were away from the

group of angels that looked like a bunch of squids that just inked. "Think of things that bring you down. Thoughts and feelings you avoid. Pull them into you and embrace them. Then push them out."

I tried. I thought of how I'd walked in on my dad crying over my picture the other day, or how guilty I felt that Uncle Richard still blamed himself for my death. I concentrated on those depressing thoughts and feelings, but I didn't feel anything building up inside me. It was just me feeling kind of depressed.

I sighed. "It's not working."

Rajesh stared at me for a minute. "Why are you here, David?"

"Because this is where you said to meet you. At this weird football field. Is that supposed to be the mascot painted on the wall over there? It looks like a pregnant unicorn."

"No, that's graffiti." He looked to be struggling to keep a straight face. "It does kind of look like a pregnant unicorn. But you're changing the subject. Why do you want to be a demon hunter?"

I shrugged. "I want to help. I don't like the idea of that *thing* loose on the earth, especially when my family is still alive."

"Yeah, that's what you said in your interview. But out of all the angels in The Resting Place, do you think you're the most qualified for the job?"

"Probably not . . . Definitely not. I'm sure a bunch of people could do way better." I could afford to be honest now that I'd already made it in.

"So why you? Why not leave it to the rest of us?"

Was he trying to make me feel stupid? Because it was definitely working.

I sighed, hating admitting this aloud. "I guess I just want to make up for what I did. It's kind of my fault he's loose . . . If I had been able to hold him there a bit longer, Hermes would have gotten there in time and then Malum wouldn't have gotten away."

Raj kept looking at me, his mouth pulled to the side. "That's not it either," he decided. "I think you know that deep down that there was nothing you could have done. Malum is more powerful than any one angel on their own. Even more powerful than your buddy Jake over there. So no, that's not why you joined the demon hunters. I think you would have joined even if you hadn't encountered Malum. Don't you?"

I shrugged. I'd never really thought about it.

He started pacing in front of me, though I'm not sure if I could really call it pacing since he was more just floating back and forth. He looked like a mall cop on an invisible Segway.

"Come on, David," he said. "What is your motivation? We need to figure this out if we're going to make any progress."

"I already said I want to help and make up for my mistake. And I want to keep my family safe."

"Other than that. Why you? Why not leave it to the rest of us?"

"I don't know."

"Come on, think!"

"I said I don't know!"

Rajesh got all up in my business. It was the closest anyone had come to threatening me since Malum. Or before that, to be honest. I wasn't interesting enough when I was alive to get on anyone's bad side and I'd never been in a fight. I mean, unless you count the time when I got so into Super Smash Bros that I punched my friend Chris in the face and then he attacked me. But that was just kids messing around and being stupid. Rajesh was supposed to be a mentor and now he was freaking out on me.

"Dude, what the heck?" I said.

He put his hands on my shoulders and said, "Spit it out! Why are you here?"

"I just want to do something with my life!"

There's an awkward pause as my yell carried over to the rest of the task force and they glanced over at me.

I grimaced. "Okay, poor choice of words—"

"No, no. I think that was the perfect choice of words." Rajesh released me and smiled. "Expand on that."

I groaned. "I don't know, Raj. I guess . . . I just died

before I really accomplished anything. I didn't even graduate from high school. I don't resent that I'm dead at all—I genuinely like being an angel—I just hate the fact that I never made anything of my life. I guess I was kind of hoping to do something worthwhile as an angel since I didn't do anything useful as a mortal, but all I really do is file papers. It's like no one trusts me to do anything important. I thought maybe the demon hunters could be my chance to be something more."

Rajesh smiled sympathetically and put a hand on my shoulder. Then he pushed me away and said, "Well, you're right. You really are useless. You've never done anything right, have you? We only let you in because we're desperate, and because I felt bad for you. There's nothing special about you and you'll only bring us down. Your life was completely pointless and there's no way to fix that."

I wilted as his words pierced me right where it hurt. "Ouch."

"Oh, don't be such a baby, you know you're no good to anybody." His face was cruel and smiling and made me feel about one inch tall.

Defensiveness and anger crept their way into my voice. "Okay, that's enough."

"Why, does that upset you? You don't like that I'm calling you a loser?"

"Yeah! I mean, no! I mean, whatever!"

"How does it feel to have someone point out just how

unnecessary your existence is?"

My hands balled up into fists. "I really want to punch you right now."

"Good! But I'm an angel and that's not going to hurt me, is it? So how are you going to hurt me, David?" He closed in on me. "I don't think you can do it."

I breathed in through my nose and closed my eyes trying to control myself. This ball of hopelessness and anger welled inside of me.

"You can't do anything right . . . " he said in a cold voice.

My eyes flashed open. I let out a growl and a puff of Darkness came out my nose. I yelped and jumped back.

Rajesh grinned. "Don't lose it! Gather it up and shoot it at me. You know you want to. Do it, or I'll just keep going on about how pointless you are as a person."

I grimaced and gathered up the ball of Darkness inside of me, then shot it from my hands. The explosion of black smoke shot him past the twenty yard line and I was left staring at my hands, immediately filled with conflicting feelings of guilt and pride. I just created actual Darkness! Was this a good thing or a bad thing? And was it worth that psycho freak-out moment with Raj pointing out all the reasons I'm a total failure?

Rajesh floated back, a weird mixture of pride, chagrin, and sympathy on his face. He approached me slowly. "I'm sorry for what I said. I promise I didn't mean any of it."

I was still kind of ticked so I just scowled and nodded. Rajesh put a hand on my shoulder. "I only said those things to try and coax the Darkness out of you, all right? You are *not* useless. You lived a very important life and enriched the lives of everyone who knew you. And your efforts here in The Resting Place are very important. I promise, you've made a difference to people both dead and alive. You have a very earnest and kind spirit that inspires others to be their best self. You are a very valuable angel and this task force would not be the same without you."

I didn't know what to say to that, so I didn't say anything.

A part of me was overwhelmed by how amazing Raj was at acting like a demon. Was this what he expected from us when we went undercover? Could I ever be that convincing? Did I want to be?

"Do you think you could do it again without me being a jerk?" he asked.

I nodded emphatically, not interested in having my self-esteem clobbered again. I closed my eyes and called to the Darkness inside, then projected it onto my hands.

"Nice work!" Rajesh held his hand up for a five, and I slapped his hand, forgetting that I was still holding a ball of Darkness. Rajesh flinched back and shook out his hand like I'd shocked him. The part of me that was still salty about all the crap he'd just said couldn't help the satisfied smirk that came over my face. Raj chuckled and patted my back. "Come on, let's go join the others. Nice work today, Dave."

Was it nice work though? We just did the work of demons. I've seen demons at work, and what Rajesh just did when he was whispering those negative thoughts to me was very demonic. And then it was like he was tempting me to do something bad. And then I created Darkness. I knew that we were doing this all for the greater good, but it just didn't sit well with me. Maybe the Darkness was already affecting me. They said using it would bring me down and that we'd all want to quit eventually. I understood what they were saying now. This kind of sucked.

chapter 11
CHOICES

After the weird training session, Jake and I decided to take some free time for ourselves. Angels are allowed to do that every now and then, we just have to sign out at The Resting Place so people know where we are if we're needed. Jake could tell I was pretty down, so he came up with this dumb idea to cheer me up.

We floated down in the middle of a Brazilian Jiu Jitsu tournament. There were dudes on the mat wrestling each other to the ground and people cheering like they were losing their minds. Jake and I stood in the middle of the mat and Jake went, "Up next we have Jake versus David! What is your weapon of choice?"

He held the fake microphone out to me.

Without a word I gathered Light into my hands and mentally shaped it into a Lightsaber, holding it back as though ready to fight.

Jake paused. "An elegant weapon from a more civilized

age."

He formed his own Lightsaber and we began our dramatic dance of death. The BJJ competitors rolled through us when we got in the way, but we ignored them. As we struck each other, we pretended that the crowd was cheering for us.

After a dramatic, childish battle, I fell to the mat and began dying a ridiculous, drawn-out death. When I was done fake dying, I sat up and said, "Is it wrong for dead people to play dead?"

Jake snorted. "If anything it's wrong for living people to play dead. Either way, I won." He faced the crowd and screamed, "Jacob Williams is undefeated!"

The crowd screamed as one of the BJJ dudes won his match and Jake pretended it was for him, pumping his fists in the air.

"What should we do now?" I asked.

He shrugged. "I dunno. We could watch the idiot box in someone's house. My brother's in the middle of this one show that's not bad. Or we could try to knock things over in your sister's house to freak her out."

Sometimes angels can move things with our minds if we try hard enough. And screw with electricity, though generally that's more of a wanderer or demon's agenda. I once made the mistake of practicing this skill in my parents' house and they both ran into the room when a vase shattered as it hit the floor, leaving a sparkling sea of glass on the tile. I felt bad for scaring them, but then my dad was like, "Very funny, David," and I smiled wider than I ever had since I'd died. I mean, I knew he was just joking to make himself feel better—stuff falling over without anyone being there is scary to mortals—but he was right about it being me. It was the first time anyone in my family actually acknowledged that I was there.

"Whaddya think?" Jake asked, elbowing me.

I shook myself from my memories and gave him a look. "We're not supposed to haunt people."

"Oh please," he said, raising an eyebrow. "You're the one who keeps putting Rocco's toy trucks by Elena's bed so she steps on them when she gets up in the morning."

I couldn't help an amused snort. "That's different. I used to do crap like that when I was alive. That's just my way of letting her know I'm still here. Also, it's funny."

DAVID, I HAVE AN ASSIGNMENT FOR YOU.

I sighed. "Sorry, Jake, I gotta go. Hermes is calling. I'll see you later, kay?"

"Later."

I apparated over to The Resting Place and Hermes was waiting for me. He looked concerned.

"I need you to go see your brother," he said. "He's about to do something drastic."

"What happened?"

"Nothing's happened yet, but he's in an argument with

Chelsea and she's going to leave him if he doesn't fix this."

I pinched the bridge of my nose. Sam had been making some questionable choices lately. I knew it wasn't my fault, but I couldn't help taking some of the blame. I felt like my death kind of screwed him up. Also, I was his guardian angel. I was supposed to stop him from being dumb, but he never listened to me.

"I'll see what I can do. Thanks."

Hermes gave me a pat on the back before I popped into Sam's house. He was pacing in his bedroom while his pregnant fiancée was crying and trying to get David, their two-year-old son, to go play in the other room so she could speak privately with Sam. In case it isn't obvious, they named their son after me. It was both embarrassing and an honor. But it's also kind of weird. I know I'm dead, but it makes me feel extra dead to have someone named after me.

I floated down next to Sam and put a hand on his shoulder. *"Sam, don't do anything stupid. You can fix this, okay?"*

Chelsea came into the room with red-rimmed eyes. "You can't talk to him like that. He's your son."

Sam's face twisted in annoyance. "All I said was for him to go away so I can get some work done."

"You told him he makes your life difficult and that you were sick and tired of him!"

Sam threw his hands up. "Well, I am!"

"How could you say that? He's your son!"

I cringed and stood next to Sam. *"Take it back. Take it back right now. You know you don't mean that."*

But now that Sam had said what he seemed to have been keeping in for a while, he took courage and continued on. "I have a demanding job and I don't understand why you can't keep him away from me while I'm working! You're his mom. You handle him all day by yourself. Why do you act like it's too much to take care of him once I get home? You get lazy just because I'm around because you think you can push all the work onto me."

"You're his father! He just wants to spend time with you! He loves you so much and you treat him like you don't even want him around!"

I stood directly in front of Sam, willing him to hear and listen to me. *"SAMUEL GARCIA, DO NOT SAY—"*

"Maybe I don't want him around!"

I hung my head. He was blowing this. Then I narrowed my eyes at a little cloud of Darkness I saw in the corner of the room. I growled as I noticed the demon there, probably putting those cruel words into his head. "Get out of here!" I said, shooting her with a beam of Light which barely missed her.

The demon emerged from the corner. I'd seen her before and she was by far the most annoying demon I'd ever encountered. No matter how many times I cast her out, she just kept popping up like bad acne. Her platinum blonde hair hung down to her unrealistically tiny waist, and she had the kind of cocky smile of a woman who knows she's beautiful. Everything about her was exaggerated: her big blue eyes, her voluptuous lips, the hourglass shape of her body. An aura of Darkness glowed around her, shadowing everything within two feet of her. She smirked and laughed a tinkling laugh that set my teeth on edge. She started floating around the room, losing all pretense of subtlety. When she passed behind Sam, she whispered, *"Tell her you resent being a father."* Darkness puffed from her mouth as she spoke. *"Tell her you think she keeps having kids to rope you into marrying her."*

"No, don't say that!" I said as I shot the demon with another jet of Light. This one hit her and she screamed like a girl that just got splashed with water while sunbathing.

"Get out of here, demon," I growled.

The demon lady gave me the finger so I shot her with another ball of Light. Finally she disappeared, but not before saying, *"It's too late anyway. He's mine, and I'll just keep coming back."*

I spun back around. I wasn't sure what I had missed while I was dealing with the infestation, but the silence was palpable.

"So," Chelsea whispered, "is this why you won't follow through on our engagement? I got pregnant and suddenly you didn't want me anymore. Is that what happened?"

"*No, it's not,*" I said, trying to work on Chelsea, since Sam wasn't listening.

"Yeah," Sam said. "I wanted you and only you. I told you that from the start. Then you had to get pregnant, and now we have kids and I never wanted that. I told you I didn't want kids, Chelsea! You knew this!"

Chelsea closed her eyes as tears streamed down her face. She took a deep breath, then looked back at Sam. "Well fine. You got your wish. I'm leaving."

She slammed the door behind her.

"Good!" Sam yelled.

"*Go after her, you idiot,*" I growled. "*What is wrong with you?*"

DAVID . . . Hermes spoke into my mind. *POSITIVE LANGUAGE ONLY. REMEMBER, WE NEVER MAKE A PERSON FEEL WORSE. HELP HIM TO SEE HIS MISTAKE AND GIVE HIM HOPE THAT HE CAN FIX IT.*

I nodded and went to Sam. I stood directly in front of him and spoke as loudly and as clearly as I could. "*Sam, I love you. You're my brother and I will always love you. You know who else loves you? Chelsea and David. They're your family. You have hurt them, but you can make it right. You know Chelsea doesn't want to leave. She wants you to run after her. So do it. You can turn it around right now. If you give your kids a chance and get to know them, you'll love them too, just like you love Chelsea. Go after her, Sam. Make it right. It's not too late.*"

Sam scowled at the floor, not moving, and it was almost like he was listening to me. Then he shook his head, talking to himself, but it felt like he was responding to me. "No, we don't want the same things. It's better that she leaves. I'm not good for her. She'll be happier with someone else."

I opened my mouth to argue, then stopped as I saw how his face had changed. He was trying not to cry. He didn't want this, but he thought it was right. And he might have been right. Chelsea probably would be happier with someone else. Someone who would love her and her kids unconditionally. Someone who would actually pay attention to her. I still thought that person could be Sam, but he'd made his choice. He didn't want that, and I couldn't convince him otherwise.

I put my hand on his shoulder. *"At least say goodbye. At least tell her you're sorry. Don't let her leave feeling like you never loved her to begin with."*

For the first time that night he listened. I watched as he raced to the driveway. Chelsea had already somehow packed her bags and was getting David into his car seat. Maybe she'd had the bags packed for a while. Before she got into the car, Sam stopped her.

"Wait . . ." He swallowed, not meeting her eye. There was a long, painful silence before he got up the courage to say, "I hope you find someone who wants the same things you do."

Chelsea glared at him. "I hate that you've given up. And I hate you."

She got into the car, slammed the door, and drove away, tears streaming down her face. I didn't blame her for her anger. He was breaking her heart and had been breaking her heart for a long time.

Again, I couldn't help but feel like this was my fault. Maybe if I had caught the demon earlier, he wouldn't have said what he said. Maybe if I had convinced him more often to spend time with his family, he wouldn't be in this situation. Maybe if I'd recruited the rest of my family and convinced them to talk to Sam they might have had a greater influence. But none of this changed the fact that Sam made his choice. And there was nothing I could do about that.

I felt a sudden warm feeling inside. *YOU DID WHAT YOU COULD, DAVID. I'M PROUD OF YOU. WITHOUT YOU, THE DEMON WOULD HAVE HAD MORE INFLUENCE AND SAM WOULD HAVE BEEN MUCH CRUELER. YOU SHOULD FEEL PROUD OF THE GOOD YOU ACCOMPLISHED TODAY.*

I smiled. For an angel who's really good at chastening, Hermes is really good at picking you up when you're down.

chapter 12
TEAM OF WEIRDOS

"Listen up," Ying Yue said.

Our task force was back in conference room nine sitting in our little AA circle again. We seemed to have shrunk, so I counted the bodies and there were only seven of us, not including Ying Yue and Rajesh. The weird thing was, they hadn't even set up chairs for the other three.

"Aren't we missing people?" I asked.

"Some have chosen to leave," Ying Yue said. She made no effort to hide her disappointment. "We lost one on that first day, and two have left since our last training session. We said in the beginning that this task force would have its own set of challenges, and many would not find themselves up to the task. "

"It's not just that," Rajesh said, jumping in to defend them. "They left on moral grounds. It didn't feel right for them to become involved in the powers of the Evil One. Which is *completely* understandable. I'm surprised we have as many angels as we do."

I shifted in my seat, feeling uncomfortable with this discussion. How could angels speak so casually of Darkness?

"Are they right?" Jake asked bluntly. "I mean, is this moral?"

Rajesh sighed. "I understand the confusion. Let's put it this way. Is it evil for a police officer to carry a gun? Is it wrong for a soldier to kill in battle? Tanks, swords, bows and arrows, firearms—are weapons themselves evil, or is it how they are used? We use our weapons to bring us closer to capturing Malum, who is evil and is causing widespread panic. There were three school shootings yesterday. Today, the number of kids kidnapped off the streets has almost doubled. Several nations are on the brink of war. What's more evil—what Malum is doing, or what we are doing?"

I frowned, hating that argument.

"Moving on," Ying Yue said, ever time-conscious. "Rajesh thought today's training session should be more of a discussion. That we should get to know one another better. It has come to our attention that most of you don't even know each others' names. While I fear we don't have much time to waste, I agree that having a close connection with your comrades can raise morale. We probably should have started with this in our first meeting. Who would like to introduce themselves first?"

"I will," Jake said. He'd never been shy. He was obviously that popular guy at school slapping everyone's hands and fist bumping everyone in the hallways. And I'd have been the one trailing behind, not cool myself, but cool by association. "My name's Jake. I'm a guardian angel and a defender. And I met my best mate on the day I died." He grinned and punched my shoulder.

I felt like he was laying it on a bit thick with the trying-to-cheer-me-up thing. I mean, I knew I'd been kinda down lately, but I wasn't that depressed. I'd just been having some dark thoughts, worrying that I'd never be worth anything, blaming myself for my family's problems, and beating myself up that the world's most powerful demon was lurking the earth because of me.

Okay, maybe Jake needed to lay it on thicker. I'd only used Darkness that one time and it was already screwing with my brain. No wonder those guys quit.

"I'm David," I said next, because I kind of had to after Jake's little 'best buds' declaration. "I'm a guardian and a front desk worker, and . . . um . . . " I couldn't think of anything interesting about myself. "I don't know, I'm kind of lame."

Jake elbowed me.

"I mean, I'm a nerd." Before Jake could elbow me again, I said, "I don't say that as a put down, just a description. I like nerdy things like *Harry Potter* and *Star Wars* and *Lord of the Rings*. That kind of thing."

I saw a few appreciative nods around the circle and thought, *All right! Fellow nerds unite!*

Ugh . . . This was why I was still single.

"Who'll introduce themselves next?" Ying Yue prompted.

"I will." A man with a long, dark ponytail stood. He looked like he thought he was a pirate. Or George Washington.

"My name is Frederick Davis," he said with a British accent. "I was a soldier during the time of the American Revolution."

Whoa. That was like two hundred fifty years ago! And he's still here?

I don't know how much of this I'm allowed to talk about, but The Resting Place is not the final stop in the afterlife. The real heaven comes after this. The Resting Place is just a stop along the way where you get your house in order before you move on. To pass on to the next place, we go to the Main Office and have an interview with . . . you know . . . The Big Man. Then together you decide if you're ready to move on, or if he thinks you need more time. We schedule the interviews ourselves, so it's totally our call when we pass on. Everyone's different, obviously. Some people pass on within a year of dying, while others wait another twenty years or so for their loved ones to join them, but *two hundred fifty* years? I couldn't understand why anyone would wait that long.

"So you were on the side of the Brits?" this lady next to me asked.

"Of course. That was the correct side."

The man next to Frederick clucked his tongue. He also had the colonial ponytail, except his was blond. "Now, listen here Frederick, we've discussed this. We shan't have taxation without representation."

Frederick rolled his eyes. "Oh, not that ever-repeated phrase."

"Do you two know each other?" Jake asked.

"But of course. William here is my dearest companion, aren't you, old chap? And we killed each other." Frederick patted William's shoulder and smiled.

Jake and I shared a look, because it seemed like our weird friendship death connection had been one-upped. Ying Yue and Rajesh exchange a confused glance as well. You don't meet a lot of murderers in The Resting Place. Something about killing people being frowned upon.

"Don't say that, Frederick," William said. "We can't know for sure."

"I am quite sure that we did, my patriotic friend. I looked you in your eyes as I pulled the trigger. I felt the musket ball enter my chest at the same time mine entered yours. We arrived in this here Resting Place within minutes of each other. It is quite apparent to me that we are casualties of one another."

"Oh, so you were on opposite sides of the war," Jake

said, finally understanding.

That made more sense . . . Not murderers, just soldiers.

"And you're friends?" the lady next to me asked incredulously. I'd just noticed she had an accent. Was it Russian?

"Of course!" Frederick said indignantly. "Why shouldn't we be?"

"If it's not too personal . . . How have you not passed on yet?" I asked.

"Fair question, young lad. We could have passed on long ago, had we chosen to. However, William and I have a competition to see who can last longer on this side before passing on. We want to do as much good as we can before approaching those pearly gates. This will also determine once and for all whether the loyalists or the patriots have more endurance and passion."

"We already know the answer to this, Frederick," William said tiredly. "The Americans won the war."

"Only with the help of the French!"

"All right, maybe someone else?" Rajesh suggested.

Frederick respectfully bowed and took his seat.

"I'll go," the girl next to me said. Yeah, I was pretty sure it was a Russian accent. She stood up and folded her arms. "The name's Natalie."

"Tell us about yourself, Natalie," Rajesh said.

"Most of my family is here but we didn't all die

together. One was a car crash, another a skiing incident, and then there was the freak dumpster accident . . . "

"Dumpster?" Jake asked.

"I taught kindergarten, then worked in a prison, then lived with some sailors for a while catching lobsters. You know, just normal stuff like that. Also, I like llamas."

She sat down and I had to avoid looking at Jake or I was going to start laughing.

"My name is Ted," the next guy said. "I'm an usher."

An usher is an angel who guides spirits into The Resting Place. Usually family members do that, but some people don't have close family on the other side. It's a cool job, but not one I'd want. You have to be super zen and chill, because people tend to freak out when they realize that they're dead.

"Anything else?" Rajesh asked.

"I was an accountant when I was alive." Ted shrugged and sat down.

"That leaves you," Ying Yue said. She was looking at the last person left in the circle, the little girl I noticed on the first day. She looked like a five-year-old. I thought Raj and Ying Yue might have been a little reckless in accepting a little girl into the demon hunters, but one look at her terrifying glare from beneath her red bangs was enough to change my mind.

"I'm Daisy," she said darkly.

"And?" Rajesh prompted with a smile.

"I like biting."

I covered my face and laughed. Jake's shoulders shook from uncontained laughter. *I like biting*? I mean I got she was, like, five, but seriously? I didn't know how, but somehow this little girl was going to kill us all.

chapter 13
TALKING TO DEMONS

Raj took me along with him on a practice undercover mission about a week into training. I was just supposed to observe what he did and not talk. We traded out our white robes for typical street clothes. Raj was radiating Darkness like an aura around his body and I tried to imitate him. I closed my eyes and embraced my fears and sorrows, and pretty soon I was glowing negative too.

Raj took me to this alley between two rows of houses in a sketchy neighborhood. A stone wall separated the houses from the alley, though it was broken in several places as though someone had taken a sledge-hammer to it. The street lights in the distance flickered and two people shouted at each other from a house to the left while a TV blared from a house to the right. Not exactly a welcoming atmosphere. A woman all alone sat crying against the wall, looking as though she had nothing left to live for. A demon chuckled, fascinated by how her crying intensified whenever he whispered something in her ear. It took everything within me not to go to the woman and comfort her.

The demon noticed me and Raj. "Beat it."

"Relax, man," Raj said. "I'm just showing this newbie the ropes. Thought I'd show him some good demonizing in action."

"Newbie?" The man took in my age and looked at me skeptically. "What did you do?"

"Why do you care?" I snapped.

"Just curious."

I took a step forward. "It's none of your business."

I wasn't sure where all this angst was coming from. Turned out when I went undercover I got deep in it.

The demon scowled and his hands started glowing with Darkness. Raj put a warning hand on my shoulder and held the other hand out toward the demon. "You'll have to forgive my young friend here. He's still learning that just because we're demons it doesn't mean we're complete barbarians."

He gave me a look like, *Tone it down, dude.*

"You better keep that kid on a leash," Demon said. "No one disrespects me in my alley."

"Of course not," Raj said. He looked around to see if anyone was watching, then leaned in and said, "I'll let you haunt my alley if you give me some information."

Demon narrowed his eyes. "What do you want?"

"Have you heard about the breakout? Looks like Malum is loose. I'm trying to track him down because he's taking all my victims."

"Malum?" Demon looked almost scared. "You're trying to track the Prince of Darkness? Good luck with that."

"So you haven't heard anything?"

"No, now tell me where your alley is. I'm getting tired of this old hag."

Raj grinned and wiggled his fingers. "No thanks." And we apparated to the next demon.

This time we went to someone's house. A demon was hanging out behind the couch as some dude stared at his phone. I didn't know much about demons, but I was starting to think they had assigned mortals, kind of like guardian angels do. Or maybe they just claimed mortals. That sounded more like a demon to me. I got this weird image in my head of little kids rushing to the candy that fell from a piñata, trying to gather as much as they could and elbowing anyone who got in their way.

"Hey!" Demon Lady turned around and flipped her hair. "Like, what the heck? This one's mine!"

Raj went through the whole spiel about showing me the ropes and Demon Lady grinned at me.

"Hey, baby demon. So what's your deal?"

I gulped. "Deal?"

Raj subtly pushed me behind him and said, "So, you heard anything about that Malum outbreak?"

"Say what?" Demon Lady looked around, then disappeared in a cloud of Darkness.

"All right, one last stop." Raj took my hand and we disappeared again.

This time we were in the back of what looked like a strip club.

"Um, we're not going in there, right?" I asked, my voice going up an octave. "Not to be a prude or anything, but I'm pretty sure angels aren't supposed to do that."

"Shh." Raj pointed to a dude leaning against the wall, glowing negative. Then he looked down at me. "Your Darkness went out."

"Oh, yeah." I recreated my aura of Darkness and felt that terrible depression like a literal weight on my shoulders.

As Raj approached the demon he said, "Yo, Randall!"

Randall perked up and grinned at Raj. "Jimmy! Good to see you man!"

They gave each other a bro hug and Randall noticed me hanging out behind Raj.

"Who's the kid?"

Raj looked back at me and said, "Newbie. Just showing him the ropes. Hey Nick, this is my friend Randall. Randall, Nick."

I shook Randall's hand and managed to keep my mouth shut this time.

"So what's new?" Raj asked.

"Oh, you know, just trying to gather more victims." Randall shrugged. "They keep dying on me and going to that stupid Resting Place and then I have to find someone new."

"Forking angels," Raj muttered.

Raj didn't actually say "fork" and I jiggled my pinky around in my ear to make sure I'd heard him right. Hermes is pretty strict on language in The Resting Place and I hadn't heard language like that in a while. For some reason it made me want to giggle.

"What about you?" Randall probed.

"Nothing much," Raj said. "I'm just a little nervous."

"Why?"

"Did you hear about the outbreak? It sounds like the Son of Evil is roaming the earth again."

"Seriously? He's out?" Randall cursed.

"He creeps me out, man," Raj said in a low voice.

"Yeah, well, thanks for the heads up. I'm gonna go in, you wanna come?" he gestured to the strip club.

"Nah, I'll see you later."

Once Randall was out of the way, Raj took my arm and we apparated back to The Resting Place.

"Okay, what did you learn?" Raj asked as we reviewed

back in our conference room. It was just me and him and our room full of chairs.

"Demons are territorial?" I guessed.

He frowned and nodded as though that wasn't the answer he was looking for, but he was trying to be polite. "Yes, but what else?"

"Don't threaten them or they get mad?"

He sat across from me and said, "Come on, David, you're smart. You can do better than that."

"All right . . . Well, I think other demons are actually afraid of Malum. Also, I think maybe it was a bad move to come right out and say you were looking for him?" I winced apologetically. "You should have gotten to know them. Gotten close before expecting them to immediately open up. Like with that Randall guy. I'm guessing you've met him before, because he acted like you were old friends."

Raj grinned. "Exactly. When you take your first solo mission, make sure you build up a rapport with the demon before interrogating them. And don't mention the name Malum right away."

I nodded.

Build rapport. No mentioning Malum. I can do this.

Yeah . . . I definitely did the opposite on my first solo mission.

chapter 14
FAILED MISSION #1

Rajesh and Ying Yue assigned me to this random sports bar for my first solo mission where we've seen a lot of demon activity. Why demons are hanging around a sports bar, I don't know. Demons hang out wherever they want. Maybe drunk people are easier to manipulate. Or maybe they're just really into football.

For my disguise I went with a moody college kid, which I guess is what I would be now were I still living. I traded out my white robe for a blue hoodie and some jeans. Then added a backwards hat, just because I'd always wanted to wear a backwards hat, but if I ever did that when I was alive, my siblings would have teased me to no end. Apparently, I was not cool enough to sport the "whatever" look.

Demons are great at subtlety, that's how they get away with things, but they don't really follow any set of rules. They sometimes reveal themselves to mortals, and unless a mortal touches them, they can't tell the difference. That's why on this day I was going to let myself be seen. It was terrifying and felt wrong on so many levels, but in order to get tight with the demons I had to act like them.

When I approached the door, I had to pantomime opening it with my hand when in reality I was just moving it with my mind. A dude nodded at me when I entered, making me freeze. This was the second time I'd been seen by a mortal since dying and it rooted me in place for a minute. Then I nodded back and navigated through the bodies until I found a bare piece of wall I could pretend to lean against.

I took in the room. There was a wall of five TVs all playing different sporting events. Most people were crowded around the TVs screaming at athletes that couldn't hear them, but a few sat at tables and ate cheap appetizers, while others lounged against the bar, getting drunk. There were five people at the bar. Two men laughing with each other, one guy on his phone, and a really beautiful girl getting hit on by a balding middle-aged man.

He reached out to put his arm around her shoulders, but she flinched away so dramatically, the guy lost his balance.

"Don't touch me," she snapped.

"Hey, it's all right, baby. I won't hurt you." The guy reached out to pat her hands, but she folded her arms before he got the chance. I narrowed my eyes at her. Either she was super creeped out by this drunk guy—which, if she was, I didn't blame her—or there was another specific reason she didn't want him to touch her.

The dude left, but not before trying to smack her butt. I wanted to step in and defend her so badly, but there were two problems with that: 1) She'd already moved out of the way, and 2) I was supposed to be acting like a demon, and a demon would never stand up for someone.

The girl sighed and plopped back down on her stool. I took a seat a few stools down from her and subtly watched her for several minutes. I had a theory, but I needed to see it proven true before I approached her.

As she got up to leave, she gave herself away. She didn't even touch her drink. Bingo.

I sidled up on a stool next to her. "Can I buy you another drink?"

She raised an eyebrow. "I have one right here."

"Ah, that's right. My bad."

We stared at each other.

"So are you gonna drink it?" I asked.

"Actually, I was just leaving."

"Without paying for your drink?"

She gave me an annoyed look, slammed a bill down, and started walking away.

Before I could check if it was real money, I raced after her. I couldn't lose this lead. I needed to bring something back to the team, so I took a huge risk and reached out for her arm. She jolted when she felt me pull her back. I resisted a fist pump. *Totally called it!* If she was alive, I wouldn't have been able to do that. Now that I was closer, I could see her dark aura. It was faint before, either because she was trying to hide it, or because she just wasn't doing anything. Auras are stronger when you're using your Light or Darkness.

She narrowed her eyes and her lips tightened. "This is my bar. Find your own."

"I was just looking for some help, all right? Then I'll be out of your hair. I'm looking for Malum."

I mentally slapped my forehead. I mentioned Malum before building up a rapport! That was literally what Raj told me *not* to do!

"Malum?" She barked out a laugh. "Good luck with that."

She started to walk away, but I grabbed her arm again. "Turn your back on me again and I will blast you with some world-class Darkness."

The hardness in my voice surprised me. I was better at acting like a demon than I thought I would be. Either that, or I was coming across as really stupid. Probably the latter.

The demon narrowed her eyes. "What do you want with the Prince of Darkness?"

Well, for starters, I'd just like to know his location. Then I can get a crap-ton of angels down here pronto to incarcerate him in a holy prison so he doesn't destroy the entire world.

I grinned. "Oh, you know. I've just always wanted to meet my pops."

Meet my pops? Crap, where did that come from?

"Demons don't have families, idiot."

"They do if they used to be alive."

Her eyes widened. "You're not a native? You're a *monster?*"

Luckily, I knew what she was talking about, since I actually paid attention to Ying Yue's lecture on using the correct demon lingo. There are two types of demons. Most of them have been demons since the world began. It's just what they've always been. In the "Red Zone," what most people call Hell, they call those demons "natives" since they've been here from the start. On the other hand, evil people that die and become demons are basically celebrities. It takes a certain level of wickedness to *become* a demon. They call those "monsters." They're as rare as they are evil. And I'd just claimed to be one of them.

I casually leaned against the wall and smirked. "One of the original monsters. Why, you into that?"

I wanted to facepalm myself. How embarrassing could I be? Even if I wasn't coming across as a total dufus, it felt weird to flirt. It was such a human thing. And I was really bad at it. I wondered what Grandma would say if she could see me now. Would she gasp in shock because I was trying to flirt with a demon? Or would she squeal and clap and tell me to make eyes with her. Sadly, the latter seemed more likely. She didn't care who or what I dated at this point.

When the demon didn't answer right away, I nudged her arm with my elbow. "Heard that my old man busted out. I've never met him. He obviously wasn't much of a family man when he was alive, and the whole time I've been dead he's been in prison. I guess I'm curious. Thought maybe the Prince of Darkness himself could give me a few pointers."

She stepped away. "Yeah, well, monsters are generally puffed up imbeciles, so I don't spend much time around them. I have no idea where your 'pops' is, Nemo, so I suggest you run along."

Nemo?

(Side note: she didn't say "imbecile" or "run along," but as an angel I might get in trouble for using language like that. I'll let you use your imagination to substitute.)

Before I had time to respond, she disappeared into a cloudy puff of smoke.

Well, I've accomplished nothing.

chapter 15
AVOIDING CONSEQUENCES

I decided to go visit my dad before I reported back to the demon hunters. Was I avoiding the consequences of my totally failed mission? Obviously. But I'd come back when they called. Also, I missed my dad. It had been a while since I'd checked in on him. Judging from the angle of the sun, I assumed he was driving home from work.

Another cool thing angels can do: we can sense where people are. It works best if we're really close to them—personally, not spatially, or that would defeat the purpose—so instead of searching his house and office and every road in town looking for him, I just sort of followed his "scent" and ended up in his car booking it down the freeway.

He looked the same as ever. A couple of wrinkles had become more prominent on his forehead, and his light brown hair was continuously receding, but he was still the same old dad, humming happily as he drummed his steering wheel. Dad has always been one of those annoying people that seems happy all the time. Even when he's alone and has no one to pretend for. I'm not sure how he does it. I mean, don't get me wrong, he gets sad sometimes, but it doesn't take him too long to bounce back.

I mentioned angels can sometimes mess with electronics. I'm not always the best at this, but I stared at his phone and willed his Spotify shuffle to play our song next. As soon as his awful Bee Gees song ended, that 4-part harmony of Bohemian Rhapsody took its place and Dad grinned. We used to jam out to this all the time. I mean, who didn't? Dad started singing and I laughed as I butchered the harmony and pretty soon we were both singing opera to the top of our lungs. Dad played the piano with his fingers and I rocked out to my guitar solo. By the end of the song we were both giggling like little girls at a sleepover. Then all at once we both sighed and sat back in our seats.

"I miss you, David," Dad said at the exact same moment I said, "I miss you, Dad."

I smiled sadly at him. We were on the opposite sides of death, but we had a connection there, both of us secretly hoping that the other was listening, but doubting it was actually true. Like we were pressed up against a wall, feeling that there was someone there on the other side. After a pause, he started talking, the way he always does.

I just sat and listened as he told me about his day and what was going on at work and home. He told me about Ginger's birthday party and how he was worried about Sam. He even asked me how I was doing and paused for me to answer. I think that people with an imagination as big as my dad's find it easier to have faith. Like, because he can imagine a world where I am sitting here listening to him tell me about his day, he's able to believe it, at least a little bit.

DAVID, YOU'RE NEEDED BACK AT HEADQUARTERS.

"Later, Dad," I said as I apparated back to The Resting Place.

"First off," Raj said to us in the conference room, "we want to keep you all in the loop. Unfortunately, but not surprisingly, angels monitoring the situation have seen a substantial increase in crime since Malum's been released. We don't have enough evidence to pinpoint Malum's location, since many of these heinous crimes happened simultaneously. Malum obviously has other demons on his side. Within the last week, there were two shootings, both with numerous casualties, and one in which the shooter has not been apprehended; a serial killer was tried, deemed "not guilty" and set free, and has since raped and killed another innocent victim; a church building was burned with five hundred people inside, about fifty died; and several members of that congregation sought revenge by burning down houses of their attackers. Let us all take a moment of silence for the mortals left behind who were affected by these tragedies."

I leaned onto my thighs as I let it all sink in. I was having a hard time breathing. The more I thought about what Malum was doing in the world, the stronger my memories became of the demon with his hand around my throat. Those terrible memories and fears he showed me. That total helplessness. If I were a mortal, could he have used me to perform one of those atrocious acts? Deep down I knew the answer was yes. I was not strong enough to fight him off. So what on earth was I doing here?

Ying Yue broke the moment of silence first. "So now you see the importance of your missions. Each of you can bring us one step closer to tracking Malum down. So. How did your first missions go?"

Ying Yue stared us down as we all shared our experiences of our first solo missions. Most of us failed to get any information, which made me feel a little bit better about my own failure. Only Daisy made any headway, which made sense because she's terrifying. She basically put a demon in a chokehold until he agreed to be her friend.

Ying Yue and Rajesh had the whole good cop/bad cop thing down like nobody's business.

"We cannot afford failed missions," she said. "Most of you made careless mistakes. Frightening the demons off by pushing too hard, accidentally radiating Light instead of Darkness, blowing your cover. You guys are better than that."

"The good thing is," Rajesh said, "we can learn from our mistakes. Also, you can learn to improvise to fix your mistakes when you make them. David? Where did you go wrong?"

I grimaced. Of course he would single me out. "I pushed too hard, I guess. I mentioned Malum too quickly before getting to know her."

He looked around the circle. "Overall, bad move. Did not work out."

"Thanks," I grumbled.

"But did you give up?"

"No . . ."

Rajesh gestured toward me. "David here improvised! He realized he mentioned Malum too soon and made up a story to cover up his mistake. He wasn't just some strange demon snooping for information about the Prince of Darkness. David here claimed to be Malum's son!" He laughed and slapped my back. "Genius."

"Does he even have a son?" asked Natalie.

Ted quietly chimed in, "He was alive once, so it's possible."

"It still didn't work," I said.

Rajesh held up a finger. "Yet. I bet if you try that same demon again, she'll let you in eventually. I'm gonna keep you on her as an assignment."

I shrugged. It was fine with me. I was glad for another chance.

"Hey Raj," Jake said with his hand up. "I've an idea."

"Let's hear it."

Jake gave me a look like he was nervous to say something without my permission and I held my hands out and shook my head. I had no idea what he was talking about.

"So David and I met this medium not too long ago and I think it would be cool to have her keep an eye out for us. I mean, she would be the ultimate spy. She's a mortal. Demons would have no reason to be wary of her."

Raj and Ying Yue shared a look.

"Could be risky," Ying muttered.

"Could be worth it," Raj muttered back. "How did you meet her?"

"She's a friend from high school," I said. "I was checking in on my cousin and she saw me, so we chatted for a bit. But Jake already asked her if she'd help us out and she said she didn't want to get involved."

"Persuade her," Ying Yue said.

"We'll send Frederick with you," Raj suggested. "He's charming and persuasive."

Frederick tipped an imaginary hat. "Thank you, good sir."

And suddenly I was roped into begging my mortal-medium-kind-of-friend into joining, or at least consulting, the demon hunters.

"Don't leave yet," Ying Yue said as we all started to get up. "Meet us at the football field. We're going to practice more Light and Darkness. We still need to whip you all in shape. We will not have another reporting session with this many failures."

"Now remember, your job is to blend in," Raj said walking around us in the middle of the football field, the pregnant unicorn supervising from afar. "Demons, as you might have learned, can be very territorial. Sometimes they lash out with Darkness if other demons get too close. Your instinct if that happens will be to defend yourself with Light, which they hate. That is the most effective way to get rid of a demon, and can be used in emergencies, but that would obviously blow your cover. So today we'll learn how to fight Darkness with Darkness."

He had us all sit on the bleachers as he and Ying Yue pulled two of us at a time to practice a Darkness battle. I couldn't stop tapping my foot with anxiety. I hated this kind of attention. At least when Raj pulled me aside the other day no one else was watching. Or, they had the decency to pretend they weren't watching.

He pulled Natalie and William first. They stood about ten feet apart, Raj behind Natalie and Ying Yue behind William. Natalie started forming Darkness on her hands, and it looked like William was struggling to create it. Then suddenly he formed an old-fashioned musket of Darkness and actually shot her with it. The Darkness bullet threw Natalie on her back and she sat up slowly massaging her chest.

"Ow," she said, scowling. Then she was on her feet shooting a formless column of Darkness that knocked him off his feet.

"Not bad!" Raj said. "Who's next?"

Ted and Frederick volunteered next. Frederick, for variety, formed an old-fashioned sword and began circling Ted with precision. Ted surprised us all by creating his own sword and engaging in a pretty entertaining sword fight. Frederick scored the first hit, right in Ted's gut and Ted doubled over for a minute. Then Ted stood up and jumped back into the fight, eventually striking Frederick on the neck, a move that would have killed him if he was alive and these were real swords.

We all stared at Ted, who shrugged. "I took fencing in college."

Daisy stepped forward next and I looked over at Jake. I wish I could say I was reluctant to fight her because I didn't want to hurt a little girl, but really I was just afraid of her. Jake shrugged and stepped forward. Jake, like a stereotypical Aussie, threw a boomerang of Darkness at her head, which unfortunately did not come back. Daisy ducked, and when she stood back up she shot him with twin beams of Darkness from her eyes. All of us on the bleachers screamed and stood up.

"What the crap!"

"My word!"

"With her *eyes*?"

Daisy's face cracked into an evil little smile, then she walked back to where she was sitting without a word. I couldn't help but laugh at Jake's shocked expression. He was flat on his back staring up at the sky. I'd have gone down to help him up, but then that would've drawn attention to me. I was hoping Raj forgot about me and I wouldn't have to do this.

"David! You're next," Raj said. "You can go up against Ying Yue."

I groaned. I should have volunteered earlier. Now I was really gonna get my butt kicked. I grimaced as I passed Jake on my way down and he gave me an "it was nice knowing ya" look.

Ying Yue and I stood in front of each other. She had the look of a tiger about to pounce, and I gulped involuntarily, feeling my Adam's apple bob up and down. Before I could come up with a creative weapon, Ying Yue threw a ball of Darkness at me. My arms came up to protect my face, and I cringed inward, but the ball just bounced off my shoulder. I grinned and stood up straighter, but Raj shook his head.

"David, you're radiating Light. Turn it off. This is a

Darkness battle."

I sighed and did my best to turn down my aura. That sentence sounds like something my dad would call "hippie garbage," but it is difficult to turn off your Light. Glowing is something we just naturally do, like breathing. We can stop it, but it's uncomfortable. Also, you don't usually *want* to turn it off because it's a natural shield against Darkness. That's why demons don't stand a chance against angels. Other than Malum, who doesn't fall into the same category as regular demons, they can't hurt us unless we let them. But at that moment I needed to let myself get hurt . . . I concentrated on how much I sucked and how much Ying Yue was going to totally destroy me and soon I was glowing negative instead of radiating Light. Then she formed a whip that slapped me and wrapped around my legs. I fell flat on my face.

"Again," Raj said.

I got to my feet, scratching at my legs. Darkness is itchy.

Before I could get my bearings, Ying Yue shot me with what I must admit was a really cool Darkness bow and arrow. It hit me right in the chest, and hurt. Not only that, but it tasted like despair and sadness, like she just emptied someone else's pain down my throat. Which is gross, because backwash.

I rubbed my chest. "That didn't feel good."

"Again," Raj said.

"Seriously? You didn't make anyone else go more than once." But Ying Yue was already coming at me with a sword before I even finished my sentence. I sucked in all my frustration, then pushed it out of me, forming it into a shield, which Ying Yue's sword bounced off of. She came at me a few more times and I did my best to block her. Were it a real sword, she would have scratched me a few times, but so far I had escaped what would have been serious injury.

Then she changed tactics, creating a ball and chain that she'd be able to whip around my shield. I did the only thing I could think of: I tackled her to the ground, knocking her right on her back. The ball and chain fell from her hand and then I did something really weird. I radiated Darkness all over my body, so thickly it became a blanket, which I peeled off myself and wrapped around her like a straight jacket and somehow stuck to the ground. Ying Yue's entire body was trapped, and she struggled, unable to move anything but her head. I stood up, breathing heavily and it took me a moment to realize that I'd won. Ying Yue looked just as surprised. Then she smiled for the first time since I'd met her.

"Nice!" Raj said, holding his hand out, and this time I made sure to wipe the Darkness off my palms before I returned his high five.

Ying Yue turned on her Light and my Darkness melted off her. She stood and dusted off her robe as Raj walked by and said, "I told you," elbowing her in the arm.

Jake came down from the bleachers and fist bumped me. "Good on ya, mate!" He was surprised in a way that was almost insulting, but I appreciated the way he was still supportive.

I shrugged. I knew I'd just done something good, kind of, but I couldn't help feeling self-conscious. I still didn't understand why Raj had me fight her in the first place. Why was he always singling me out? Did he know I would win this time? I knew he had our best interests at heart, but there was still a lot about him I didn't get.

At least I'd won over Ying Yue. Who knew the best way to earn her respect was to throw her on her back?

chapter 16
FRESHMAN BIO

I showed Frederick to Sandra's classroom when the time came to go talk to her. She wasn't in there, so we just hung out as Frederick inspected the posters on the walls. I noticed there were lab tables in the back of the room with microscopes. This confused me, because I thought Sandra taught history. She must have shared the classroom with another teacher. Or she was just given a classroom that used to be some kind of science.

Sandra and I had both biology and chemistry together in high school. A memory came to mind as I stared at those lab tables with the stools that spun around.

I was in freshman bio and had missed most of the explanation of our experiment because I fell asleep. I was still getting over a super crappy cold and could barely keep my eyes open. An eraser plopped onto my desk and I jolted upright. It hurt my cheek which had stuck itself to my desk and I may have drooled a bit. As I wiped my face I looked around for who threw the eraser and saw Sandra trying not to laugh.

"Thanks," I mouthed, handing the eraser back to her.

She made a show of wiping my drool off on her jeans.

"Any questions?" Mr. Ronald asked. "All right, get to work."

"What's happening?" I asked Sandra. I looked around myself bewildered as everyone got up and paired up as they headed toward the lab tables in the back.

"It's dissection day," Sandra said. "Did you really not hear anything Mr. Ronald said?"

I frowned and shook my head. I just woke up and now I had to cut open a frog? Was I still dreaming?

"Come on, sleepy," Sandra said, pulling my arm toward a table. "I'll take pity on you and be your partner."

"Um, thanks?"

We approached an open table and I gagged from the smell. There was a laminated diagram laid out with directions for how to properly dissect the frog. There was even another page where we were supposed to deposit different parts of his insides, like some sick, backwards puzzle.

"Ugh, I can't even," Sandra said, turning away from the poor dead frog. "You do it."

"We're supposed to do it together."

"I don't like dead things," she said, staring at her toes.

I shrugged and relented, picking up the scalpel and feeling like an evil scientist. I still couldn't decide if this was interesting or disgusting. There were equal amounts of squeals and excited gasps around the room as my peers dissected their amphibian victims and giggled at each other's reactions.

"It's not that bad," I said under my breath.

"Oh, huh-uh. I took notes for you all last week when you were sick. You are not allowed to give me crap."

"Fair point."

I leaned down over the frog to try and figure out where I was supposed to slice, but the formaldehyde smell made me gag.

I covered my nose and backed away.

"Here, I'll distract you," Sandra said, still facing away from the frog. "Did you hear Vicky is asking Brad to homecoming?"

"I thought it was guy ask girl?"

"It is," she said with a snort. "But I mean, it's Vicky. What Vicky wants Vicky gets."

"Can you say the name Vicky one more time?"

"Vicky."

I raised an eyebrow at her and she laughed.

"Are you going to homecoming?" she asked, looking casually down at her nails and then back to me.

"Nah."

"Oh," she said with a shrug. "Yeah, I probably won't

go either." She bit her lip and glanced at me, then looked away.

"Oh my gosh," I said, blinking out of my flashback. "She totally wanted me to ask her out!"

"Beg your pardon?" Frederick asked, bending close to a microscope.

Why didn't I ask her out? I liked her; I thought she was really cute and smart. I honestly couldn't think of a single valid reason not to have asked her out. I guess I just thought I had more time . . .

I wondered what would have happened. I never did go to a high school dance. I probably would have gone to my senior prom had I made it that far. Would Sandra have said yes if I'd asked? My eyes glazed over as I daydreamed of how I might have asked her. Would I have tried to be bold and creative, or would I have just blurted it out in the hallway during passing period? Sadly, the latter sounded more like me.

I jumped when Sandra walked in, and the door slammed shut behind her. She sighed when she saw us. After forcing herself to walk over to us, she raised her eyebrows and blinked. "Yes?"

Oh my gosh, that's such a teacher way to approach someone, I thought. *I wonder if she calls her students by their last names like Mr. Feeny.*

Frederick took charge. Good move.

"Allow me to introduce myself. Captain Frederick Davis, miss," he said, tipping a three-pointed hat that he'd just created out of thin air. "May we have a moment of your time?"

She covered her face and groaned. "I said I didn't want to get involved." She removed her hands and glared at me.

I held my hands up. "Hey, it wasn't my idea. Jake's the one that blabbed."

She took a deep breath and sat on a desk. "All right," she said patiently. "How can I help you?"

Frederick smiled. He had this superpower smile that made everyone relax around him and instantly think that he's a very kind and handsome man. "Good lady, we were wondering if you would share information with us. A woman of your talents must have a vast store of knowledge."

She smiled slightly at his flattery. "What do you want to know?"

"Have you heard the name Malum?" I asked. "Or Prince of Darkness? Or Son of Evil?"

She scowled at the ground as she thought. "Not that I can recall."

"Would you let us know if you hear anything from spirits who maybe don't know you're listening?" I asked. "We're trying to track this guy down."

"Why?"

"We needn't frighten you with the details," Frederick

said. "Suffice it to say he's a demon who needs to be stopped."

"I'll keep my ear to the ground," she said.

I smiled at her thinking about frog dissection day.

"What?" she asked.

"I'm sorry I didn't ask you out to homecoming."

I wasn't sure what possessed me to say that, but it was out and I couldn't take it back.

Sandra smiled and finally she looked like the girl I knew, not this tired teacher who couldn't get rid of all the ghosts. "Don't flatter yourself, David."

I smirked at her. "Would you have said yes?"

She rolled her eyes. "Probably. If you didn't bug me to death." She gasped and covered her mouth. "I'm so sorry."

For a minute I was confused, then I remembered how touchy mortals are about death, despite the fact that they throw the word around all the time. I snorted. "The word 'death' does not offend me. My name is David, and I am dead. Also, you just joked about your own death, not mine."

She bit her lip. "I'm still sorry."

"It's not a big deal. Everybody dies."

"It's sad for us, all right?" She looked genuinely upset and then I felt like a jerk. I had to remind myself of what it was like to be mortal. When you're mortal, death is the scariest, most horrible thing that could happen. I mean, the worst-case scenario in every situation is, "We're all gonna die!" And then if someone you love dies, it's like the end of the world.

But that's not at all what it's like on the other side. To angels, death is kind of exciting. A celebration. Another angel recruited. Kind of like the equivalent of birth for mortals. New beginnings. A fresh start. And it's so inspiring to see that first expression people have when all their earthly cares just melt away. It's weird how that happens. Everything that seemed so difficult is suddenly irrelevant. Even wars, apparently. I'd be willing to bet that the Revolutionary War was the most important thing in the world to both Frederick and William. Alive, they would have hated each other. Alive, they killed each other. And now they were friends.

"Well, we should probably go," I said to Sandra. "You said once that you don't like dead things . . ." I trailed off and gestured toward me and Frederick, "so we should probably get out of your hair."

Sandra blinked at me a minute, then her shoulders started to shake and she smiled, a familiar laugh bursting through.

"You always were a dork."

I grinned. I'd missed her smile more than I'd realized.

chapter 17

IT'S A DATE

I was starting to feel like someone who has to actually schedule things in a planner. That's such an Elena thing to do. She even has little cupcake stickers for birthdays and stuff. But seriously, how was I supposed to keep tabs on all four members of my immediate family, make it to all the demon hunter meetings, go on missions to spy on my assigned demon, get to front desk duty on time, and find time to check in with Sandra too? It was a good thing that I didn't have to sleep.

After Frederick and I reported back to Raj and Ying Yue, they sent me back to check on my demon and see if I could get anywhere with her. She was sitting in the same place she was last time in the same bar. Why did she hang out there? Was there a specific person she was haunting, or did she just really like grimy sports bars with fat, middle-aged men?

"So this is, like, your place?" I asked, taking a seat next

to her.

"Run along, Nemo."

Again, she did not say "run along." She did say "Nemo," though . . . I really hoped that nickname wouldn't stick.

"My name's David." I mentally slapped my forehead. Did I seriously just give her my real name? Oh well, there's a million David's in the world. Doesn't really give much away. "And you are?"

"Leaving."

She got up to leave just like before, and I rolled my eyes. Why did she always run? Probably because demons aren't usually so chummy. She obviously didn't like me being friendly. I tried to think of what would get her attention.

A plan formulated that I hoped wouldn't get me in trouble at The Resting Place.

Before she disappeared, I turned invisible and knocked a dude's beer over, causing it to spill all over another dude's crotch. He was an enormous biker probably a foot taller than me. He looked around for who spilled the beer and made him wet his pants. I leaned in close to him, then blew Darkness into his face like someone smoking a cigarette. I whispered into his ear.

"That guy right there. The one in the stupid baseball hat. He did it to you on purpose. He's looking for a fight. You should give it to him. You look like a little sissy girl who wets her pants. Beat the crap out of him to show him who's boss."

The guy growled and punched the guy in the face. The other guy punched him back so hard that he fell into another guy who dropped his beer. Pretty soon there was an all-out brawl with black eyes and beer bottles broken over people's heads just like in a movie. I was horrified at what I'd just done. As an angel, this was the opposite of what I was supposed to do. But the she-devil was watching so I materialized next to her and barked out a laugh as though I found this all incredibly amusing.

She smirked. "Okay, not bad. Are you assigned to one of those guys?"

"Nope." I let my lips pop on the P. "I don't really follow assignments. I do what I want."

She was aghast. "But you have to follow your assignment!" I took a mental note that demons are assigned specific mortals. "If you mess with mortals other demons are assigned to it can totally unbalance everything."

I cocked an eyebrow. "So?"

She blinked and looked at me in an impressed sort of way.

Ha! Look at me, being impressive! I thought. *Mom would be so—no, no, mom would not be so proud. This is a demon lady. Bad call, Dave.*

"So, you wanna get out of here?" I asked her.

"And do what?"

"Compare notes on all the people we've tortured?"

She looked at me like I was stupid, and I didn't blame her. Compare notes? Really? That's not what demons do. I had no idea what demons do other than tempt and torment people, but it definitely wasn't that.

I wanted to get her out of this place so I could talk to her one-on-one. Trick her into thinking we were buddies so she'd tell me stuff.

An idea came to mind. It was almost Halloween. . .

"We could go haunt a fake haunted house and scare the people that work there because stuff's happening that they didn't orchestrate."

She stared at me for a moment, then narrowed her eyes. "I don't trust you."

"Good," I said. "I don't trust you."

Inexplicably, we smiled at each other, coming to some kind of agreement.

What we agreed to, I had no idea. But something possessed me to say, "It's a date."

Before she could say another word, I disappeared in a cloud of Darkness and transported myself back to headquarters.

I was choking on the Darkness when I arrived at headquarters. It concerned me that it was easy to create this time. It just sort of flowed out of me, but no matter how easy it was to make, I still hated it. Ever since using Darkness that first time, I'd been having terrible thoughts and it was getting worse. Memories flowed through me. Mom crying over my casket. The crunch sound when I died. A memorial they made for me at the high school. The crunch sound. The things Rajesh said to me that he didn't mean but I was now starting to think were true. The image of me tempting those men at the bar, looking like a demon myself. The crunch sound.

I slapped myself on the face, trying to snap out of it.

"You okay, *mijo*?" Nana Maria asked.

I jumped. I hadn't even realized I'd landed right next to the front desk. Nana paused across the counter mid-file.

"Uh, yeah," I said.

"You look as white as a ghost."

I forced a smile. "Ha ha."

"You need a report?"

I shook my head. "I was on a mission. We report those to our task force leaders, not here." I shuddered thinking about what she'd think of me if I filled out my report here and she decided to peek.

She folded her arms and gave me a concerned look. "Are you sure you're all right?"

"Yep! I'm me. I mean good. Goodhello! I mean . . . Goodbye!"

I disapparated to conference room nine to check in

with Raj or Ying Yue, whichever one was there. Jake walked out when I arrived, looking a bit shaken himself. It looked like this job was taking its toll on both of us.

"Hey, mate!" he said with his typical arm punch. "Whatcha doin' this arvo?"

"Nothing," I said. "Wanna do something? I could use a distraction."

"Me too."

"I'll wait down the hall."

My report to Ying Yue was pretty uneventful. I expected her to scold me for what I had done, but she congratulated me, which made me even more uncomfortable. I'd rather her yell at me.

"David, I know this is weighing on you," she said. "You have a really strong conscience, so naturally you feel guilty for what you did. That's a good thing. It's part of the reason we wanted you on our task force. Someone who can do these things and not feel conflicted about it would be someone I'd worry about. But your firm morals allow you to keep sight of what is good and right. I trust you to know the difference between what is necessary and what crosses the line."

I blinked and sat back in surprise. *This is the most positive thing she's ever said to me.*

"So what do I do?" I asked.

"I want you to follow through with this demon. Continue to get close to her and get her to open up. You thought she was hiding something. Figure out what she knows."

I nodded and left. Jake was waiting for me in the hallway. We walked around until we found a bench and both sat down with a sigh.

"How's it going?" I asked.

"Not great," he said. "The demon they assigned me to is a real . . . I can't think of a word bad enough. He preys on children."

I cringed.

"Yeah. There was this tiny ankle biter who ran away and got lost and I just sat back and laughed as he tormented the poor kid and got him even more lost. It was the worst thing I've ever done . . . I laughed as he basically kidnapped this child. I led the boy back home when the demon finally left, but I still can't shake myself of how dirty I feel. I should have blown my cover to save the kid sooner. Right? I don't know. It feels dangerous when you don't know what's right anymore."

I felt really stupid for my self-pity, because it was starting to sound like Jake had it worse than me.

"Did you at least get any info out of him?" I asked.

"Not much. I guess Malum is unpredictable. Also, all the other demons hate him. I'm still trying to find out why, but when this guy brought him up, he seemed real scared."

I'd come to the same conclusion. But why would demons be afraid of another demon? Did he prey on them too?

"What about you?" he asked.

"Well, it looks like my first date's gonna be with a demon."

Jake threw his head back and laughed as I told my story. Even though it had been a terrible experience, having him laugh about it made me feel lighter. I found that I could laugh about it too.

"What do I do?" I asked.

"Are you nervous because it's a date or because it's a demon?"

"Both!"

Jake grinned. "I can't believe you're the one whose persuasion technique is seduction."

"I'm not trying to seduce her!"

He laughed again, then turned toward me. "Not that you actually like this evil demon, but you need to get her to like you. Whatcha gonna do? Take her out for a cuppa, and just pretend to drink it?"

"No, I'm not taking her out for a 'cuppa'. We're gonna go haunt haunted houses."

He frowned and nodded. "As far as demon dates go, that's not bad. Whatcha gonna wear?"

"I don't know. That blue hoodie I've been going around in with the backwards hat."

"Show me."

I magically changed my clothes and Jake started

shaking his head. "No. That's the outfit of a kid *trying* to look cool. Let's see . . . Lose the hat and trade the hoodie for a white t-shirt."

"A white t-shirt? Really?"

"I'm not done yet. Trust me."

I sighed and did as he said. He inspected me. "Okay, now add a leather jacket and some aviator sunglasses. Darken your jeans."

I looked down at myself and frowned. "This looks like the exact outfit Zac Efron wore in *17 Again*."

Jake grinned. "I know. Now mess your hair up a bit. Girls like that, for some reason."

"What makes you the expert on what girls like?"

He smirked. "I had some serious game back in high school."

I snorted. I don't know why it was funny. I had no doubt all the girls in Jake's school were super into him, it was just the way he said it. Almost like he was making fun of himself, but secretly very proud.

I quickly changed back into my white uniform before Hermes caught me walking around in street clothes.

Jake slapped his thighs and stood. "You wanna do some random acts of kindness to make up for all the bad we did today?"

"Wanna race?" I asked. "Whoever helps the most mortals before we're called back for a meeting takes my next shift at the front desk."

"You're on, Garcia."

I was gone faster than I could finish this sent

chapter 18
SANDRA'S INFESTATION

I decided to start with my family. It was Saturday morning and I found Sam was asleep on the keyboard of his $1,500 big screen computer. The lamp on his desk cast a yellow glow over Sam's sleeping form, clashing with the natural light peeking through the blinds in the window behind him. I wished I had the ability to take a picture, because he looked ridiculous. He was sitting there with his slacks unbuttoned and no shirt. It had likely been removed last night since stress makes him sweaty, so he's often topless in his office. His arms were curled around his head, the way he's slept since he was a child, looking as though he expected the ceiling to cave in on top of him. His drooling face was simultaneously pressing down on several keys on the keyboard, so the email he was writing said,

Jonathan,

I was just kljjjjjjjjjjjj jjjjjjj jjjjjjjjjjjjjj jjjjjjjjjjjjjjjjjjjjjjjjjjjjjjjjjjjjjjjjjjjjjjjjjjjjjjjjjjjjjjjj

jjjjjjjjjjjjjjjjjjjjjjjjjjjjjjjj;rigwijg;oAJJJJJJJJJJ JJJJJJJJJJJJJJLiiiiiiij . . .

I really wanted to press "send" and see what Johnathan would say back, but that wouldn't have been very helpful to Sam. I was pretty sure he worked Saturdays because that was one of the things he and Chelsea always argued about. I checked his watch. He was definitely going to be late if he didn't get up now.

I leaned down close to his ear, took a deep breath, and shouted, "*Wake up!*"

Sam gasped and startled awake, his drooly cheek making a gross squelching sound as it unstuck from the keyboard. He looked around himself in confusion, wiping the drool from his cheek. Then he checked his watch and swore, rushing off to get dressed.

"*You're welcome!*"

One.

Next, I checked in on Elena. She was putting on makeup in the bathroom, singing to some pop song on the radio that I didn't recognize. Unlike Sam, she was, thankfully, already dressed for the day in her name brand jeans and an olive green V-neck t-shirt that she could have found at Goodwill but probably cost fifty bucks from Nordstrom. Her hair was thrown into one of those messy buns that makes everyone think she just woke up like that, when she probably spent thirty minutes perfectly tying and pinning it into place, using magical hair products to give it more volume. Various makeup products were splayed across the counter, and she held up the mascara tube in front of her mouth as she sang. She didn't look like she needed any particular help, but everyone can always be a little happier.

"You look beautiful today," I said in her ear. *"You're an awesome mom and your husband is lucky to have you."*

I cringed, wishing I'd left off that last part. The "husband" thing was a bit of a sensitive subject right now. Her husband, Charlie, was in the army and was currently deployed overseas. He'd been gone for about two months.

To my relief, Elena's eyes didn't start watering. She smiled at herself in the mirror, checking herself out from different angles. "I look hot!"

I threw my head back and laughed. That was what she'd gotten from what I said?

Two.

I checked in on Dad next and found him passed out on his bed with his arm thrown over his face, breathing like Darth Vader. There was a humidifier and a bottle of Nyquil on the night stand, and tissues littering his entire room. The humidifier was running low on water and was making an annoying sucking sound like someone trying to drink out of a straw when there's nothing left.

I bit my lip. *This could be risky . . . but it might work.*

I crouched down by the humidifier, and using all my concentration I mentally unscrewed the lid on top and floated the cap onto the night stand. Then I took a water bottle next to his bed and hovered it over the opening. Water dropped on the floor as I tried to pour it in the hole, but most of it got into the humidifier. I set the water bottle down and floated the cap back into place. It wasn't screwing on though. I tried doing the hand motion of screwing it clockwise as I concentrated, but it barely moved. With a frustrated growl, I twirled my whole body in a circle, like an angry pirouette, and somehow that worked. The cap screwed firmly into place.

The humidifier stopped making the sucking noise and my dad continued snoring, completely unaware of anything that just happened. I nodded in satisfaction.

Three.

I checked in on Mom next. She was out for her morning jog along the trail by our house. Again, she didn't really need anything right then, so I just kind of waited until a moment presented itself as I floated along next to her. When she stopped to take a break, I felt the urge to hug her, so I did. Sort of. I hugged her as well as an incorporeal dead dude can hug a mortal.

"I love you, Mom. And I'm doing just fine."

There was no way she could have actually felt me, but when I pulled away, she was in tears. *Oh no, did I make her sad? Maybe I should have left her alone.* I wished I could know what was going on in her mind. Did she really feel me there? As an angel, I was usually too busy helping others to feel sorry for myself, but I felt a rare pang of longing for my old life when I could hug and talk to my mom whenever I wanted.

"Sorry . . . I didn't mean to make you sad."

Before I could get a better read on her, she spun around and gasped. A black Labrador who'd escaped her leash started running down the path and barking. My mom screamed and ran away, continually looking behind her. She's scared of dogs. Luckily dogs are scared of me. They hate spirits because they can sense us, and sometimes I think they can see us, but they definitely can't smell us and that's what freaks them out.

I stood between the dog and my mom. "Hey, puppy!"

The dog skidded to a stop and barked once, then whined.

"Let's go this way!"

I headed in the opposite direction of my mom and the dog barked like crazy and chased after me until we reached her owner. I looked back to see my mom with her hands on her knees taking a relieved breath.

Four.

I knew it might lose the kindness race for me, but I got the idea to check in on Sandra next. Likely this would turn into a longer conversation because I couldn't just pop in and out—I mean, she could see me—but I was curious to know if she'd discovered anything. I used my spidey sense to locate her and apparated over to her apartment complex. She'd just gotten out of her car and was getting the mail. I wondered where she just came home from on a Saturday morning. Maybe making copies at the school to prepare for next week? I decided to just float up to her floor and wait by the door for her. It looked like a nice place from the outside. They had a gated pool and a workout room on the first floor. I wondered if she had roommates or if it was just her. Would it bother her that I came to bug her at her own place? I wondered if I should have met her at the school like I did last time.

Before I could change my mind, Sandra reached the top of the stairs, mail in one hand and a large tote bag in the other hand with the words "THIS IS A TOTE BAG" printed on it in big block letters. I smiled at her weird sense of humor, so I was grinning like an idiot when she noticed me. She stopped short and blinked. "You're waiting outside?"

"What do you mean?" I asked.

"Most dead people don't worry about doors."

I shrugged. "It felt rude to just barge in."

She raised her eyebrows. "Well, you're the first one to ever give me that courtesy." She tucked her mail under her arm, unlocked the door, and gestured me inside.

When I floated into Sandra's apartment, the first thing I noticed was not the squeaky clean surfaces or the cinnamon candle smell. It wasn't the pictures of her and her mother around the apartment, or even the inviting bookshelf in the corner with a mixture of books I had and had not read. The first thing I noticed was that she had company. *Lots* of company. Her house was infested with wanderers.

"Hey, Bill," she said to a middle-aged man sitting on a barstool at her counter. "I brought you some more math problems for you to solve."

She set out a worksheet she must have taken from one of the math teachers at the high school. Bill created a pen and paper out of thin air and began furiously working out the problems.

"Patty, I called Mark to give him your message, but he didn't answer," she said to a woman sprawled out on the couch.

Sandra stopped in the living room and put her hands on her hips. "Asher and Oliver, off the fan now." I looked up and saw two little boys hanging from the fan blades as it twirled around.

I counted nine different wanderers hanging around her house, not quite haunting it, but still totally taking over the place. Did she ever get a moment alone, or was she always surrounded by the dead?

"*Híjole* . . ." I whispered. "This is the most haunted house I've ever seen. What are they all doing here?"

Sandra looked at me and smiled tiredly. "It's refreshing

to bring someone over who can see them all."

"No, seriously, is this normal?"

She sighed and plopped down on a kitchen chair. "Yep. Ghosts follow me around all the time. These guys just decided to take up residence in my apartment so they wouldn't have to follow me everywhere. I guess they like that I can see them. I try to help them cross over, but some of them are really stubborn."

"Are they bothering you?" I asked.

I closed my eyes and willed the Light to flare up in my hands. It took longer than usual and I had to concentrate much harder before anything happened. It flickered on the palms of my hands like a flashlight running out of batteries. It also kind of hurt, like I was forcing my body to do something it didn't quite like. Shoving food down my throat when I was already full, or picking a scab. I'd never struggled to create Light before. Was the Darkness already affecting me that badly? Eventually, before I could really freak out, I felt the familiar lightness and contentment and both my hands flared up, glowing balls of Light in each palm.

I looked at Sandra and gestured toward the wanderers. "Do you want me to get rid of them?"

She scowled at me. "Of course not. They need help and it's my job to help them."

"Technically it's the angels' job to deal with wanderers. We have this group called the Rescuers. They go around trying to help the dead who are in denial and—"

"I know," Sandra interrupted. "I'm in contact with them. I'm basically an honorary member."

I blinked as I tried to make sense of what she just said. "But you're not dead."

"No duh."

I smiled slightly. That was like her catch phrase back in high school. Kind of her go-to response to everything I said. It was probably an appropriate response because I'm not that smart.

"Throw him out," a wanderer said from the couch, flipping through channels on the TV with his mind.

Sandra rolled her eyes. "Ignore Terrance. He doesn't like angels."

But I couldn't. Because this "wanderer" was radiating an aura of Darkness. He wasn't a wanderer at all. He was a demon.

I still had a couple balls of Light glowing in my hands so I threw them at the back of his head.

The demon turned and growled at me. "Stupid angel . . ." Then he disappeared in a puff of smoke.

Sandra rounded on me. "What the heck was that? What is wrong with you!"

"He's a demon. I was getting rid of him for you."

"Why would you just assume . . . I was finally starting to get somewhere with him and now you scared him away!"

My mouth popped open. Was I hearing her right? Was she trying to *help* a *demon*? There was no way she could be that naive. Demons are evil and they have evil intentions. They tempt and torment mortals and influence them to become the worst version of themselves.

"You do understand what a demon is, right?" I asked. "You can tell the difference?"

"Yes, I know what a demon is, but no I can't tell the difference. All you dead people look the same to me. My job isn't to judge you, just to help you."

I let out a huff of air. There was no way she was lumping me in the same category as wanderers and demons. Demons spend their afterlives hurting mortals and wanderers just make their lives difficult. Angels dedicate our time to selfless service. We help, not hurt.

I could see from her crossed arms and the firm set of her mouth that there was no use arguing with her. I'd come here for a reason and I figured I should probably get to the point before I wore out my welcome.

"I just came to see if you'd heard anything about Malum. Your demon friend say anything?"

She rolled her eyes at my tone. "No, I haven't heard anything. But if Terrance, 'my demon friend,' ever comes back, I'll ask him. Is there anything else you want?"

The way she said that gave me pause. Like she was used to asking what people wanted from her, and while happy to help, she was also tired of it.

A realization hit me like a fastball to the chest. Obviously she couldn't visually tell the difference between angels, wanderers, and demons. How angels radiate Light, demons Darkness, and wanderers nothing. For some reason her gifts didn't extend to seeing our auras. The only reason she knew I was an angel was because of Jake's little indignant tirade back when Sandra first met us. But she shouldn't have had to rely on our auras to know what we were. Our actions should have been enough.

Yet, I couldn't think of a single time since I ran into her that I'd actually done something to help her. I'd been asking things of her, just like all the spirits hanging around in her house. And the other angels she'd met? I bet the rescuers were constantly asking her to use her gifts to help them with their missions. No wonder she couldn't tell the difference between angels and wanderers. When it came to her, we were always using her. Asking her for things without any thought of her feelings and capabilities. She was mortal and she was doing the job of an angel. That had to be tough with all those mortal limitations we angels don't have to worry about. The dead must have been such a burden to her.

I sat down in a chair across from her and said, "Sandra, do you have a guardian angel?"

She scowled and blinked, confused about the subject change. "I don't know."

"They'd be a family member. And they would be

someone to offer guidance and comfort when you need it."

She sat back and thought on it. "Maybe my aunt Tamara? She shows up every now and then, but she spends most of the time telling me what to do. I've just sort of tuned her out by now. She's gotten kind of naggy."

I'm sure guardian angels would be really annoying to mortals if they knew we were here. I mean, no one listens to all the advice they're given to their face. One of the reasons angel whispers work is that mortals think the ideas we give them are their own, which makes them more likely to listen to them. It's a sad view of humanity, but mankind is known for being prideful.

"I'm not going to tell you what to do," I said, "but she can definitely help you when you need it. That's her job. That, and to offer counsel. Unfortunately, you can see her, so she doesn't get the benefit of being anonymous, but you can bet that if she's telling you to do something, it's probably the right thing to do."

Sandra blinked at me, seeming to say, *I thought you weren't going to tell me what to do.* Aloud, all she said was, "I'll keep that in mind."

"And I'm sorry for casting out that demon without asking you first. Maybe he was listening to you, I don't know. But this is your house and I should have asked first. Just be careful, all right? Their job is to deceive and I'd hate to see you get hurt. I really love your attitude of trying to save everyone, but the sad truth is that not everyone wants to be saved. That's kind of what a demon is. It's someone who was given the opportunity to choose light, and they chose darkness instead."

She nodded and looked away. "Anything else?"

"Yeah, do you need help with the wanderers?" I held up my hands, stopping her before she started yelling at me again. "Not casting them out, helping them cross over. I mean, this is a really big job to expect from one mortal. Not that you're any less capable than an angel, but you do have a few limitations we don't have. Like a full-time job and the need to sleep."

She sighed and shrugged her shoulders. "This is how it's always been. There are countless wanderers around the world. These are the few I've been asked to help."

I thought about wanderers and what they were by definition. Aimless would be the best word to describe them. They're hopeless and sad and in complete denial. They don't want to move on to the next step because that would mean that their life really is over, and they don't realize that it actually gets better from there.

Admittedly, I'd never been the best at helping wanderers cross over. They're kind of annoying to be honest. They just screw around and make my job difficult. But sometimes people just can't move on. The best way I've been able to convince wanderers to join us in The Resting Place is to help them realize that they still have a purpose. Just because their mortal life is over, it doesn't mean that *they* are over. Once they see what they can actually contribute, they soften up, because it feels good to be needed. It gives their afterlives meaning.

"Sandra, have you ever asked your wanderers to help *you?*"

She raised an eyebrow. "How could they help me? And why would I ask them for help when they're the ones that need help?"

"I have an idea," I said with a smile. "But I need to run it by Raj and Ying Yue first."

"Who are—"

"I'll be back."

And I disappeared in a puff of Light, too excited to use the door.

chapter 19
DEMON DATE

I couldn't find Raj, so I tracked down Hermes to run my idea by him. I assumed he had some influence on the demon hunters since he's in charge of everything, but he just shook his head at me. "The demon hunters are in charge of the demon hunters. I cannot give permission for missions specific to your task force."

I sighed. "Really? Well, can you tell me where Raj or Ying Yue are? Or should I just wait until our next meeting to bring this up?"

Hermes smiled. "Oh, the impatience of youth. I could tell you where they are, but they are both visiting family right now, so I think it's best you wait until your next meeting."

"All right, thanks."

There were a number of things I could do while I was waiting. Check in on my family, volunteer at the front desk, even though I wasn't on duty, meet up with my demon. When I was alive and I had a bunch of homework to do, I usually would start with the worst homework assignment to get it out of the way. I figured if I applied that to this situation, I could get my demon date out of the way. The idea made me queasy.

"What about Jake?" I asked Hermes. "Is he visiting family?"

Hermes closed his eyes tapping into his spidey sense. "No," he finally said. "He's watching his friend from high school play video games. Would you like me to call him back?"

I snorted. Kindness race my butt.

"Yeah," I said. "If you don't mind. Thanks."

I felt so dumb that I had to depend on Jake at a time like this, but I was the farthest thing from cool and I needed some pointers for my demon date. So I waited as Hermes used his super telekinesis to call my friend back to The Resting Place. A moment later, Jake popped into existence next to me.

"Hey, mate. You called? I helped twenty-one by the way. Did I win?"

I rolled my eyes. "Yeah, I only got to five. What did you do, just hang out at a mall or something and help every random stranger you saw?"

"Yeah! So what's up?"

Hermes was listening, so I give Jake a "let's talk over there" gesture with my head. Jake walked with me and finally I said, "Dude, I'm freaking out about this demon date. I have no idea how to act. I obviously can't be myself. I need her to like my fake identity, but I'm not cool enough to know how to even fake being cool. How do you get a girl to like you?"

I could tell Jake was fighting it, but a laugh squeaked out anyway.

"It's not funny!"

"Dorky David seducing a demon."

I gagged. "I am not trying to *seduce* her."

This made him laugh even harder. Then he sighed. "Okay, so this girl already said she didn't trust you, so you defo don't want to come off too strong. Have fun, then at the end of the night go for a walk or something. Try holding her hand. Tell her something personal and see if she starts talking. Just make sure you're actually listening. Girls hate it when guys don't listen to them. They get really mad and then you can't figure out what you did wrong and then they get even more mad."

I raised an eyebrow. "Is this a lesson you learned from experience?"

He pursed his lips. "Maybe. I was a stupid teenager, give me a break."

I laughed and he shoved my shoulder.

"Does all of this apply to demons?" I asked.

Jake shrugged. "I've never dated a demon, but I'm pretty sure it's the same concept as dating a mortal. They have all the same feelings we do."

I covered my face with my hands and groaned. "I can't do this."

"You got this, mate."

"No, I do not 'got this, mate,'" I said, butchering his accent.

Jake chuckled. "Just think to yourself: what would Jake do?"

I gave him a look. "Didn't you just say girls used to slap you all the time?"

"True. Maybe I'm not the best example. Just be yourself. She'll be right."

What would Jake do? What would Jake do?
What *would* Jake do?
After changing my clothes into the young Mike O'Donnell outfit, I apparated over to the bar and waited hesitantly by the door. She was in her usual place, totally visible to all the mortals around her. I wondered why she did that. Most demons liked to be sneaky and invisible, but she was always visible for all the world to see.

I couldn't help freaking out a little and my mind was a tornado of questions.

How do I approach her? What if she says no? Is it bad if I want her to say no? I can't believe Raj and Ying Yue are encouraging this. I can't deceive a demon! And gross, what if she kisses me? What if she wants me to kiss her? What if she doesn't want me to kiss her?

I mean it's a first date, that would be moving way too fast. Or is that normal? Also, is what's normal for mortals what's normal for demons? I'm gonna barf and I don't even have the ability to do that.

"David."

I jumped about a mile in the air. She was standing right next to me. When had she gotten there? "You scared the crap out of me," I said clutching my heart.

She just smirked.

"I still don't know your name," I admitted.

"Sheila," she said. "So do you have a place in mind?"

I almost asked, "For dinner?" but then I remembered our plans. We were going to go haunt fake haunted houses. And I'd totally forgotten to find one.

"I thought I'd let the lady choose," I said as smoothly as I could. Jake would have been laughing his head off if he were watching. I was so not off to a great start.

"I was hoping you'd say that," Sheila said, "because there's this one place I've really been wanting to go to."

"Taco Bell?"

"Um . . . what?"

I grimaced, mentally scolding myself for showing my weirdness too soon.

"Is it the scariest place you could think of?" I asked.

"Nope," she grinned. "It's one of those corny kid ones. You know with creepy clowns and fake severed hands hanging from the ceilings? No one would expect a real demon to pop up in one of those."

My stomach turned queasy. She wanted to terrorize kids? The super scary haunted houses are expected to be terrifying. This was so much worse.

"Love it," I said, with a fake grin. "Lead the way." I held my hand out and she smiled, putting her hand in mine.

"Make it so they can't see you yet," she said. "We're gonna pop up as a surprise."

I made myself invisible and she teleported us there in a cloud of smoke. I had to turn around so she didn't see me choking on the Darkness. That stuff's the worst.

We were in the middle of a parking lot of costumed teens laughing and texting as they hopped from booth to booth, trying to win stupid prizes from rigged games. Popcorn bags and soda cans littered the asphalt. There was a corn maze to the left where some kids were playing Marco Polo. The haunted house was just a few trailers connected to each other, and while I couldn't see inside yet, I could already hear the recorded evil laughs and frightened teenagers screaming. A group of friends pushed each other out the exit, yelling and giggling at each other.

A girl in a Harley Quinn outfit shoved her friend dressed as a sexy nurse. "You were so scared!"

"Was not!"

A kid dressed as . . . a potato? . . . laughed. "Did you just live stream that?"

The nurse squealed. "Oh my gosh, don't you dare post that."

"It's a live stream, smart one. It's already posted."

Sheila looked over at me with excitement on her face. "Ready?"

I forced a smile and nodded, letting go of her hand.

We floated through one of the trailers together. The inside was dark and misty from a fog machine. Recorded laughs and cries played from speakers hidden behind ugly, headless mannequins. A creepy doll popped out of the wall next to me and I screamed, making Sheila laugh. I almost screamed again when I noticed how she'd transformed herself. Gone was the olive-toned skin and coppery hair. She was now pale as a sheet with black hair hanging in front of her face like that girl from *The Ring*. I followed her lead and made myself look like a vampire.

"This okay?" I asked, turning toward her.

"You look like a little kid's Halloween costume," she said, and her voice was low and gravelly, making me jump again. She looked like a demon. I mean, she *was* a demon, but now she looked and sounded the way mortals expected them to be—evil incarnate, rather than just vengeful dead humans.

Before I could change my vampire costume to match Sheila's expectations of terrifying, two middle-school-aged girls squealed as they ran from the previous trailer to ours, an evil cackle carrying through the tent flaps.

Tentatively, they made their way through the headless mannequins, looking around themselves, anticipating something popping out at them. Sheila floated through the girls, making them shiver, then she blew on one of their necks. The girl squealed and looked behind herself but couldn't see anyone there. Then Sheila made herself visible and the girl screamed. Her knees give way and she collapsed into her friend, who was also screaming bloody murder. Sheila grunted garbled nonsense and started crawling after them on the floor. The girls picked themselves up and stumbled past me, crying. From the smell, I was pretty sure one of them peed her pants. I wanted to go after them and make sure they were okay, but I forced myself to stay where I was.

Sheila straightened up and held her hands out as if to say, *Hello? Why are you just standing there?*

I smiled and nodded as I came up with some way to contribute to the most terrifying haunted house these kids had ever seen. Instead of a stupid vampire, I made myself look like a "ghost." I hate that word. I guess technically I am a ghost, but the connotation is different. According to pop culture, ghosts are pale hollow-eyed apparitions that moan as they drag their chains behind them. So I made myself look like that and stood in front of the exit. I planned to make myself visible right as they were about to walk through. Then when they tried to push me out of the way, their hands would go right through me. Then they'd know I was a real "ghost." Or just assume I was a really convincing hologram.

A group of teenage boys guffawed as they stalked into the room, trying to act completely unaffected in front of their friends.

"This is so lame," one of them said.

Another one shrugged as the doll popped out of the wall.

"It's made for babies," another said. "I heard there's a better one down the road."

Then Sheila blew on one of their necks and they shivered, turning around. "Not funny, Noah!"

"I didn't do anything," Noah said.

Then Sheila appeared and the four boys screamed as high and loud as the girls who had just passed through. They ran to the exit and I appeared out of nowhere, yelling like a crazy person. It happened just as I had predicted it. They screamed even louder and tried to shove me out of the way, but their hands went right through me. One of them cried as he ran through my body and out the door, followed by his friends who could see that there was no other way out.

Sheila flipped her hair out of her face and laughed. I did my best to make my face look like someone who was having fun, but I couldn't make my smile meet my eyes. I held my hand out for a high five and Sheila slapped it.

Another group came through before Sheila and I were

in our positions. We were still visible, and while we frightened the kids, they thought we were just people wearing costumes. Then Sheila disappeared and did her little breath trick, sending the kids sprinting to the exit like their pants were on fire.

If I was alive and working in the haunted house, this would have actually been kind of fun. It would have just been some silly prank, and while I would be scaring people, they'd know it was just me. But Sheila and I were the real deal. We were the evil ghosts and demons everyone secretly fears and I couldn't help but feel sick to my stomach at the nightmares these kids were going to have because they met a legit demon that day. Sure, their friends would laugh it off and their parents wouldn't believe them, but deep down they'd know they saw something evil. Is that what I was now? Was I evil?

After an hour of scaring the bejeebers out of everyone who came through, I just couldn't take it anymore.

"I'm bored," I said, removing my fake costume. "Let's go check out the corn maze."

Sheila shrugged and transformed back into herself. "Sure."

We made ourselves invisible again and floated through the trailer and crowds of people until we got to the maze. After her little display, the last thing I wanted to do was touch my demon date, but I took her hand, like Jake told me to do, and we walked together.

"That was a blast," I said, with my permanently fake grin. "You were terrifying."

She smiled. "You were all right, I suppose."

"Tell me something," I said, trying to think of something personal to talk about. "How come you always reveal yourself to the mortals at that bar? Most of us like to work in subtle ways."

We walked through a guy kissing his girlfriend up against the haystacks. Unlike the kids in the haunted house, they had no idea we just passed by.

"The bartender just got dumped by his girlfriend of eight years who looks just like me," she explained. "He's the mortal I'm assigned to, so I just go in and sit at the bar, reminding him of everything that he's lost."

"Ouch. That's harsh."

"I know, right?" She grinned. "I don't even have to tempt him to do bad things, because just the sight of me makes him angry and depressed."

"That's pretty genius."

"Now you tell me something," she said. "Why do you care so much about finding your dad? No offense, but he's . . . Well, everyone hates him."

Think of a good lie, think of a good lie, think of a good lie . . .

"Well . . ." I started, clucking my tongue as I waited for the magic words to just pop into my head. They didn't. "I want to be like him," I finally said.

She raised an eyebrow. "You want everyone to hate

you?"

"Yeah."

She looked at me like I was totally crazy, which I probably was. "Why?"

"Well, if they hate me, at least they're thinking about me. I'm always overshadowed by my dad. Maybe if he taught me to be like him, people would notice me too."

All right, that wasn't terrible as far as lies go, I thought. *And it sounds really personal, which Jake said was the best way to make Sheila open up.*

Sheila almost looked like she felt bad for me, which was crazy because she was evil. Her eyebrows came together in a contemplative scowl. She sighed loudly and leaned back against a barrel of hay.

"I might be able to hook you up," she said, looking down at her toes.

"What do you mean?"

"I may be in contact with him. I could mention you want to meet him and see if he's interested."

My eyebrows almost met my hairline. In all the scenarios of tonight I played in my head, I never imagined it ending like this. She could set up a time and place for me to meet Malum. Me, David, face to face with the Son of Evil. Again. I knew I should have been excited. We'd been trying to root out his location since he escaped and this would be the perfect opportunity. We could set up an ambush and have him captured in no time. But the minute

I started to imagine this meet-and-greet, I felt the fear seeping through me again and I froze, staring ahead of me in terror as I remembered what it was like when he had his hands around my throat, whispering every terrible thought I never even thought to have. That feeling of wanting to run, but feeling so stuck in my nightmares that I couldn't even remember how to move. New nightmares joined the old ones that were already too dark to discuss. These new ones had me as the bad guy, working with Malum. Father and son laughing as humanity screamed and the world burned.

"David!"

I blinked and shivered out of my momentary paralysis. Sheila was looking at me like she'd been saying my name for a while now and was a little freaked out. I frowned, thinking how odd it was that *I'd* just freaked out a demon.

"Sorry," I said.

"Are you okay?" It weirded me out that she actually looked concerned.

"Yeah, I just . . . " I trailed off, too drained to even come up with a lie.

Another problem with this situation came to mind. Did Malum even have a son? How were we going to swing this if I showed up claiming to be his son and he knew I wasn't him.

Somehow my brain kicked back on and I said, "Yeah, I'd like to meet him, but could you not mention I'm his son? Maybe just say you know someone who wants to join him."

She looked at me suspiciously. "Why don't you want me to mention you're his son? Also, wouldn't he know once he sees you?"

"I've never actually met the guy," I said. "I was the bastard son he never knew about."

Sheila considered this, then nodded, accepting my story. "All right."

"Thanks," I said, so relieved I actually smiled.

Sheila smiled back, and then just stared at me, stepping closer. I panicked. *Oh no . . . is she going to kiss me? Is she waiting for me to kiss her? What do I do? What would Jake do?*

I steeled myself and inwardly cringed.

Without thinking I grabbed her face with my hands and kissed her. I didn't have a lot of kissing experience—okay, I'll be honest, I didn't have any—but even without other comparisons, I could confidently say this one was *disgusting*. Her Darkness seeped through her lips and into my mouth. It was like kissing someone who'd just taken a drag from their cigarette. Except instead of smoking weed or crack, they're smoking pure evil. I tried not to gag as she wrapped her arms around my shoulders and neck and pulled me closer. I tried holding my breath, but it didn't help. I was swallowing Darkness and it poured down my throat, filling me with evil thoughts and questions and total despair. I thought I was going to faint.

Finally, I couldn't take it anymore and I pulled away, trying to hide my grimace. She gave me this seductive look and for a confusing second, I kind of wanted to kiss her again.

"I still don't trust you," she whispered.

"I don't trust you either."

Then I disappeared in a puff of Darkness.

When I got back to headquarters I barfed Darkness. It spewed from my mouth for a whole thirty seconds. When it was over, I jumped around shaking my arms and legs, trying to get it all off me.

I wished I had a bedroom where I could shut the door, flop on my bed, and process what on earth just happened. I wasn't sure what I expected to happen when I joined the demon hunters, but it certainly wasn't this. I had just kissed a demon and now I had a meet-and-greet with the Prince of Darkness. *Me*. David. The kid who cried when Sam told me Elena was an alien and we would have to send her back to her mothership. The kid who was afraid of "pool sharks" until I was, like, ten years old.

The guy that froze up and did absolutely nothing when Malum escaped.

chapter 20
DEPRESSED ANGELS

Conference room nine was exactly the same as it had always been, but the people in it were not. Mainly it was spending so much time with demons and Darkness, but there were also the terrible atrocities that Raj had just reported were Malum's doing. Another school shooting, a terrorist attack, serial killers actually joining forces for mass killings.

I felt myself curling up inside, wishing I could hide under a blanket and block it all out. Fear spiked, making me twitchy and jumpy. I eyed every shadow, positive that Malum would materialize from it and lunge for my throat. By looking around, I could see I wasn't the only one negatively affected by all this crap. Jake was quiet, Frederick and William weren't debating, and Daisy wasn't a little girl anymore.

I may have mentioned that angels can look like whatever we want, but most of us choose to look the way we did before we died. As much as people complain about their appearance, after a lifetime of looking like you, you tend to get attached. I wasn't sure exactly what it meant that Daisy didn't want to be a little girl anymore, but it made me sad. She still had her red hair and bangs and that scary glare, but now seemed overwhelmed and tired. I guess she just didn't feel like a child anymore. Her experiences had aged her, and her appearance reflected that.

Ying Yue created a whiteboard and a marker. "All right, let's compare notes and write what we've learned, then we can talk about next steps. Let's start with William."

William sighed. "I regret to say that I have nothing yet to share. The demon I have been following has been resistant to me. I need more time."

Ying Yue frowned and nodded. "Frederick?"

"I am still building a rapport with my demon, but I do not believe she is privy to any special information. She appears frightened by him. I've come to the conclusion that Malum often terrorizes and uses other demons. Perhaps Helga has experience with this. I will return with more information next time."

Ying Yue turned and wrote: *Other demons frightened of Malum.*

"Natalie?"

Natalie shook her head. "Nothing yet."

Ying Yue's face tightened, trying to hide her disappointment.

"Ted?"

Ted lifted his head. He'd been leaning his forearms on his thighs, his head in his hands. He took a deep breath and said, "I think this time is different than the last time he escaped."

"How so?" Raj asked.

"Well, last time he just caused panic and terror, right?"

Raj nodded.

Ted swallowed nervously. "My demon mentioned something about a change in management. He said he and a group of his friends were supporting him. I don't know much more than that."

"My demon mentioned that, too," Jake said quietly. "Something about a plan to take over."

"A revolution?" William asked. "Against whom?"

Daisy looked up with her typical glare. "The Evil One."

The room was silent. What did it mean? A change in management? Malum wanted to take over from the Evil One? Could he do that? Why? And why would some demons think he'd be better in charge? Couldn't they already do whatever they wanted?

Ying Yue turned and wrote: Possible Motive - take over from the Evil One.

She acted unaffected by the strange and frightening news. "David?"

I'd been dreading this. I was starting to seriously doubt whether I should actually do it. Meet Malum? Me? First of all, I'd mess it up somehow. Freeze, blow my cover, I don't know but I'd do something wrong. Second of all, I didn't want to. I was sick of all the Darkness and evil surrounding me all the time. He'd figure out my secret and then he'd attack me and I knew I wasn't strong enough to fend him off.

And yet . . . I knew I couldn't pass up this opportunity. People were depending on me.

I sighed. "My demon is in contact with Malum. She said she might be able to hook me up with a meeting with my 'dad.'"

The room was completely silent and they all stared at me, their faces a combination of awe and terror. Were they frightened for me? Or worried I'd screw it all up?

Jake turned on me. "You held that back 'til the end?"

"Don't worry," I said, knowing Ying Yue was about to point out the huge flaw. "I told Sheila I was a kid Malum didn't know about. I told her not to mention the whole 'son' thing."

Rajesh's face finally broke into a typical grin and he slapped me on the back. "I knew it!" he said. "I knew my instincts with you were right. David, you are a game changer! We'll come up with a plan for you to meet him and set up an ambush. Don't do anything yet, don't even contact your demon until we have a plan." He turned to

Ying Yue. "We should go talk to the other task forces. Set up a meeting with Hermes."

She nodded and they disapparated, leaving the six of us to stare at each other with dumbfounded expressions.

I groaned and put my head in my hands.

"You got this, mate," Jake said, patting my back. "C'mon, let's go for a walk."

We sat on our bench, and I unloaded everything that had happened on my date with Beelzebub. How I acted like a demon and scarred some kids for life. How I deceived a demon and still felt bad about it. My nasty kiss with Demon Breath. How scared I was about meeting Malum again. It was a lot of me talking and I felt bad. I was sure Jake had his own demons to deal with (no pun intended), but he just listened as I went on and on like some dude laying out on a futon while he spilled his guts to his therapist.

"She'll be right, mate," Jake said when I was finally done. "I was wrong before. You are a demon hunter. Your instincts out there were ace!"

I nodded, mentally disagreeing.

"You want a distraction?" he asked.

I shrugged, then shot him a look when I realized something.

"What?"

"Distraction has three syllables."

He counted on his fingers to check. "Well, I've cactused that rule, haven't I?"

"You're weird, man."

"That's why we're mates. Now, I'd love to hear you whinge on all arvo, but my little brother has his first footy game today."

I sat up. "Really? Man, that kid's getting old. Wait, footy's rugby, right?"

"The only sport worth playing! I'm stoked!"

I smiled. "You gonna get out there on the field and play with them?"

"Defo."

"Well, have fun. Don't die this time."

He slapped me upside the head, and I cringed. "Too far?"

He just rolled his eyes. "Shut it, sneezy. And don't kiss any demons while I'm away!"

chapter 21
SANDRA IS GRUMPS

With all the craziness going down, all I really wanted to do was talk with my mom. I used to talk to her about everything. I know most teenage guys like to keep to themselves, but my mom and I were kind of . . . friends. I mean, obviously she told me what to do and I had to listen, but other than that, we would just kind of hang out. Some nights after dinner, we would sit and talk until Elena would get bored, and dad would say something about yard work, and then it was just me and mom, chilling and talking about everything and nothing.

We couldn't really do that anymore, but every now and then I'd catch her in her car venting to nobody and I'd pretend she was venting to me.

I hope I'm not giving an inaccurate representation of my parents. I've only shared the good stuff. Obviously, they would fight sometimes, and we'd get into arguments, just like all families. There were moments when I got really angry or upset, I just don't remember them. The living romanticize the dead, and we tend to do the same thing for the living. Is that such a bad thing? Really, it's just focusing on the good in people. We should do that anyway.

I decided to visit Mom. I wasn't on front desk duty for another hour, so I had some time. And then I could stop by and talk to Sandra about the idea I forgot to bring up in the last demon hunter meeting.

When I got to the front office, it was just as packed as the first day of school. Probably because Mom wasn't there and Yvonne was all by herself. After a moment of confusion, I put the pieces together. My mom probably caught whatever my dad had over the weekend and was taking the day off. Good for her. I decided to check on her at home after I talked with Sandra.

It was first period, so I was able to check on Dani too. I melted through the door, startling Sandra, and froze.

"*Sorry*," I mouthed. Then I pointed at Dani as my excuse for why I was there. Sandra just pursed her lips and turned away. Still mad at me about how I acted at her apartment, probably.

Dani's sign language interpreter was just standing at the front of the room, not even bothering to translate anything Sandra was saying as she lectured about the Cold War. Interpreter lady was glaring pointedly at Dani who wasn't even paying attention.

Dani was smiling at her lap, which I assumed meant she was texting. I don't know how kids think they're being slick by texting under the desk. Nobody just smiles down at their crotch like that.

"Hey, cuz. You should pay attention," I said. *"Don't text and learn."*

I was glad she couldn't hear me because that was probably the lamest thing I'd ever said. I leaned down to get a closer look at who she was texting. Some dude named Tyler.

Tyler: hey boo

Dani: im so bored!

Tyler: i think miss johnson skipped her coffee this morning

Dani: she looks grumps

Tyler: im grumps

Dani: follow me to the closet by the bathroom after class and ill make you un grumps

Ugh, gross . . .

I looked up. Sandra did look a little grumpy. She kept glaring at the back of the room, and I soon understood why. Moaning Myrtle and Dr. Crowe had just appeared. I expected them to start knocking stuff over or banging on the walls, but instead they floated over to Sandra as she was teaching and moaned in her face. Sandra did her best to ignore them, but they kept circling around her, being really weird and annoying.

"*I'm with a class,*" Sandra said out of the corner of her mouth.

They didn't care. They were just demanding attention in the rudest possible way. I tried not to intervene, but I felt really bad. She was valiantly pressing forward in her lecture, but the two wanderers were getting so loud, I couldn't hear a word Sandra was saying.

Unable to stand it anymore, I floated over to them and said, "Come on, guys. You can talk to her later. She's teaching right now."

They ignored me.

"Here, if you want someone to listen to your problems, I'd be happy to help," I said. "Let's just go somewhere else."

They continued to ignore me.

"Guys, come on. You're being really rude." I took their arms and tried to drag them away, but that turned out to be a bad idea. They turned their attention toward me and screamed bloody murder. I could see Sandra fighting the instinct to cover her ears.

I took a deep breath and closed my eyes, trying to create Light with my hands. It hurt just like it had before, only worse. I'd used so much Darkness on my date with Sheila and it was definitely affecting me. I winced as the Light sputtered and finally flared to life. As soon as I was holding the little orbs, the pain was gone, and I felt like I'd just laid my aching body in a nice, warm bath. I held up my hands and looked at Sandra for permission. I was prepared for her to glare at me or get mad, but she just nodded as she changed the slide on her Power Point.

I blasted the two ghosties, who wailed as they were blown into the next room. Sandra smiled and gave me a grateful nod. Okay, so maybe she wasn't still mad at me.

Sandra droned—I mean lectured—on for the next forty minutes, and I tried to get Dani to listen, but I couldn't blame her for not paying attention. The lesson was a little dry. I was relieved when the bell rang and all the teenagers bodily shoved themselves through the door. When the class was finally gone, leaving blessed silence in their wake, I sat myself at the edge of Sandra's desk.

"Don't you want to see what Dani's up to?" Sandra asked as she pulled a bag of chips from a lunch box that said "Treat yo' self."

"Not really," I said. "She's making out with Tyler in a closet somewhere. At least, that's what they were texting about."

Sandra rolled her eyes. "I knew they were dating. They're always shooting glances at each other across the room. So, what can I do for you, Mr. Garcia?" She paused and looked me up and down. "Just out of curiosity, and if you don't mind me asking, how did a white guy end up with a name like Garcia?"

"I'm half Mexican."

"No, I'm talking about your dad. He's where the Garcia name comes from, isn't he?"

"Oh, yeah, we have no idea," I said with a shrug. "My dad did a DNA test once and he was like 70% British and the rest was French and German. So, it really doesn't make any sense."

"Huh. Weird." She popped a chip into her mouth and leaned back in her chair. "So why are you here?"

"First, I wanted to apologize. Sorry for barging into your apartment and being all, '*I am a holy angel and must cast out all evil! Fear my righteous indignation!*'"

"That was a great impression of yourself."

"Thanks."

"Especially that weird voice you used. Spot on. I always thought you sounded like an anime character."

I laughed. "Shut up. Anyway, I came here to share my idea with you for your wanderer friends."

Sandra had just popped another potato chip in her mouth when a voice over the intercom said, "*Teachers and staff, please excuse this interruption. We are having an emergency meeting in the media center. If you are not with a class, please come immediately. If you are with a class, please continue as usual, then come to the media center as soon as you are available. Thank you.*"

Sandra and I exchanged confused glances. I followed her as she power walked to the library, cutting through a gaggle of freshmen laughing hysterically over something that probably wasn't that funny, their braces flashing in the fluorescent lights. I knew this meeting wasn't my business, but I was curious. Sandra actually held the door open for me when we got there, which I thought was pretty cute. She knew I could just float through, but she was being polite and treating me like a person.

It was pretty standard, as far as libraries went. The perimeter of the room was covered with bookshelves and cheesy posters of celebrities trying to convince kids that it's cool to read. The left side of the room had rows of old, crappy computers while the right had a bunch of tables with chairs. The teachers didn't sit. They all stood around whispering, a tension permeating the air. They didn't know what was happening, and I could tell this kind of impromptu meeting in the middle of the day was far from typical.

Eventually the principal walked in, and the room fell silent. Teachers tensed as they took in Principal Newman's red eyes and blotchy face.

"Teachers." Her voice cracked and she cleared her throat. "Gloria Garcia was in a car accident this morning. I just received word from her husband that she's passed away."

chapter 22
FLORES Y FRIJOLES

"No," I whispered. "No, no, no, no, no." I brought my hands to my head and shook it back and forth. We did not need another death in the family! It was terrible when I died. They were all broken for a long time. And now Mom? This was going to kill them. How could this happen?

Teachers all around the room brought their hands to their mouths as their eyes filled with tears. Already people were mourning her death. I was still too shocked to even cry about it.

Sandra brought her phone to her ear, the way she did when she talked to dead people in public. "David, I am so sorry," she whispered, her eyes watering and threatening to spill over.

"Don't be sorry for me," I said, tears finally coming. I looked down as they fell and disappeared before hitting the ground. "Be sorry for my family who just lost a wife and a mother. My family who has already dealt with so much. A family of five is now down to three and—"

I froze and gasped as a crucial bit of information clicked in my brain. I felt a really inappropriate grin spread across my face.

"Wait a minute. *I'm* dead." I grabbed Sandra's shoulders, forgetting for a minute that I couldn't touch her. My arms went right through, but I didn't even notice. I was too busy spinning in circles and saying, "*I'm* dead! Don't you know what this means?"

Sandra looked at me like I'd started laughing at someone's funeral, but I was too impatient to stick around and explain.

I should have checked on my family first. That's what a good angel would have done. They were receiving the worst shock a person could get, one that would affect them for the rest of their lives. If ever they needed me, it was now. But I just couldn't help myself. I hadn't talked to or hugged my mom in ten years and I was not waiting another second.

I apparated over to the front desk and flew to the front of the line. Rudely shoving someone out of the way, I slammed my hand down on the bell over and over, demanding immediate attention. "Gloria Garcia. Maiden name Ramirez. Which door?"

I could tell by Adrika's scandalized frown that she was about to tell me to get to the back of the line, but luckily Grandma Gertie was also working the desk. She smiled and checked the clipboard before saying, "Door number five, sweetheart."

You don't technically need to go through a door to get to The Resting Place, but we have doors spaced around the perimeter for new arrivals. I guess walking through the door is supposed to be symbolic of something.

When I got to Door 5, there was already a crowd gathered round in anticipation. I wondered why Hermes hadn't called me back sooner. I should have been here first. I landed in the back of the crowd just as Nana Maria opened the door and ushered my mom into The Resting Place.

I could barely see her through all the bodies, and I let out a frustrated growl. A bunch of dead Rarmirezes were beginning to approach her with smiles and welcoming arms. I'd have just floated over everyone, but angels don't crowd like mortals do because they aren't constrained by gravity. They all floated at different levels, so there was someone above, beneath, or in front of me wherever I turned. I tried to make my way through the crowd, but there were too many people. Eventually I dropped to the ground and just started shoving people out of the way, pleading, "Let me through!" The crowd parted for me as people realized that this kid just needed his mom *right now*.

"*Mom!*" I yelled when I could finally see her.

She gasped and turned as I sprinted toward her, tears

flying from my face.

"David?" she cried. Her face was so overjoyed she looked distraught. "Is it really you?"

I barreled into her, and she threw her arms around me. She smelled like lemon bars and garden dirt and home. The familiarity felt like falling into a well broken-in recliner. These were the arms that held me as a baby and picked me up when I fell down. The arms that tied my shoelaces and neck ties and fidgeted with my collars. The arms that hugged me too tight. The arms that had to be pried off of my broken body when I died. She squeezed the living daylights out of me and kept repeating "my David" over and over and kissing me all over my head and face.

"Oh, my boy, I missed you so much!"

"Me too," I said, my head buried into her shoulder. "I can't believe you're here."

I'll admit it. I bawled like a baby. Because here's the thing about being dead: it's not as sad for us as it is for mortals. We still get to see our loved ones whenever we want. We're as much a part of their lives as we were before. But it wasn't until my mom was there hugging the afterlife out of me that I realized how much I'd missed her. It makes a difference to be seen and heard and touched.

My mom rubbed my back and said, "This is the best and worst day of my life."

I pulled away, wiping my own eyes. "I hate to break it to you, Mom, but your life is over. These are all dead people," I said, gesturing around me.

"David," Nana scolded. "Be sensitive or I'll get the *chancla.*"

"Sorry," I said. I forgot newly dead people weren't used to the word "dead" being thrown about so casually. "Can I come with you on your tour?" I asked Mom and Nana.

I knew what came next. Nana would show her around, drop Mom off at the front office for her interview with The Big Man, and then she'd meet Hermes who'd give her a job. Then would come the depressing part of attending her funeral, which really sucks because funerals are awful even when you're dead.

"I forbid you from leaving my side ever again," Mom said, squeezing my hand. I couldn't stop looking at her face. That little wrinkle between her eyebrows, the way both sides of her hair curled to the left, her dark brown eyes that almost looked black. It's not like I hadn't seen her in a long time, but it was different seeing her next to me. Almost like she'd been the ghost before and now she was real.

Of course we had to be interrupted.

DAVID, YOU'RE NEEDED ELSEWHERE.

I scowled. *C'mon, Hermes. Can't it wait? My mom—*

JUST DIED, LEAVING BEHIND A FAMILY WHO NEEDS

COMFORT AND REASSURANCE.

I'll admit something really selfish here. I didn't want to go comfort my family. First of all, I knew there was nothing I could do to make it better. It was going to suck for them for a very long time and there was no changing that. Second of all, I knew it would bring me down, and with all the Darkness I'd been using lately it was going to be really hard to bounce back. I didn't think angels could suffer from depression, but I felt it peeking its head around the corner, waiting for the right moment to latch onto me and never let go.

But I knew this wasn't about me. So I sighed and said, "Actually, Mom, I've gotta go. I'll meet up with you when you're done with your tour and stuff."

"Where are you going?" she asked, her face filled with concern.

"I gotta go do my job," I said with a grin.

Mom smiled. "You got a job?"

"Actually, I've got three jobs. You'll get assignments too. But yeah, I'll see you later and we can catch up. A lot has happened recently. Like a lot, so we should chat, okay? See you soon!" I kissed her cheek and disappeared in a puff of Light, admittedly showing off a bit.

I'll spare you the specifics of the first day. I don't really want to talk about it. It was really sad, which doesn't even begin to give justice to what everyone was going through, but I just don't really feel like reliving it.

The next couple of days were a lot of crying and hugging and comfort food. My house was overrun by Ramirezes and flowers and beans. (Not together. The neighbors brought a lot of flowers and my family brought a lot of beans.) I was just kind of there, more in the way than anything. Hermes was right that I should have been there, but I wasn't really needed. Another thing people don't often realize is that guardian angels aren't just dead people. Living people can be angels too. You see it a lot when people die. Families, friends, and neighbors band together and help each other and us angels don't have much to do. It's after the funeral when we come into play. When friends and neighbors move on with their lives while those that lost someone are still hurting.

The day after Mom died, I did a short shift at the front desk before heading back to my dad's house. I talked to Raj briefly who told me I was excused from demon hunter duties until after the funeral. That was nice of him. Dad, Elena, Sam, Tata, and a bunch of aunts and uncles were sitting around the dinner table making funeral arrangements. Rocco was in the family room watching a Disney movie with some cousins (they weren't first cousins, but our family's so big we just call everyone cousin), and Ginger was in the corner sitting by herself doing nothing, which was very out of character.

"You okay, Ginny?" I asked.

She stared down at her lap.

I patted her knee, looking around for someone to come talk to her. Dani was curled up on the couch texting her boyfriend, I assumed. I thought it was time she put her phone away. I knew what she was doing. She was seeking comfort in her friends because she was worried her family wouldn't understand. Young people do that. I did that. I still do, to be honest. I don't know why we don't realize that if you just talk to your family, you'll find that they understand better than you think.

"Hey, Daniella, do you see Ginger over there?"

Dani blinked and briefly glanced up from her phone, then went back to texting.

"You should put your phone down and go see if your cousin's okay."

Dani looked up again, frowned sympathetically, then went back to texting.

I raised my eyebrows and folded my arms. *"Put your phone away now, or it's mine. I don't want to say it again."*

Yikes, I thought. *Sandra's teacher voice is rubbing off on me.*

Dani sighed and ripped her eyes from her phone before setting it aside. She walked over and sat next to Ginger.

Awesome Elena had learned sign language as soon as she heard Daniella was deaf. I tried too, but I sucked at it. And I didn't have a lot of time to practice with her because

I died when she was four. Anyway, Elena taught it to her kids when they were born. I really admired her for that. I mean, we don't even see Dani that often, but I know it meant a lot to her.

You okay? she asked in ASL.

Ginger shook her head.

Are you sad? Dani asked.

Ginger nodded.

Want to tell me why?

Ginger finally lifted her head and started responding in sign language. *I never got to give Nana the picture I drew.*

Dani gave her a sad smile. *Do you still have it? Will you show it to me?*

Ginger nodded and pulled out a folded piece of paper from her pocket and gave it to Dani. It was a picture of a rainbow unicorn with a speech bubble that said "i luv yoo!" Dani smiled at it and said, *We should give it to her.*

How? Ginny asked.

We can mail it to her.

Ginger's eyes widened. *But she died. She doesn't have a mailbox.*

Sure she does. We'll put it on her casket when she is buried, and if we close our eyes and cross our fingers, the picture will show up in her mailbox in heaven.

Aww, I thought. That was actually kind of sweet.

After that conversation, Dani and Ginger went and got

some ice cream from the freezer and ate it outside, away from all the people. I could see a cute little friendship budding. It's funny how you can know someone a long time and never really get to know them. Then one day you realize you have all this stuff in common and they become your new favorite person. Kind of like how I went to Sandra's school since kindergarten, but we never even talked until we were lab partners, and never really hung out until I died.

I spent the rest of the day giving people ideas and words of comfort and sometimes I just kind of sat around, listening to conversations. For a while I closed my eyes as I listened. I've always loved listening to people talk, especially people I love. When I was alive there were times when I'd be getting ready in the morning and I'd hear my family laughing and joking out in the family room, and I'd just sit against the door, close my eyes, and listen. I didn't want to join them, because it would spoil the moment. And there's something nice about listening to people without having to worry about your own reaction. Some of my favorite memories were long car rides when Mom and Dad thought I was asleep so they'd talk to each other in hushed tones about things they wouldn't have said in front of me. I got to hear a different side of them. A side that didn't have to put on the adult front of always knowing what they're doing. I got to see their human side—and we all know kids don't always see their parents as humans with feelings. They're a different species altogether. A sort of compassionate robot species that has no weaknesses and always knows what to do.

I lay on the couch at home, enjoying one of those rare, beautiful listening moments. There were tears and laughter. I counted how many times I heard someone say "*Ay mijo!*" or "*Ay mija!*" and lost count after twenty-three. I also lost count of how many times my dad asked someone else how they were doing when you could tell by his eyes that he, himself, was not okay.

I didn't mean to pry, but he went missing for a while on the third day, so I went to check on him in his room. He was just sitting on the edge of his bed, staring at nothing. His leaking eyes were glazed over in a look that mixed shocked with distraught.

"I miss you, Gloria," he whispered. "It's only been three days, but I miss you so much it hurts."

He sniffed and started crying and it broke my heart. My dad is one of the purest people I've ever met and seeing him weep is one of the worst things I've ever seen. Like stomping on a butterfly or torching the Mona Lisa. It's just *wrong*.

Hey, Hermes? I asked. *I know Mom's still new at being dead and is learning the ropes and all, but is there any way we can get her over here?*

Before I had time to think of a more persuasive

argument, I heard someone yelp behind me and say, "Well, this isn't right." The voice was strangely muffled.

I spun around. "Mom?"

"Where am I?"

From the sound of it she was hanging out in the insulation between two rooms

I laughed. "Mom, I think you landed in the wall."

"Oh . . . I think you're right. How do I get out?"

"You just float through it."

Mom tentatively stuck her head out of the wall and gasped. "Oh, my word!" Pretty soon her body followed, and she spun around, testing out her floating ability. "This is weird."

I smiled. "Yeah, it takes some getting used to."

"The guy in that place told me I should come here. What's his name?"

"We call him Hermes. Yeah, I asked him to. Dad was talking to you, and I thought you'd like to be here. He's not doing so hot."

Mom's face fell as she floated closer to Dad. "Oh Sam . . ."

She tried to put her hand on his face, but it went right through. She gasped and almost started crying herself.

"It's okay, Mom," I said quickly, floating over to her.

"What can I even do for him if he can't see or hear me?" she asked, her lip trembling.

"You're right. He can't see or hear you. But he can feel

you here if you try and if he's paying attention. And Dad's great at paying attention."

"What do you do to let him know you're here?" she asked, trying not to cry in front of me.

"Like this." It was awkward having an audience, and I never thought I'd be the one teaching Mom, but I knew the confusion and helplessness she felt. So, I sat next to Dad on the bed and started talking to him like nothing was wrong. I told him about my day and about my jobs, and I told him I loved him. Dad listened quietly, staring morosely at the floor.

"Mom's here too," I said. I looked up at Mom, then smiled and winked. "Watch this." I worried I'd get in trouble because what I was about to do would probably fall under the category of "haunting," but I was willing to risk it. I hijacked his phone on the nightstand and mentally fiddled with it until it started playing "Bohemian Rhapsody." Dad's head shot up as he grabbed his phone. He looked around and said, "David?" I did a little more angel hocus pocus until his phone played "The Power of Love" by Celine Dion. It was sort of my mom and dad's song, as embarrassing and cheesy as that is. They used to sing it at each other across the house and it was mortifying.

When dad heard the opening notes of the song, he gasped. "Gloria?"

Mom smiled and cried and just started spilling everything to him that she'd been feeling since she'd died, and vice versa.

It wasn't long until I started to feel like I was intruding on something private. I left to give them some privacy and check on the rest of the family.

chapter 23
WHITE MEXICANS

As much as I'd dreaded it, and as depressing as it was, I actually kind of enjoyed those couple days leading up to the funeral. I just like it when the whole family is together. It's sad that it takes someone dying for it to happen. Also, it had been a long time since me, Sam, and Elena were in the same room with each other. It didn't happen often, but every now and then we used to all subtly end up with no plans on a Saturday night and stay up late playing Disney Monopoly, watching *Star Wars* or *Indiana Jones* (depending on which version of Harrison Ford we felt like at the time), and arguing about stupid stuff.

We once had an argument over which one of us was the most Mexican, which is hilarious because we're all super white. We're what I call "white Mexicans." Basically, that means that we have a foot in that culture, and it's a big part of us that we cherish, but it's nothing compared to first- and second-generation immigrants. If we actually went to Mexico, we'd just come across as a bunch of Americans. Also, the white thing is literal in mine and Sam's case. I don't know why Elena was the only one that came out looking like Mom.

On the night of that ridiculous argument—over which of us was the most Mexican—we were all sitting on the carpet in old pajamas with most of the lights off except for the glow of the TV and a lamp shining on our Monopoly board.

I took a bite of my fudgesicle and said, "We all know I'm the most Mexican. I can speak Spanish. Kind of. Well not really, but more than you guys."

"That doesn't make you more Mexican," Elena argued, her pink braces glowing in the dark. "You learned it from school and stuff, not from your family."

"What, you're saying you're more Mexican?" I laughed, causing me to drool a bit of fudge.

Elena blinked and said dryly, "I'm brown and my name is Maria."

"That doesn't count. You go by Elena, and you don't even say it right. It's *el-EN-uh*, not *uh-LAY-nuh*."

"What about me?" asked Sam, putting a castle on the *Toy Story* space. Elena groaned and threw a Cheeto at his head.

I picked it up and ate it, just to gross out Elena. Then, I pointed at Sam with my fudgesicle. "You're not even in the running, *guero*."

Sam narrowed his eyes at me. "Don't even go there, *Baby Blues*. Plus, I eat the most like a Mexican. Which one of us eats *menudo* on New Year's and actually likes it? I have the appetite of a true Mexican. I can take the spice better than you two, and I eat a lot. I ate almost as many *tamales* as Tata last week."

"And you'll get a *panza* just like Tata if you keep it up," I muttered.

"I like *menudo* . . ." Elena said weakly.

I shook my head. "You like the watered-down version without the hooves and stomach and crap."

"They don't put crap in *menudo*," Sam said, the corner of his mouth twitching.

I rolled my eyes. "You know what I meant."

That's when Mom walked in and, subtly joining the argument, popped a yellow *chile* into her mouth, showing off what a real Mexican looks like. Then her eyes watered, and she swore, coughing into her hand. "That was hotter than I expected." She ran to the kitchen for a glass of milk.

You see now why I'm so lame? Given my family of weirdos, I had no chance at being normal. But that's okay, normal people are boring. The point is, it was nice to have everyone together for a change. Just like old times.

I went to the funeral with Mom the next day and it was packed. People were parking a block away. Part of this was because I have a huge extended family, but also because my mom knew a lot of people, having the job she had. A huge chunk of the teachers and staff from school were there, along with a handful of high school kids. I saw Sandra as she found her way to a seat and she waved at me. Then she smiled and tentatively waved at Mom, who freaked out, so I had to explain the whole Sandra situation to her.

"Hmm . . ." Mom smiled and looked at me suspiciously.

"What?" I asked.

"She's cute. And she can see you . . ."

"Yes, such a high bar, being able to see me." I rolled my eyes. "Why are all the older women in my life obsessed with setting me up with someone? Come on, let's find somewhere to sit."

At first Mom and I just floated in the aisles, but once people started speaking it got real depressing real fast. Uncle Richard, who was still blaming himself for my death, spoke first. At least his sense of humor came out a little and made people chuckle a few times when he shared some embarrassing situations his sister got him into when they were little. Mom and I hung out in the back most of the time.

When a cousin got up to sing a song, my mom turned away and gave me an expectant look. "So, are you going to tell me about this little cloud over your head?"

I wanted to cry. She hadn't seen me in over ten years and still she knew me well enough to recognize when something was wrong. So I told her everything. And by everything, I mean *everything,* starting from the day I died. Sadly, it didn't take long to sum up most of the past ten years of filing papers. I spent the majority of the funeral talking about everything that had happened since Malum got out. The outbreak, the attack, signing up for the demon hunters, despite what everyone else said. I paused during my story to give mom a chance to laugh at me. When she didn't, I said, "Wait, you're not going to comment on that?"

"What would I say?"

"That I'm not a fighter. That I'm too young. That I'm too *David.*"

Mom smiled and cupped my cheek in her hand. "You have a strong heart, son. I think you can do anything, including fight demons."

I looked away to wipe my eyes before continuing my story. I told her about using Darkness and how scary and depressing it was, I told her about Sheila and my demon date (which made her laugh hysterically), and I rounded it off with the fun revelation that I would have to face Malum again and how I was freaking out about it.

It felt so good to talk to her. But a part of me knew this little respite from the crazy was coming to a close. And I was right. Once the funeral was over, Hermes contacted me, telling me I was needed in conference room nine.

I gave my mom a hug and a kiss on the cheek. "Sorry, but I gotta go now. Duty calls."

"Good luck, son! Give 'em hell."

I snorted at her beautifully crafted irony.

chapter 24

GUESS I'M AN EVIL SCIENTIST

Everyone in conference room nine sat with their chin or head in their hands like they were too tired or weary to sit up straight. I felt great, personally. Hanging out with my family and seeing my mom was just what I'd needed. Also, I hadn't used Darkness in a while, so that "cloud" Mom had sensed had all but dissipated. I felt bad for being all chipper while everyone else was depressed, but not enough to change my mood.

"Here's your job," Ying Yue said standing before the whiteboard. "Each of you needs to discover which side your demon is on. If they support Malum, get close to them in order to get information out of them."

"What if they don't support him?" Natalie asked. She looked tired. How could an angel look tired when she didn't need sleep? I understood the feeling though. It had been nice to set all this down when I went to go deal with the family stuff.

"Get close to them," Ying Yue said. "If this comes down to a fight, we might be able to count on some demons to fight on our side."

Nobody said anything, but I could almost hear the skepticism in everyone's thoughts, probably because that sounded either ridiculously hopeful or insane. But we didn't have much to work with at the moment, so we kept those thoughts to ourselves.

Ying Yue picked up a clipboard and began reading off lines of notes she'd made with Raj, checking each line with a pencil. "William, we're assigning you a new demon since you were attacked last time. Good work defending yourself with Darkness though. Your cover is still intact. Frederick, keep working with Helga. Ted and Jake, your demons seem to know a lot about this Malum movement. See if you can meet up with each other's demons. If the four of you joined forces, it would be easier to infiltrate Malum's supporters. Daisy, I know you only terrorized that park to stay on your demon's good side, but don't get too carried away or we'll have to pull you out. Natalie, you need a new tactic with your demon. He's clearly not responding to you trying to bond over your love of *Twilight*." She looked up at Natalie. "Which is a bit outdated anyway. And goodness gracious, why? I'll admit the books were compelling, but Edward and Bella have a horrible relationship. What message is that sending all the young girls out there reading those books? And the movies were terrible. Even Robert Pattinson hates *Twilight*." Ying Yue blinked, noting our amused glances at her random outburst. She cleared her throat. "Find a new tactic." She looked down at her clipboard and paused, then looked at me. "David, we need you to get a time and place from your demon. Our plans depend on when and where you're meeting. Once we know that, we'll be able to flesh out a plan for an ambush."

I gulped and nodded. It was nice to be reminded that all these plans hinged on me not screwing up.

Raj stood and said, "Overall, nice work, everyone. Now, I know you're all technically trained already, but people don't stop working out once they're healthy, do they? We're going to continue to work on strengthening both your Light and Darkness. I'll meet you all near the pregnant unicorn."

No one laughed at that, because she'd become such an integral part of our training sessions, overseeing us with her maternal, lopsided eyes.

I pulled Raj aside during our training session to tell him my idea for Sandra's wanderers. He looked at me skeptically. "I'm not sure they'd be much help. If anything, they'd be a hindrance."

"I won't tell them our plans. We'll give them their own jobs."

"I don't know . . . "

"What can it hurt? If it doesn't work, we'll just let it go and move on."

He pursed his lips, considering. Eventually he sighed. "All right, but you'd have to train them. We can't spare any more task force leaders. Are you sure you want to add that to your plate?"

No, I really didn't, but this wasn't about me, so I just nodded and said, "Yeah, no problem."

Raj looked at me like he saw through my fake confidence, but let it go.

"All right everyone, listen up," Raj said, directing his attention back toward the group. We gathered around him in a semi-circle. "Today we're going to work on fighting more than one opponent. We'll work in teams. At some point, maybe today if you're ready, we'll challenge you to fight two opponents at once on your own."

"I pick Jake!" I called. Natalie muttered something I didn't understand, which I assumed was Russian for like "darn you, you little man boy!" Jake grinned cockily, gratified to be fought over. I'd have been annoyed by his smug face if I wasn't so relieved.

At first, we fought demons versus demons, both sides using Darkness. Jake and I went up against Ted and Natalie first. Before the fight, Jake pulled me aside to talk strategy. I'd forgotten for a minute that he was a defender. Fighting demons was his job, and he was good at it, but I had no idea that he was that smart. Neither of us really talked about our jobs much. Probably because my job was so boring and his job was so cool that it just came off as bragging.

"All right, first, we take stock of our enemy," Jake whispered. "What do we know about them?"

"Natalie's weird and Ted looks boring but is secretly cool."

Jake gave me a look. "I meant their fighting abilities, not their personalities, ya fruit loop."

"Right," I said. "Well Ted's good at fencing, but that's pretty much it. And Natalie has a lot of 'fight me' in her, but it's mostly show. She's not very creative."

"Right," he said. "I've never seen Natalie create any kind of weapon. She just throws balls of Darkness at her enemy. I reckon she's never used any kind of weapon before. Ted knows how to fence, but he's stuck in that box. So, we start the fight and pretend they're winning to make them confident, then we get fancy on them and make it impossible for them to rely on their typical fighting styles. I'll go after Ted. I'll start by sword fighting him. He should have no problem beating me, so I don't even have to pretend to lose that one. I'll make sure I end up on my back, then I'll shoot him with a Darkness gun. Then I'll do that blanket thing you did with Ying Yue and pin him to the ground. You just throw balls of Darkness at Natalie and let her hit you a few times. Then make a shield to cover you and tackle her to the ground too." He slapped me on the shoulder. "Should be easy as."

"Easy as what?"

He shrugged. "I dunno. That's the whole sayin'."

"All right, well . . . good plan."

I felt like I hadn't really contributed anything, but I was cool with that because the plan worked. We took down Ted and Natalie easily. Rather than making me feel good though, I felt terrible. I think it was all the Darkness we'd used. It took every good emotion and flipped it. Instead of feeling victorious, I felt guilty. I hadn't used Darkness in a while and I'd forgotten how suffocating it was. I pushed through though and I was glad I at least had Jake on my team.

After Ted and Natalie, we went up against Frederick and William. It didn't matter how much we strategized, those two were unbeatable. Not only were they soldiers when they were alive, but they had a lot more experience as angels, they were best friends and knew each other better than Jake and I, and it turned out they were also defenders, something Jake simply forgot to mention to me. They clobbered us, but I'd like to think Jake and I put up a good fight.

After we'd fought every other team (Daisy had been paired up with Raj and they totally kicked our butts), Raj and Ying Yue decided to give us a completely unfair challenge.

They had me and Jake go up against the two of them.

But if that wasn't enough, they were both radiating Light and made no move to switch to Darkness.

"Wait," Jake said, "you want us to fight you as angels? That's not fair, a demon could never beat an angel. Light is always stronger than Darkness."

"Why would we ever need to fight an angel anyway?" I asked.

"To keep your cover," Ying Yue said. "You can't know every single angel in The Resting Place. There will likely come a time when an angel comes across you and your demon and doesn't know you're secretly an angel. They'll try to cast you out. You're gonna need to put up a good fight to keep your cover."

Jake and I glanced at each other. We'd never thought of that. "Give us a sec," Jake said.

Once we were out of earshot I said, "It's not like we actually have to win. If we're in that situation, shouldn't we want the angels to win?"

Jake shook his head, scowling. "We *have* to win. We've lost the last two fights; we need to win this one."

It turned out that while Darkness made me feel like giving up, it made Jake even more stubborn.

"All right, well, you said yourself that we can't win," I said. "We just need to hold out as long as we can."

Jake growled and kicked at a rock on the ground. His foot went right through it, which made him even angrier, and I thought I heard him swear. As long as I'd known

Jake, I'd never really seen him angry before. It felt wrong. And he had this look like he wanted to really hurt someone, which secretly kind of scared me. I didn't like seeing this side of Jake so I racked my brain for some way we could get this victory for him.

I thought about what I knew. Darkness couldn't penetrate Light. But Darkness could cut through Darkness. I knew this because whenever we had Darkness battles and I was hit, I could feel their Darkness melding with mine. If Darkness could cut through Darkness, could Light cut through Light? Had anyone ever tried that? It wasn't like angels ever fought each other. But even if Light could cut through Light, it wouldn't hurt the angel. You'd just be adding more Light to the Light they already had. It would be like trying to hurt someone with kindness.

I sat down and contemplated a seed of a thought growing in my head. It may be cheating, because we were supposed to be fighting as demons, but at the moment I cared less about a fair fight and more about victory for Jake.

I approached Jake who stood with his jaw and fists clenched, trying to come up with a plan, but clearly coming up empty.

"I think I have an idea," I said hesitantly.

Jake spun on me and sneered. "*You* have an idea? The wuss that froze and did nothing when Malum got loose? You think you can come up with a plan better than me, an actual defender?"

"Hey," I said, taking a step back. Jake had struck a chord. My face fell and my shoulders slumped and all those thoughts of my own uselessness came back in full force. Really, who was I to try to win this? If Jake couldn't come up with a plan, there was no way I could. I couldn't do anything right. That's why I'd been at the front desk for the past ten years. No one could trust someone as pathetic as me with anything more important.

Jake's sneer fell away, and he looked absolutely mortified. "I'm so sorry! I didn't mean that, I promise."

"It's fine . . . " I said, trying to shrug it off.

"What's your idea?" he asked me.

"It's stupid. It probably won't work."

"Listen." Jake put a hand on my shoulder. "It doesn't matter if it works. I don't really care if we win. But I still wanna hear your idea, because I'm sure it's ace."

I nodded and smiled tentatively. That was the Jake I knew. I don't know if he really thought my idea would work or if he was just trying to humor me to make me feel better, but regardless, it did slightly lessen my feelings of uselessness. "Okay. Again, it probably won't work, but I don't think anyone's tried this yet, so who knows. Make a ball of Darkness in your hand."

Jake obliged and held it up for me. Now came the tricky part. We'd been using Darkness for hours now, and I seriously doubted I'd be able to produce a drop of Light, but I gave it my best shot.

I closed my eyes, thought of where Light came from, and willed it to appear in my hands. It was agony. It felt like someone was pulling a knife out of a stab wound, but all over my body. I sucked a breath in through my teeth, unable to hide how much it hurt. I heard Jake say something in a concerned voice, but I pushed through until my hands finally lit up like candles.

That was by far the worst I'd ever felt trying to create Light, and I worried that it would just keep getting worse until I couldn't do it at all anymore. If I lost my ability to create Light, they'd pull me out of the demon hunters. It was there in the contract I'd signed.

I took a second to gather my breath, then shoved the two balls of Light together and flattened them out like pizza dough.

"Drop your ball of Darkness in the middle," I told Jake.

He did as I said. I wrapped up the ball of Darkness in my blanket of Light. The Light dimmed slightly but didn't disappear. It just turned into an outer layer of the ball of Darkness. Unless you compared it to a normal ball of Light, I doubted anyone would be able to tell the difference.

Jake studied the weird ball of Light and Darkness in my hand. Before he could say anything, I told him my plan. A grin slowly spread across his face. It wasn't condescending and it wasn't surprised. This made me feel like maybe we had a chance.

We made another ball of Light and Darkness and I hid them both in my pockets. We approached Raj and Ying Yue and told them we were ready. I could tell everyone had gotten bored and antsy while Jake and I planned. Natalie was tapping her foot and Daisy muttered, "Finally!" Jake and I ignored them. We each created shields of Darkness and took our places.

Raj blew his whistle, and the fight began. I started by throwing a ball of Darkness at Raj, then ducking down behind my shield, purposefully looking weak and scared. It wasn't hard. Then Jake freaked out on them, shooting beams of Darkness from both his hands and screaming a crazy war cry. The Darkness didn't hurt them, but it got their attention away from me as I cowered behind my shield. Once Raj's back was turned, I pulled out the glowing ball from my pocket and threw it at his back, making him fall forward on his face. Then I threw a second one at Ying Yue's chest.

She gasped and put a hand to where I'd hit her. "Ow," she said, more surprised than anything. Jake threw our remaining two balls of Light and Darkness at each of them, knocking Ying Yue over and throwing Raj back down just as he'd started to sit up. Ying Yue sat up warily and held up her hands. In a confused voice she said, "Victory to Jake and David." Raj winced and stood.

"How did you do that?" He asked me. I thought it was weird he asked me and not Jake, like he knew it was my idea.

"We hid a ball of Darkness inside the ball of Light," I said. "The outer layer was able to cut through your Light aura, so the Darkness was able to hit you."

Raj blinked. Then he threw his hands up and shouted, "How have we never thought of that?" He started pacing back and forth on his invisible Segway. "I wonder if it would work the other way . . . " He paused and created a ball of Light in one hand and a ball of Darkness in the other. I had no idea how he did that and it was probably the most impressive thing I'd ever seen him do. To be able to create Light while still holding on to Darkness? And it didn't even seem to hurt him. That more than anything proved that this guy had some serious years on me.

He shook the ball of Darkness out until it flattened, then wrapped it around the ball of Light. "Catch," he said as he threw me the ball. Then he turned off his aura of Light until he started glowing negative. "Do your worst," he said.

I shrugged and threw the ball at his chest. He was thrown flat on his back and didn't move for a moment. "Ow," he said, winded. It sounded more like a squeak than anything. It was like that part in *The Avengers* when Hulk throws Loki around like a rag doll and Loki just lays there, all the air knocked out of him.

Jake whooped and pumped his fists, "Look what you discovered, mate! This is a whole new way of fighting demons! It's fair dinkum genius! Of course Light pushes demons away, but it can't hurt them because the Darkness aura keeps it from actually hitting them. But this way causes actual pain! The kind of pain like when we try to make Light while radiating Darkness, because the two can't exist in the same place! I can't wait to share this with the defenders."

Raj stood and smiled at me proudly. I felt really awkward because of the attention and also because I hadn't really discovered it. Raj was the one that flipped it to be a Darkness ball filled with Light.

Then I heard a whoop from the bleachers and a shrill, "That's my boy!"

I spun around and blushed. "Mom? What are you doing here? This is a demon hunter meeting."

She put a finger to her lips. "I was never here." And she disappeared.

I turned around and all the other members of my task force were staring at me wondering who the crazy lady was.

I grinned and said, "My mom died a few days ago," by way of explanation.

They all nodded and said things like "that's awesome" and "congratulations."

I've said it before and I'll say it again. Death is *so* not the same on the other side.

After our little discovery, Raj brought everyone in and taught them how to make the Light and Darkness balls.

"We can't keep calling these Light and Darkness balls," Jake said. "It's a mouthful."

"How about Larkness," I said, cracking a smile. "Or Dight."

"That sounds stupid," Jake said. "We should call them 'angel killers' and 'demon killers.'"

"We're already dead," Daisy said.

"So?"

After that, the names stuck, even if they didn't quite make sense. Angel killers had Light on the outside. And demon killers had Darkness on the outside.

It was a lot harder for us to make them than it was for Raj. We still struggled to switch back and forth, so most of us helped each other, one creating Darkness while the other created Light. Frederick and William created a little canister they filled with demon killer musket balls. Ying Yue made a quiver full of demon killer arrows.

Overall, it was a pretty successful training session, and despite the Darkness I'd been using all day, I felt a little proud. I'd actually done something right.

chapter 25
OSCAR THE GROUCH'S CAR

I caught Sandra after work as she was walking to her car.

"Hey, I was wondering if I could talk to you about something."

She looked around for people. Then, noting a few other teachers in the parking lot, she put her phone to her ear. "Sure, what is it?"

"It's kind of a long explanation. Can I . . . would it be weird if I caught a ride with you to your place?"

Sandra bit her lip. "Umm . . . Hang on. Stay where you are."

She dropped her bags on the ground and began frantically moving stuff around in her car, her legs sticking out of the driver's side. I hoped she wasn't cleaning up on my account. I mean, it didn't matter if there was stuff in the seat when I could just float through it.

"Okay . . . Just, don't judge, all right?" she said, finally emerging from the driver's side.

I shrugged and floated into the passenger's seat.

"*Hijuela mañana . . .* " I said under my breath.

"What does that mean?" Sandra asked as she got in and shut her door.

"It means, wow, your car is just beautiful."

"Shut up," she said, slapping my shoulder. It was a familiar reaction from high school, and she forgot that her hand would go right through me.

Seriously though, I was so confused. Her apartment was pristine, so was her classroom. The inside of her car was a dump. Her back seat was covered with books, water bottles, a broken stool for some reason, shoes, binders. There was an empty box of Eggo waffles by my feet and an old Wendy's bag. Even her cup holders were filled with junk: loose coins, bobby pins, receipts. It was bad.

Sandra blushed. "I clean up for company. I don't usually have company in my car."

"Are you telling me you keep your apartment so clean because you want it to look nice for all your wanderers?" For some reason that was kind of sweet. And creepy if you think about it. People lived with her without her permission, and she not only let them, but catered to them.

"They're my guests," she said, sticking her keys in the ignition. "Now what did you want to talk about?"

"It's actually about your wanderers," I said. "What if we gave them a job?"

She raised an eyebrow as she turned and checked behind her for cars. "A job." She said it so flat it wasn't even a question; it was just one of those statements where people skeptically repeat what you say to make you sound stupid.

"Think about it," I said as she started pulling out of the parking lot. "Why are they wanderers in the first place? It's because they're afraid of death and of moving on. They're so stuck in this bubble of fear and denial that they kind of lose all sense of purpose and identity. If we gave them something to do, it might snap them out of it. They'd feel wanted and needed. We could show them that death really isn't the end."

She frowned as she thought about it. "What kind of job?"

I grimaced, worried about what she'd think about this. "What if we made them demon hunters?"

Sandra was silent so I kept talking.

"Look, we need some serious help. We have this big plan that sort of rides on me not being a giant wuss, and if that doesn't work, we'll need some backup. Recruiting your wanderers is a win-win situation. They help us demon hunt and in turn they get pulled out of their little funk and hopefully cross over to The Resting Place."

Sandra still showed no emotion on her face as she thought about it. "Who would train them? Who would be in charge?"

"Well, they're your wanderers, so you'd be in charge of them. You'd be like their task force leader. But I could train them. I know how to use both Light and Darkness, and I could teach them everything I know about demon hunting."

"How would I lead them if I, myself, don't know anything about demon hunting? Also, I don't know your guys' big plan. How do we all stay on the same page?"

"I'll act as the liaison between the demon hunters and you guys. I'll visit and give you updates and send messages back and forth."

We reached a stoplight and Sandra looked over at me. "You think it would work?"

I shrugged. "I honestly don't know, but even if they aren't any help to the demon hunters, at least they'd be able to do something useful with their afterlives and maybe remember who they really are."

She smiled, then turned away as the light turned green. "Okay, I'm in. Now you wanna tell me about this big plan that rides on you not being a giant wuss?"

I told her bits and pieces and was as vague as possible. I didn't tell her how Malum got out or my role in it. I didn't tell her about Sheila or my upcoming meeting with my "dad." I just told her that a really bad demon had gotten loose and I was part of the plan to capture him.

I'm not sure why I didn't want to tell her everything. I guess I just liked this odd sort of friendship we had, and I didn't want to change the way she thought of me. For all she knew I was brave and bold and totally crushing it as an angel. If she knew how I'd let Malum go, or the way I was laughed at by everyone when I said I'd join the demon hunters, would she see me that way too? Maybe she already did. Either way, I wasn't ready to admit my mistakes. She was the only one I knew who had no idea just how much of a disaster I was.

When we reached her apartment, I did my best to walk up the stairs with her, rather than just float to the top. It took some concentration, but I think I pulled it off. Then she held the door open for me when we got there, which made me smile. It was cute, all right? She wanted to treat me like a person and didn't know that I could open doors myself, even if I usually just float through them.

"Hey, Bill, I got you some more math problems," Sandra said to that one guy who always sits at the island barstool. She set a worksheet out in front of him and smiled. He eagerly created a piece of paper and pen for himself to work out the problems.

She walked to the living room where a despondent middle-aged woman was watching *The Nanny*. "Patty, I called Mark, but he didn't answer, so I just left a message."

Then she put her hands on her hips and frowned up at the two boys hanging from the fan as it twirled them around like a merry-go-round for dead kids. "Asher and Oliver, off the fan now." It was actually pretty impressive that they were able to hold on that well when they couldn't physically touch it.

I frowned and raised an eyebrow.

"What?" She asked when she saw my face.

"Déjà vu much? That was the exact same thing you said to all of them last time. What, do you just repeat the same conversations every day when you come home?"

She nodded, dropping her "THIS IS A TOTE BAG" bag on the table and sitting down. "I've learned that wanderers do best with routine and repetition. When things get switched up on them, they freak out."

"Encouraging," I said, thinking about how I was about to switch things up on them.

"Don't worry, they might not even listen to you," she said.

"You've really got this whole encouragement thing down."

She laughed then turned toward her nine wanderers in various positions around the room. "Hey guys? This random angel has something to say to you. I think his name is David or something?" She looked over at me expectantly.

Yikes. This was awkward. I wasn't prepared for any kind of speech. I had no idea what to say. They wouldn't even look at me, how could I get them to listen?

I looked around from wanderer to wanderer. "Hey guys . . . My name is David. And I have a job for you if you want it."

Silence.

"It's a job with the demon hunters."

Cricket, cricket.

"You know, spying and catching bad guys?"

I looked at Sandra who just shrugged her shoulders. Of course I couldn't just rely on her. The reason these wanderers were still here was because she couldn't get through to them. Not that it was her fault they were there in the first place, that was their choice, I just meant she was at as much of a loss with them as I was.

Maybe words weren't going to get them to listen. Maybe it had to be with feelings. They needed to remember what light and warmth felt like in order to want it too. I groaned inwardly. This was going to hurt.

"Excuse me a minute," I said to Sandra.

Sandra raised an eyebrow and gave me a look like: *Bailing so soon?*

I just smiled awkwardly and floated through the front door.

Once I was alone, I closed my eyes and willed the Light to form in my hands, then waited for the pain. Oh, it was bad. It still felt like someone pulling knives out of my body, except stronger than before.

Please, I prayed. *I'm trying to help. Please let this work.*

The pain got sharper and I cried out. I shoved one of my fists into my mouth, so Sandra wouldn't hear me, and fell to my knees.

And then it was gone. My body was filled with warmth, like sinking into a bath, and my shoulders slumped forward in relief and exhaustion. A single ball of Light was shining in my hand. I got shakily to my feet, breathing heavily. I wasn't sure why, because I didn't technically need to breathe, but my body still reacted the way it would have if I were alive.

I cleared my throat and straightened up before I floated back through the door. Sandra looked partially concerned and partially freaked out. She'd heard me scream. Great…

"Bill, right?" I said to the math nerd. He didn't respond, so I set my ball of Light in front of him to see what he would do. He blinked and looked at it curiously. Then he held his hand out as though he wanted to touch it.

"You can touch it," I said. "Hold it, even."

Bill hesitantly took the ball of Light in his hands and gasped, his eyes watering the same way mine did every time I used Light.

"It's beautiful, isn't it?" I said quietly. "And it feels like home, doesn't it? You know why?"

Bill looked at me and shook his head.

"It's because of who it comes from."

"Who?" Bill asked me. Sandra gasped, understandably so. Wanderers rarely speak. Their identities are so lost they sort of forget how to.

"I think you know," I said solemnly. "Do you want to

learn how to make Light too?"

He nodded eagerly.

"I'll show you," I promised. I almost took the Light from him to go repeat the process with the other eight wanderers, but then I had a better idea. "Why don't you go share it with someone else?"

Bill looked intensely into the Light and nodded. He floated slowly over to Patty and knelt next to her on the couch. He silently held up the Light and Patty blinked, seeming to come to for the first time in a long time. Bill handed the ball to her and when Patty held it, she started crying.

"What is it they're holding?" Sandra whispered. "I can't see it."

I tilted my head. "It's Light. You can't see it? Hmm… I wonder if it has something to do with you being unable to see our auras."

She didn't answer because she was staring open-mouthed at Bill and Patty. The two of them went around sharing the Light with everyone in the room, and then Bill came back and set it reverently in my hand. I'm not gonna lie, the wanderers were still creeping me out. Before they were dead-eyed zombies, but now they were all gathered around staring at me expectantly, almost worshipful. Even Sandra was looking at me like I'd done something unforgettable like push her out of the way of a speeding car.

"Okay . . ." I said, now that I had everyone's attention. "I'm going to teach you all how to make Light. I'm not sure this has ever been done before since you usually learn this once you become an angel, but who says wanderers can't make Light, right?" The answer was "everyone," in my experience, but that didn't mean they were right.

For the next hour I walked around teaching them each in turn. They were mostly unsuccessful. A part of creating Light is the intention behind it—you have to be using it for good—and a part of it is being worthy to use it. It's like the Mjölnir of the afterlife. Except, unlike Thor's hammer, more than one person can wield it at once. A lot of them just weren't there yet, and the reasons why were none of my business. At least they were listening to me now. I even had a little bit of a conversation with Bill.

All in all, not too shabby.

WELL DONE, DAVID, I heard Hermes say. *NOW IF YOU ARE AVAILABLE, WOULD YOU PLEASE RETURN FOR FRONT DESK DUTY?*

"All right, I gotta go," I told Sandra. "You heard the basics of how to do it, right? You can help them while I'm gone?"

She nodded, apparently speechless.

"You okay?" I asked.

She cleared her throat. "Yeah. That was amazing. Thanks so much."

I narrowed my eyes suspiciously. "Are you being

sarcastic?"

"No, I'm being totally serious. I've never made this much progress with them ever. You were incredible."

I blushed. "Yeah, well . . . You'd do the same in my position. Anyway, I go now. I mean, I gots to go. I mean, goodhello."

Oh, David, just stop talking! I just wasn't used to receiving open praise, especially from a girl.

I waved and disapparated before I could say or do anything else embarrassing.

chapter 26

I'M (NOT) A BARBIE GIRL

The front desk was crazy busy, and it was just me and Kam again. The lobby echoed with the sounds of dozens of angels packed into an enclosed space. I could barely hear myself think. Messenger angels kept flying around with little memos for people that we had to sort into different mailboxes. Why the messengers didn't just deliver the memos themselves, I had no idea, but it was one more thing to add to our plates. I wondered for a moment why Hermes always scheduled me and Kam when things got so busy. Was it as punishment, or was it because we were good at our job?

Let's go with the second one because it makes me feel better.

It was fine though. Secretly, I kind of liked it when things got crazy like that because I got into "authoritative mode." I know I talk all the time about how I'm lame and I don't know what I'm doing, but when you've been doing the same job for ten years straight, it's impossible not to get the hang of it. I've complained a lot about front desk duty, but really, when I'm behind the front desk, that's the only place I really know what I'm doing and the only place I can feel confident telling others what to do. The front desk is my domain and I am in charge and that feels good.

I was in the middle of reorganizing a pile of papers that had fallen when some dude cut in line, shoved a piece of paper at me, and started floating away.

"Hey, wait a minute," I said, setting my spilled stack of papers aside. "What's this?"

The guy turned and said, "I don't know, I was told to turn it in."

"This says, Rescuer Report. And it's practically blank."

The guy shrugged. "So?"

I stifled a sigh. Either he was new or lazy. I hoped it was the former. "I'm sorry, but you can't turn these in here. The rescuers have their own filing system. Try conference room five. The rescuers often meet there. Next?"

A lady stepped up and said, "Yes, I was wondering if I could rent out a meeting room?"

I pointed to the clipboard sitting on the counter. "You can sign up for a time slot there, ma'am. Next?"

"Look at you doing your big boy job!" Mom said, slamming her hands on the front desk. I knew she was trying to embarrass me, but I didn't give in.

"How can I help you, ma'am?"

"Ooh, so serious!"

"Mom . . . " I complained.

"Oh, all right. Where do I put this? It's my first report and I'm not sure what to do with it."

I smiled and took it from her. "You give it to me and I file it away."

"So, how's your day going?"

"Sorry to rush you, Mom, but there's kind of a line. Can we talk later?"

"Oh, sorry!" She blew me a kiss and flew off.

"Next?"

A big guy with a long black beard handed me five guardian angel reports.

"Whoa," I said. "You know you only have to fill out one per visit, right?"

The guy scowled. "I thought it was one per family member."

"Nope," I said, scooting away from the counter. The dude was quite intimidating. "This is fine, though. The more detail the better. But next time you can just fill out one."

I rushed to go file his reports as the line got longer.

"Next?" I said as I checked the clock. Five minutes left of my shift. Thank goodness.

"This is crazy. Is it always like this?" Jake was the next one in line.

The pieces suddenly fit together. The crazy lines. All these angels who didn't know what they were doing. We definitely have busy days, but this was not normal.

I grimaced, "I think it's been more crowded lately because of Malum."

He frowned, then said, "Oh . . . all the mass killings? Lots of newbie angels? Sheesh, that's depressing."

He handed me a report.

I shoved his report in a file and said, "Hey, you doing anything this arvo?"

Jake laughed at me trying to steal his word. "No. Why?"

"Meet me by that bench. My shift is over in like three minutes."

"Cool, man," he said in an American accent. "Righteous."

I threw an eraser at him as he floated away.

Jake took one look at me in my agitated state and smirked. "Got another demon date tonight?"

I groaned as I plopped down next to him on the bench. "Maybe. How are things with your demon?"

Jake grimaced. His shoulders slumped as he leaned his forearms on his thighs. "So, we went to see what Ted and his demon were up to because Ying Yue told us to try and get them together. They hit it off right away and started teaming up to terrorize little kids. They were haunting daycares and scarring these tiny, little ankle-biters! Ted and I almost blew our cover because I refused to knock a shelf over onto a kid. Ted saved us by getting into a fight with me. We stepped outside for a Darkness battle and our demons were so entertained they forgot all about terrorizing the kids."

"Sheesh," I said. "That sucks. Quick thinking on Ted's part, though, to cause a distraction. Are you guys gonna keep teaming up? Did they tell you anything about supporting Malum?"

He shrugged. "I don't reckon we have a choice. We didn't get any information out of them, so we'll have to try again next time."

"What are you gonna do?"

He blew air out his lips. "I reckon I'll have to meet up with Ted at some point and come up with a plan. Maybe if we show more interest in the Malum movement we can steer them back in that direction." He sighed and sat up. "So, where're you gonna take your demon girlfriend on your date tonight?"

I groaned. "I haven't even thought that far. Also, do demons change clothes? Or do they just wear the same thing all the time? Because I'm kind of tired of being Zac Efron."

He shrugged. "Then change."

"What do I wear?"

"I dunno. Ask a girl."

"I don't know that many girls . . . "

Jake frowned, then said, "Give me a sec."

He disappeared and I watched as the line going into headquarters slowly shrank. Angel lines look kind of funny because we don't stand in a line, we float. So everyone looks like they're being pulled along by a rope underwater when the line moves up. And then you have a few people who float a little higher, looking like human kites being pulled along by a string. It's all very odd at first, and then once you get used to it, it's odd that it's not odd.

Jake came back with a cute blonde girl with big wavy hair. "This is my friend, Kelly," Jake said. Then he turned toward Kelly and said, "So whatcha think?"

Kelly studied me, then actually walked around me in a circle, making me feel very self-conscious. "What's your typical style?" she asked with a high Tennessee accent. "Like what did you wear when you were alive?"

"Well, I'm not really going for what I would normally wear," I said. "I'm not sure what Jake told you, but this is for an undercover date with a demon."

"Oh! You're a demon hunter too? So you need to look like a bad boy." She grinned in a way that kind of scared me. "Challenge accepted." She rubbed her hands together. "Okay . . . let's just start with a simple gray t-shirt and build off of that. Make it a v-neck. Darken the jeans and make them skinnier. Add a leather jacket. Hmm . . . what else? Maybe add some clunky boots?"

"What are you doing?" some random girl asked as she floated by.

"We're trying to make him look like a bad boy," Kelly explained.

The girl looked at me, then said, "Make your hair longer so it's kind of shaggy."

"What if it was a black t-shirt?" another random girl asked. A small crowd of girls was starting to form as curiosity got the better of them, and of course I became more of a spectacle as more joined. They slowly closed in on me, each of them shouting things for me to change about my outfit. One of them started messing with my hair I'd just grown out, trying to style it while another turned me around and said, "This is all wrong. Lose the black t-shirt, you look like Danny Zuko." They all started arguing, crowding in on me. I felt claustrophobic and agitated, their voices an irritating buzz in my ears that just kept getting louder. Eventually I snapped.

"I'm not your Barbie doll!" I shouted.

Of course Hermes had to be floating by right then. He paused, raised an eyebrow, then floated away shaking his head.

The girls gave me some space and apologized.

"It's okay," I said. "Just one at a time."

"Ooh, what about some tattoos?" one of them suggested. "That would look cool."

I thought about it, then pulled my sleeve back and

added one tattoo to the inside of my right arm. Jake took one look and said, "Please don't tell me that's from *Harry Potter*." He covered his face with his hand like he was embarrassed for my answer.

"It's the dark mark," I said defensively. "It's what the bad guys have on their arms. They call themselves Death Eaters because they're trying to defeat death, and I'm dead. It's ironic."

"You being the linchpin in this entire plan is ironic."

"Rude," I said, putting my finger to my arm. "I'm calling Voldemort." One of the girls in the crowd gasped.

"All right ladies, let's leave the poor bloke alone," Jake said finally. He started herding them back like a policeman protecting a crime scene. "Show's over."

"Wait . . . " Kelly said. "One more thing. You should give yourself some scruff. Tough guys are scruffy."

"Isn't that lying though?" I said. "When I was alive, I was never able to grow anything."

"Your whole appearance is a lie right now, mate," Jake said.

"True." I grew myself some stubble for the first time ever and all the girls nodded, their eyes widening. One squealed.

"That's what you needed," one of them said. "Oh, and one more thing." She messed up my hair again, leaving a couple long strands hanging down on my forehead. They all smiled at me, and one of the girls waved shyly.

"Um, thanks," I said, my voice cracking. "You guys can go now."

Slowly the girls dispersed until just one was left. She leaned in and whispered, "I'm Alani. We should hang out sometime." And then she disappeared.

I looked at Jake at a loss for words. "What just happened?"

Jake chuckled. "Turns out you're a handsome bloke. Now go seduce your little demon."

I walked through the door of that old sports bar and leaned against the wall, mentally prepping myself for talking to Sheila. She had one elbow on the bar, gracefully resting her chin in her hand. Her coppery hair hung down in waves around her. She stared off into the distance with her eyebrows slightly pinched, utterly lost in her thoughts. I couldn't deny that she was beautiful. And somehow . . . I felt like she didn't know it. It was a strange thought, but she didn't carry herself like that. Some girls, even when they're sitting alone, are posing, hoping that people are looking at them. You can tell by how they smile as they look around expectantly, pretending they don't notice if someone passes them a glance, yet you can see a slight smirk in the corner of their mouth. Sheila wasn't like that. She either didn't notice or didn't care what people thought of her.

It was a strange revelation for me. I'd assumed all

demons were vain. But now that I thought of it, it would make sense that they weren't. When I was filled with Darkness, I felt like a piece of crap. I wondered if that was what all demons felt like all the time. What a nightmare.

Now I was nervous to approach her for a completely different reason. I used to be afraid of her because she was a demon. Now I was afraid of her because she was pretty.

She seemed to sense me there because she turned suddenly and smiled, patting the barstool next to her.

"What were you doing standing over there like a creeper?" she asked when I sat next to her, a smile breaking through that weary look she'd been wearing.

I wished she wouldn't smile. That made her even prettier.

"Watching you," I said. I winced at how creepy that sounded. "Like a creeper . . ."

"Why were you watching me?" she asked.

Because you're really pretty, and I was too scared of you to notice until now.

"You just looked really deep in thought," I said. "I didn't want to interrupt."

"So, where've you been?" she asked.

"Oh . . . you know. Places." I grimaced. It really didn't matter what I wore, my awkwardness seeped through all the layers like BO.

"Very informative," she said.

"I convinced a teenager to do drugs," I amended.

She frowned and nodded, impressed. "Nice."

"You?" I asked, worried for the answer.

"I almost got this guy," she gestured toward the bartender, her assigned mortal, "to sleep with a stranger to get revenge on his girlfriend. But then some stupid angel intervened."

"Oh, I hate those guys," I said, probably louder than necessary.

She glared bitterly at nothing. "I despise them. All of them and their stupid pious attitudes, acting like they're better than everyone else. They go around 'helping' people, but really they're all just helping themselves. Adding impressive acts of service to their angelic resumes so they can wind up somewhere better where us unworthy scum don't exist. Deep down, they're no better than us. Everyone's looking out for number one, especially those white robed butt heads."

She didn't say butt heads, obviously. I'm just trying to keep this all PG, because of my "stupid pious attitude."

We were quiet for a minute and eventually I said, "You wanna get out of here?"

"Yeah. Where to?"

Before I'd come, Ying Yue pulled me aside and stressed to me how important it was that I stay on Sheila's good side. She suggested something romantic to make her think I was serious . . . I laughed nervously, because nothing involving me could ever be romantic. I was too much of a dork. But I had to at least try.

I held out my hand and laced it through hers, then brought us to the most beautiful place I could think of.

It was dark out by now, but the beach looked really pretty in the moonlight. And the perk of being dead was that it wasn't cold to us, and we didn't have to worry about beach towels and getting sand everywhere. We watched silently as the waves crashed angrily against the shore and slowly crept back, white foam frothing at the tips. I've always loved the ocean, but it's always been an enigma to me. Why is it always so angry? And so mysterious, because the part that we see is only masking depths we couldn't even imagine.

"You remind me of the ocean," I blurted.

Sheila gave me an amused look. "How so?"

"Well, it's this powerful force of nature. It's wild and dangerous and angry. But it has this mystery about it that makes you think that maybe it knows something you don't. Maybe it has a reason to be angry." What the crap was I saying? The words just kept spilling out. "And it's kind of beautiful in a terrible way."

She just blinked at me for a while, expressionless. I couldn't blame her. What the heck was that garbage I'd just spouted? *Beautiful in a terrible way?* What did that even mean? Was that supposed to be a compliment? The fact that you couldn't tell was concerning.

"That was pure poetry, David," she said with a chuckle,

"but you should stick to awkward. Romantic is not your thing."

"Yep," I said, my cheeks and neck flaming red. It wasn't too surprising that she'd never been fooled by my bad boy impersonation, but it was a let-down. I'd never been Cool David; she'd always known I was just me. Which . . . hmm. Did that mean she actually liked the real me?

"So . . . " I said, trying to change the subject. "Any news on the dad front?"

Any news on the dad front? I wished I could die all over again.

Sheila looked out at the ocean and was quiet for a moment. Then she said, "He's willing to meet with you. But you have to do something for him first."

I gulped nervously. This sounded like one of those gangs or drug cartels that blackmailed or threatened people into doing terrible things for them. I did not want to be turned into a drug horse. (Is that the right term? It sounds off.)

"What do I have to do?" I asked.

"Surprise him," she said. "Do something to get his attention. Something so terrible he has no choice but to take notice. Then think about him long and hard and if he wants to, he'll show up."

My eyes widened. This was bad. It was one thing to learn how to use Darkness and spy on demons, but this would require me to actually harm people, and I was not willing to do that, no matter what the payoff. I was an angel first and foremost, and I was not going to fall into the whole "greater good" mindset that people use to justify doing horrific things.

I looked over at her curiously. "What did you do to get on his good side?"

"None of your business!" she said sharply.

My head reared back. "Wow, sorry, just asking."

We fell into another awkward silence until she scooted closer to me and leaned her head on my shoulder. "Sorry," she said. Then she reached her hand up and scrubbed my scruff. "This is new."

"You like it?"

"Oh it's very nice. Though it might get a little scratchy."

I thought she was talking about it being scratchy for me, but then she turned toward me, and based on the intent in her huge hazel eyes, I realized she was talking about herself. I gulped again, remembering the last time she'd kissed me. Kissing a demon was not an experience I wanted to repeat. But she kept looking at me and I couldn't stop staring at all the little flecks of green and brown in her eyes and her cute nose and her disproportionate lips. The top lip was slightly fuller than the bottom one. I wanted to kiss those lips.

REMEMBER WHO YOU ARE, DAVID, Hermes reminded.

Yep. Got it. This is just for the task force.

Then, remembering my talk with Ying Yue, I put my hands on either side of her face and kissed her quickly. I pulled away before I ingested any of her Darkness breath and said what had become our common farewell: "I still don't trust you."

She grinned. "Good. I don't trust you either."

I disapparated back to The Resting Place before she could say or do anything else.

I was confused. Very confused. Because Sheila was getting less repulsive to me, somehow. But knowing she had to have done something truly evil to get Malum's attention made me feel . . . disappointed? Because it meant she really was evil, and I didn't want her to be.

chapter 27
THE PLAN

"So let me get this straight," Jake said. "You, David, got your demon girlfriend to tell you exactly how to track down Malum? And to get his attention you have to do something evil?"

"She's not my girlfriend," I said defensively. "But yeah, that's the gist."

My task force looked at each other with expressions that were hard to read. I couldn't tell if they were impressed, or worried that another part of the plan depended on me.

"This is a bit of a pickle," Raj said. "You obviously can't hurt anyone, but pain and fear is the only way to get his attention."

"I have an idea," Natalie said.

"Yes?" Ying Yue asked, her pencil ready to jot down notes.

"We free the animals from the zoo!" she said with the fervor of a movie villain. Her eyes brightened with misplaced passion. "Except for the penguins. Because they will die. But we free the others! Animals loose will scare people and cost the zoo money."

Raj nodded politely. "I like where your head's at, Natalie, but I'm not sure that's a Malum-level disaster."

"We could kill them," she suggested with a shrug. "The animals, I mean. Just kill all the zoo animals."

"No killing innocent animals," Ying Yue said, disturbed. She looked genuinely offended, which was an interesting new layer to her personality. I wouldn't have pegged her as an animal lover.

"Perhaps we could cause an explosion," William suggested. "We would make sure the inhabitants were out of the building, of course."

"Good show, sir!" Frederick said, slapping William on the back. It reminded me of Jake slapping me on the back saying something like, "Good on ya, mate!" Did that make me the William of our friendship? The shorter, quieter, less popular one? The one insecure enough to need someone to tell him "Good job?" I guess there were worse things to be. William was still pretty cool.

"That wouldn't hurt anyone," Daisy said quietly. "Malum likes it when people hurt. He likes it when they're afraid."

"Unfortunately, Daisy has a point," Raj said. "There's no way to root out Malum without causing harm to mortals, and that is something that as angels we simply cannot do."

I blinked and scowled thoughtfully. Something Raj had said got me thinking . . . Something about mortals and angels.

"What plan are you brewing, *chuvak*?" Natalie asked.

I didn't realize she was talking to me until everyone was staring at me, waiting for my answer.

"Um . . . I don't have a plan," I lied. "I was just mentally asking Raj if he was for sure against the zoo animal idea. I thought it was a great plan."

Natalie smiled smugly, but Jake gave me a sideways glance. He wasn't buying it.

"I'll tell you later," I whispered out the side of my mouth.

Ted made a suggestion that I didn't hear because at the time I reached out to Raj with my mind. *Hey Raj, I have an idea. But we should talk about it somewhere else. And we should probably invite the defenders.*

I may have mentioned before that angels are telepathic. That is, we can speak to each other with our minds if we need to. Most choose not to though. First of all, regular angels don't usually have secrets so there's no reason to not just say everything out loud. Second of all, it's seen a bit as an invasion of privacy, because you're in that person's head and that's generally a private place. They may think something they didn't intend for you to hear.

Raj kept an impressive poker face. To the point that I

wondered if he'd even heard me until he said, *All right. We'll talk later.*

I guess Raj trusted me, because he set up a meeting with the defenders and demon hunters before I even told him my full plan. We met in a university lecture hall that was big enough to hold all of us. And by all of us I mean me, Hermes, the demon hunter commander (I guess she was over all the demon hunters, though I'd never met her), all the demon hunter task force leaders, the defender general, and all their captains. There were somewhere around fifty of us total. I had no idea Raj was going to invite this many people to the meeting and it made me even more jittery than before.

Raj had made the mistake of choosing a lecture hall that had fold-up seats, so we all just stood in front of the chairs. This was fine by me as the peeling yellow paint on the chairs was decorated with so much gum and other sticky residue that I didn't want to go near them even though I knew I couldn't actually touch anything. I grimaced and shook my head. These were college kids who went here. They were how old I'd be if I was still alive, and they were still sticking their gum under their seats?

I stood up straight and smiled nervously at the angels on either side of me, who nodded and then ignored me. Unfortunately, the dude in front of me was a super tall, bulky defender and I couldn't see a thing going on in the front of the lecture hall. A part of me was okay with this as I was the only one there who wasn't some kind of leader and I felt very out of place. Everyone looked so serious and confident. When they figured out this whole plan rested on my shoulders, I knew they'd be disappointed. I was a whole different kind of being. Someone who had no idea who I was or what I was doing there. I imagined them all looking down at me, thinking they could do better. Part of me almost liked that idea. I'd love for someone to take my place. Another, more stubborn part of me, wanted to prove them all wrong.

Hermes started the meeting by introducing himself, the demon hunter commander, Rashida Moustafa, and the defender general, Espen Wolff. They were in the front of the lecture hall, supposedly, though I still couldn't see a thing past the guy in front of me. Hermes then introduced Raj and had him come forward to explain the plan.

"A demon hunter on my task force has made contact with a demon who can give him a way to root out Malum's location," he started. "David, can you please explain what you were told? David? . . . Where are you, kid?"

I raised my hand and said, "Here." My voice cracked. Everyone looked around, but no one saw me until the dude in front of me turned around. He frowned at me, probably thinking, "*Good grief, this squirt's the size of one of my abs. Of which I have six. In a pack.*"

Raj smiled encouragingly and gestured for me to come down to the front next to him. I nervously floated down, glad I wasn't mortal because in my nervous state, I'd have tripped over my feet and faceplanted on the stairs.

When I reached him, I gulped and turned toward the crowd.

Raj put a hand on my back and said, "This is David Garcia, a very promising demon hunter who has shown an impressive amount of quick thinking and ingenuity. He's gotten the closest, by far, to rooting out Malum's location."

Ying Yue nodded curtly in affirmation.

I appreciated their support, but I wished Raj had skipped his introduction. It added to the pressure because now I had to actually live up to those expectations.

I cleared my throat. "So, my demon is in contact with Malum. I told her that I was Malum's son, and I was interested in meeting my dad. She said in order to meet with him, I'd have to prove myself by doing something really evil to get his attention. Then if I thought about him hard enough, he'd show up."

Commander Moustafa stepped forward. I took a step back, because the lady was rather intimidating. She looked like one of the Wakanda warriors and carried herself like she ate demons for breakfast. "We must decide what the act will be. It will need to be quite shocking in order to attract the Prince of Darkness."

"We have a problem, then," General Wolff said. He had long hair, clear blue eyes, and a Scottish accent, giving me some serious *Braveheart* flashbacks. All he needed was a horse. "How can he do this without breaking the contract and causing true harm?"

"I veto any plan that jeopardizes David's angel status," Ying Yue interrupted, a fiercely protective look on her face.

That set my heart pounding. Jeopardize my angel status? Could a person really do that?

"If I may, General," one of the defender captains said from the rows of chairs. "Perhaps we could create an illusion of some terrible act. Blow up a building with no one in it, for example."

"Malum isn't stupid," said another angel from the stands. "He'd know that no one was hurt. He feeds off fear and pain. If no one is truly harmed it most certainly will not capture his attention."

"Could we do something for real?" another angel asked. "I know we signed a contract and took an oath not to harm mortals, but if it's for the greater good, wouldn't it be worth it?" This caused some murmuring in the crowd, but she persisted. "How is this any different than war? Obviously fighting is something to be avoided, but sometimes there is no way around it, and you have to sacrifice the lives of good men and women in order to find peace."

"This is one hundred percent different than that," Ying Yue said. "Other than instances when there is a draft, men and women volunteer to join the war effort. It is their choice to risk their own lives. It is not up to us to sacrifice the lives of innocent civilians."

"Sir?" the General asked, looking back at Hermes.

Hermes had mostly been quiet. He hadn't been contributing to this conversation and I got the impression he was mostly here to oversee, rather than participate. "She's right, of course. Only God may decide when it is a person's time to die. Unless he commands us to do so, we must never kill."

I hope you don't think too badly of us for even having this conversation. Again, we don't see death the same way. Obviously, death would affect the living left behind, but to those that die, it's merely stepping into the other room. The concept of causing a person to die to us feels less like killing, and more like evicting someone from their home. Which, admittedly, is still pretty harsh.

Angels all spoke at once, arguing and discussing until the room was an unintelligible hum of voices. I tried to speak up, but nobody heard me. "Excuse me!" I tried. "Hello!"

No one was listening. They were too busy arguing over their impossible conundrum. Malum was attracted to pain and suffering. In order to get his attention, people had to be very hurt in a serious way. They had to fear for their very souls. They had to feel the way I did when he attacked me.

And I was pretty sure I had the answer.

If only someone would listen to me.

Finally, Raj put his fingers to his lips and whistled. "Everyone quiet down," he said. "David has an idea." He and Ying Yue smiled at me eagerly and I was struck by how much faith they had in me. While others looked at me skeptically, they looked at me like they genuinely expected me to have something good to share.

I took a deep breath and forced my insecurities away. This could work and I could do this.

"All right," I said, clearing my throat. "Here's my idea: I capture an angel."

The room was silent, so I kept talking.

"Look, most demons don't have any power over angels because Light always wins. But I know from personal experience that Malum's influence is greater than any demon in existence. I know I'm no warrior, but he was able to incapacitate me pretty easily, and I doubt it would take him much effort to do the same for any other angel."

I took a deep breath, trying to calm my PTSD jumpiness that always came over me when I thought of Malum attacking me.

"Now, just because he's the Prince of Darkness, it doesn't necessarily mean he's one of a kind. We could make me look just as powerful as he is if I could take down and capture an angel. No one would get hurt, but it would still look like a pretty serious act of evil. I mean, dragging an angel down from heaven? That's some pretty serious stuff. Plus, it would make me look even more impressive because it would mean I somehow broke into The Resting Place to do so, which is supposed to be impossible.

"So, what we do is we pick the time and place, get a bunch of defenders and demon hunters to hide and wait for their ambush, I drag some angel down from The Resting Place, kicking and screaming—we'd keep the plan a secret from them so their fear is actually real—and once Malum shows up the defenders can spring their trap on him, capturing him for good."

It was quiet for a long time. I thought the plan was genius, but now I was starting to doubt.

Finally General Wolff said, "I like this lad's thinking!"

The room erupted into nods and sounds of affirmation. Moustafa looked impressed and even Hermes didn't protest.

"We'll need a volunteer to act as his captive," Wolff said, turning to the audience.

"No," I protested, "It's gotta be someone who doesn't know—"

"I'll do it," a familiar voice said. My head snapped up and my mouth hung open. How had I not seen him earlier? He was right there in the second row.

"Captain Williams," Wolff said. "Excellent."

"Jake?" I said incredulously. "When did you get promoted to captain?"

"A while ago, mate."

"How come you didn't tell me?"

"We don't talk about our jobs," he said with a shrug. "I mean, for all I know you're now captain of the . . . paperwork."

And this was why we didn't talk about our jobs.

"No," both Ying Yue and Raj said together.

"Why?" Jake asked.

"First of all, you two are friends," Raj said. "Even if anyone would believe David would turn on his best friend, I seriously doubt either of you could act convincingly. You'd fall into a fit of giggles or something."

"Also," Ying Yue added, "the person David takes has to be genuinely scared in order to attract Malum's attention. He's driven by fear. The captive needs to be someone who hasn't heard the plan."

Moustafa nodded. "Let us work out the details."

We spent the rest of the evening hashing out the plan as Hermes observed and spoke up only if someone asked him a question. The more we planned the more it felt like this ambush could actually work. And it had been my idea! I had a hard time suppressing my grin. I was confident I could pull this off. Which made me nervous. When was David Garcia ever confident? I tried to push down the nagging worry that something would go terribly wrong.

chapter 28
DISAPPOINTING MCGONAGALL

Raj took me to our typical training grounds to "rehearse," even though it was still about a week away. We needed to make this capture seem real and I'd need to play my part convincingly. It seemed he thought I needed more training to pull off this stunt. He was not wrong; I was in way over my head. I'd already learned that I was a bad actor. Even Sheila knew I was nothing more than a dork.

The field looked so different without all my friends inking up the place. It took me a minute to realize that that was how I saw my fellow demon hunters now. They were my friends. I'd never imagined I'd make actual friends doing this. When I first joined it was mostly about proving myself. But I really cared about all of them, even if I was still getting to know them.

Raj and I stood in the middle of the field. "I have thoughts, but I want to hear yours first," he said. "How do you plan to capture this angel?"

"I guess I'd . . . " I closed my eyes and focused on the Darkness inside. I let it radiate around me, then I projected it onto my hands. I shaped the Darkness into ropes and tied them around his hands. "I'd do this, then I'd fly down to the place we meet Malum, then just sort of throw them down at his feet."

Raj raised an eyebrow. "So the entire operation will depend on your acting skills?"

"What do you want me to do? Actually fight?"

"David," he said. "Malum senses true sorrow and fear. Acting will not be enough."

"Okay, so I'll throw some Darkness at them."

"Wouldn't it bounce off their Light aura?"

I sighed. "Well, what do you suggest I do?"

He just raised his eyebrows and waited for me to come to the conclusion on my own.

"Oh . . . Hit them with an angel killer?"

He took a few paces back and held his arms out. "Let's see it. Do your worst."

I hesitated, looking down and shuffling my feet. "Do I have to do it right now?"

"Is there a problem?"

I really didn't want to do this. Light was always hardest to make after creating Darkness, and I was currently surrounded in it. I knew I wouldn't be able to do it, and if I did, it would hurt so bad. I didn't want to show Raj how badly this had been affecting me. I might get kicked out of the demon hunters. That was the deal right there in the contract I signed. If I lost my ability to use Light, they'd pull me out. And as much as this job terrified me, I just had to do it. This was my mission and I had to see it through.

Raj waited patiently until, in a quiet voice, I finally admitted, "I'm not sure I'll be able to make Light . . . At least not so soon after making Darkness." I looked up at him nervously. "It's been getting really difficult and painful and I'm scared I'm going to lose the ability. I think it's Malum. I think he's still affecting me. I'm worried I won't be able to face him . . . "

Raj looked at me for a while, then sat down, right there in the middle of the field, and patted the ground next to him. I sat and stared down at the grass, watching a little ant climb up a blade and back down.

"David, what are the requirements for creating Light?"

"You have to be worthy, and you have to have good intentions," I said automatically. A jolt of fear washed over me. Did this mean I wasn't worthy anymore? I'd never considered that.

"You're missing one," Raj said.

I frowned and blinked. "What?"

"Think back to your first training session. Not as a demon hunter, but as an angel. When you first learned how to use Light."

And so I did.

♦

I floated unsteadily, hovering above a small grass expanse in The Resting Place. I was trying to stand on the ground like a normal person, but it was like pushing the same poles of a magnet together. Glaring at the ground I finally got my feet to lower to the grass, then found myself surrounded by darkness. I started screaming until I realized I'd floated into the ground. Embarrassed, I slowly floated back up to the surface.

"Young man, what are you doing?" my teacher asked. Her name was Vivian, I think. There was a group of about ten new angels in the class and they all turned to look at me. Some of them turned too fast and spun a one-eighty, looking like someone who was trying to regain control of their hoverboard. Having a spirit without a body takes some getting used to.

"Sorry," I said, floating back up. The teacher glared at me, but not in a way that made me feel bad. It was like a Professor McGonagall glare that demanded you to obey, but you knew no matter what she did, she was still on your side.

"Creating Light is simple," she continued, looking back at the rest of the class. "It only requires a few important things. First, you must be worthy. As you are all angels, that's a given. Next, you must have good intentions. You cannot use Light to do anything that God would not want you to do with it."

"So how do we make it?" a little boy asked. He looked about nine and I wondered how he died. He was younger than me, and I was young enough that one of the things I was still celebrating was the fact that I didn't have homework anymore.

"Close your eyes," McGonagall instructed. "Now think about where Light comes from. From whom it comes from. Think of how much you are loved. Let that thought fill you up until you feel like you are going to burst. Then channel that feeling and project it onto your hands."

I tried, but nothing happened. Again, I tried, but achieved nothing but a grunt and a grimace. The entire training session I tried and all I could accomplish was a slightly warm feeling in my palms and a look of constipation. I kept peeking at everyone else to see if they'd be able to do it, and some were already showing flickers of Light. What if I wasn't able to do it? What if I was the only angel in history who couldn't create Light. What would they do to me? Kick me out?

I imagined Professor McGonagall—we're just embracing the name now—screaming, "He's a dud! This angel is not fit for The Resting Place! Oh, the shame!" as she fainted in horror and all the other angels crowded around her trying to revive her as they all glared over at me, pointing and saying, "You did this, David Garcia!"

"Young man?"

I blinked out of my horrible daydream to see

McGonagall standing before me, leaving the rest of the class to their own devices. They looked like a bunch of kids playing with dying flashlights that had way too many settings, including strobe light. I gulped as McGonagall raised her eyebrows.

"I can't do it," I admitted quietly. "I did exactly what you said. I don't know what I'm doing wrong."

She folded her arms and smiled. "Let me see."

I tried again, but nothing happened. I was thinking of where Light came from, I was "worthy," whatever that meant. And still, nothing was happening!

"What if I never get it?" I wondered aloud. "What if I have a disability? Maybe I have Light dyslexia or something. Can that happen?"

McGonagall chuckled. "There are no disabilities in The Resting Place. But I can see your problem quite clearly."

"What is it?" I asked.

"It's the 'what if' that's your problem, boy. You can't be afraid. Put aside your fear and believe that you can do it. You must have faith."

Back in the present, I blinked and focused back on Raj. "I know my problem," I said. "I'm afraid. Every time I go to make Light, I'm afraid I won't be able to do it anymore. I'm afraid it's going to hurt. I'm afraid I'll be kicked out of the demon hunters."

Raj smiled approvingly. "So fight that fear with faith."

I closed my eyes, thought of where Light came from, and focused on what I *knew* rather than what I was afraid of. I had never been a perfect angel, but I was trying my best, and I helped people every day. More importantly I knew that I could do anything with the help of The Big Man. It really didn't matter how strong, brave, or smart I was. I could do anything with his help.

Light exploded from my palms. And it didn't even hurt! It felt amazing, actually. I felt like I could do anything.

"Why didn't it hurt that time?" I asked Raj, amazed. "I'd just used Darkness. Doesn't Darkness screw up your ability to create Light?"

He smirked and created Darkness in one hand and Light in the other like it was nothing. "The pain comes from the Light and Darkness warring with each other inside you. You've been giving equal power to both, and both entities cannot exist in the same place, so they try to smother the other. But if you always keep more Light inside than Darkness, that isn't a problem."

I thought about that, but it didn't really make sense to me. "What about when I'm on a mission and I'm radiating Darkness? How can I have more Light if the Darkness is literally all over my body?"

Raj shifted his sitting position until he was facing me directly. Whatever he was going to say was important. "When you radiate Light, nothing can hurt you, right? It works as a shield against Darkness, correct?"

I nodded.

"Pardon how cheesy this sounds, but you need to keep that kind of shield around your heart. Keep the faith, protect yourself from those negative thoughts, and no matter how much Darkness you create—as long as it's for a good cause—it can't hurt or stifle you. It's like a warrior rushing out to battle. He might have to kill, but if he's fighting for a noble cause, it won't truly damage his soul. He'll be given the strength to do what he needs to do."

I digested that. It seemed a bit backwards from how he first taught me how to use Darkness. He kept telling me to think of everything that made me depressed. He kept yelling at me and calling me useless until I actually felt it. Until the Darkness was inside me, consuming my thoughts.

But I guess . . . I guess he was just showing me how to tap into it. I didn't need to dwell in that feeling, I just needed to know what it felt like and how to expel it from me.

Smiling at my revelation, I tried to copy Raj. Keeping a piece of Light inside me, I focused all my negativity into one hand, and lit the other hand with a ball of Light. Then I wrapped the Light around the Darkness and smiled at my awesome invention.

chapter 29

TAMALE TIME

There were still a few days until Operation Angel Bait (that's what I called it anyway), which gave me plenty of time to do some family visits. It had been a while since I'd seen any of my family members, and I felt a little guilty for that. I mean, I was supposed to be a guardian angel first and foremost, but this demon hunter stuff had kind of taken over my afterlife. Luckily Mom seemed to be pretty on top of things. I'd just finished a shift at the front desk when Mom popped up out of nowhere and grabbed my arm.

"Come with me. We're making tamales."

I blinked. "What?"

She huffed in agitation. "It's almost Christmas and the family is making tamales. Which worries me. They're going to mess up the *masa* if I'm not there! That's *my* job!"

"Oh," I said. Mom was always in charge of the *masa*. She had to have it perfect and exactly her way, so I'm sure this was going to be challenging for her to watch the family try to do it without her.

Nana Maria showed up out of nowhere. "What are you two doing here? It's tamale time!"

"We know, Mom," Mom said. "We're on our way."

We showed up at Tata Ramon's house, which was pretty packed. Sam, Elena, Ginger, Rocco, some woman I didn't recognize who was holding Sam's arm—did he have a new girlfriend??—David Jr., and Dad.

"Who's this lady?" I demanded, pointing to the redhead laughing at Sam's arm.

"That's Jessica," Mom said. "They've been dating for about a month now."

"Huh. Do you like her?"

Mom frowned and shrugged, which I'm sure had more to do with my mom than Jessica. She loved Chelsea, Sam's ex.

"And does little David hang out with Sam a lot now?" I asked.

"Hmm? Oh, about once a week, but today he's with Sam because Chelsea's at the hospital having their baby."

I held my hands up. "Shouldn't he be there for that? It's his daughter."

Mom growled and sighed at the same time. "He doesn't know. Chelsea dropped David off unexpectedly saying she had a checkup and didn't tell Sam she was in labor. I guess she didn't want to make him feel obligated.

Or maybe she was afraid he wouldn't come." She rolled her eyes. "Young people are so infuriating."

"Should I go convince Chelsea to call him?" I asked. "What hospital is she at?"

"Oh, I'll do it!"

She disappeared in a puff of Light.

"Alrighty then," I said to myself as I drifted around the kitchen. It looked like a disaster—pots of red *chile* all over the stove and counter tops, bowls of *masa*, cookie sheets of tamales, bags and twist ties, people using their wrists and elbows to grab things because their hands were covered in goo—but I knew they had a system. Tata was mixing up the *masa*, Elena was spreading it on the *hojas*, Sam was filling them with *chile*, and Ginger was wrapping them up in paper. That left Dad to look after the little ones while the tamale-making happened in the kitchen. I don't think he minded. He was laughing as loud as the boys were as they wrestled on the ground. I bet Dad was remembering when me and Sam were that little, because that's what it reminded me of.

It didn't take long for Sam's phone to start buzzing. He glanced over at it on the counter, saw Chelsea's name, and bit his lip.

"*Answer it, Sam*," I prompted.

He went back to filling the tamales.

"*Dude, answer the phone*," I said.

He continued to ignore it.

"Oh my gosh, who's phone is buzzing?" Elena complained. "Can someone please pick it up? It sounds like a chainsaw."

Sam sighed. "It's mine."

"Well, answer it!"

Sam wiped his hands off on a wet rag and took the phone into the next room. Jessica's eyes followed him suspiciously. She'd been sitting across from Sam, helping Elena spread the *masa*. Curiosity got the better of her and she frowned, wiped off her hands, and followed him.

Oh boy, I thought. *I hope she's not the jealous type…*

I followed both of them into the next room. Sam had just hung up, his face pale.

"What is it?" Jessica asked.

"It was my ex," Sam said quietly. "She's having the baby."

Jessica screamed, startling me and Sam. She jumped up and down clapping her hands. Then she swatted Sam on the shoulder. "What the heck are you still doing here! I'll drop you off, let's go!"

I chuckled. Maybe this Jessica wasn't so bad.

"Hey, Tata, I gotta go," Sam said when he got back to the kitchen.

"Oh, okay. Is everything okay, *mijo*?"

"Yeah. Uh, Chelsea's having the baby."

Everyone in the room gasped and cheered and Sam blushed. He went to the family room and said, "Hey, Dad, can you watch David for a while?"

"Sure, kid!" He grinned, just as Rocco tackled him to the ground, making him go "Oof!"

I smiled as I looked around at all the shenanigans happening. Elena wiped some *masa* on Ginger's nose, Tata was singing in Spanish, Nana was yelling at him to pay attention to what he was doing. It didn't matter that she was dead. Even if she was alive, Tata would still be smiling and ignoring her as he hummed and whistled. It was one of those moments when I didn't feel like I was there for my family; I was there for me. I needed this.

Mom showed up just as Sam left. "Did he go?"

"Yep," I said. "You know, I kind of like this Jessica. She doesn't put up with his crap."

"Hmph."

She was quickly distracted by a glass of water on the counter with a ball of something that had sunk to the bottom. "What is *this*?" she demanded of everyone. "Is this *masa*? Did you do the water test? Well FYI, it's supposed to float! Please tell me you didn't use this *masa*!"

Nana interrupted her with a scream. "Leave my family alone!" She threw a ball of Light into the corner.

Oh great. A demon was there to screw it all up.

The demon dude laughed and floated around the room, avoiding blasts of Light from my mom and Nana.

I closed my eyes and thought of where Light comes from and I felt it filling me up. My eyes watered as they always do and I smiled at the feeling. It was so nice to be able to make Light again! Once my Light was charged up, I pointed a finger gun at the demon, and shot it with a beam of Light. The demon wailed and flew out the door. It did not come back.

Mom and Nana looked over at me and I blew smoke from my finger, which made Nana laugh and Mom roll her eyes.

chapter 30

I AM A REAL SPY!

I had Mom and Nana head back to The Resting Place without me. I wanted to check up on Sandra and her wanderers first. When I showed up at her apartment, it was not what I expected. Five of them were sitting around the table playing Go Fish. Literally, that's what they were doing. Except they couldn't hold the cards in their hands so Sandra had set up privacy folders for them so they could lay their cards out on the table in front of them without anyone peeking. She was teacher-ing even when she wasn't in school.

Asher pointed to an ace with a questioning look.

"Do you have any Aces?" Sandra asked for him.

Bill shook his head.

"Go fish," Sandra said.

Asher tried to make another card float to him, but his mind powers were still kind of weak. Sandra sat one down in front of him.

I tilted my head. "Uh, what am I seeing?"

Sandra spun around. "David! Where have you been?"

I shrugged and smiled. She asked me where I've been, which meant she'd been expecting me, which meant she wanted me around. Or, more likely, she was annoyed I hadn't been around to keep training the wanderers like I'd said I would. "I've had a lot going on. Sorry. Is everything okay? Where are the others?"

Sandra left the table and gestured for me to follow her to the other side of the kitchen so she wouldn't be overheard. "I don't really know where the others are. They've been coming and going more than usual. I wanted to help train them some more, but you were gone and I wasn't sure what else to do. But they're all acting a lot more lucid. And some of them can almost do the Light thingy. I think. I can't see it, but sometimes Bill gasps at his hands and then scowls like he lost it."

"Oh, nice!" I said.

I wasn't exactly sure what I was supposed to do now. I didn't really have a long-term plan for these wanderer/demon hunters. What had Raj and Ying Yue done next? They taught us how to use Darkness. But was that wise to do for wanderers? They were on the brink of becoming angels or demons. Would using Darkness be risky for them? And I couldn't exactly teach them to be spies when they still wouldn't even talk to me.

I nodded to the laundry room and Sandra followed me.

It was pristine, like the rest of her place. She didn't even leave the detergent on top of the washing machine. And there were no clothes in sight, meaning she washed and put all her laundry away right away. There were these pink little wicker baskets where she kept all her fabric softener sheets and the wall behind the dryer had this cursive plaque saying, "Cleanliness is next to godliness."

I did not understand this girl.

She saw my raised eyebrow and folded her arms. "What? I can't be clean?"

"I'm not saying you can't be clean, but that sign is not you. You always have dumb quotes and sayings on your stuff, not scriptural proverbs."

She smiled sheepishly and pulled a wooden sign out from behind the washing machine. "Well, I did buy this, because I thought it was funny, but there's kids in the house. . ."

I leaned closer. The sign read:

> *I'm feeling a little dirty today . . .*
> *Will you do me?*
> *Love,*
> *Your Laundry*

I threw my head back and laughed so hard my abs would have been killing me if I was still alive.

"So, what did you want to talk to me about?" she asked,

shoving the sign back behind the dryer. Her lips were pursed like she was trying not to laugh, but the corner of her mouth kept twitching.

I forced myself to stop chuckling and be serious. I cleared my throat. "Well . . . the thing is, I have no idea what to do with your wanderers."

"What are you talking about? I thought you were gonna teach them how to be demon hunters?"

"Well, here's the thing . . . Becoming a demon hunter is pretty dark business and I think your friends might be a little too fragile right now for that. I mean, you have to learn how to use Darkness so you can blend in with demons, and that stuff kind of screws with your head. I mean, I'm an angel and I almost lost my ability to use Light. That's pretty bad."

"Oh," she said, a realization coming to her. "Is that why you went outside the other day to make Light and screamed and it was really weird?"

I sighed. "Yeah, that's why I went outside and screamed. I was struggling to make Light. But I'm good now! Anyway, if I've been an angel for ten years and Darkness had that kind of effect on me, I don't really want to see what it would do to your wanderers. They might actually turn into demons."

"Hmm . . . " Sandra turned a laundry basket upside down and sat on it. "What do we do now?"

I shrugged. "You're the rescuer. Why don't we focus

on getting them to cross over? Then when they're angels they can apply to join the real demon hunters if they want. Though, if our next mission goes all right we might not need demon hunters anymore."

"What's the next mission?" Sandra asked, scooting her laundry basket closer to me.

"Well, we're gonna stage a—" I froze. "You know, I probably shouldn't say. That's confidential business."

She gave me a look. "Stop acting like you're James Bond or something. It's not like you're a real spy."

I scowled. "I am a real spy. This is serious business, Sandra. I even have an Evil David alias for when I'm undercover." I transformed myself into Evil David with the leather jacket and the long hair and scruff.

Sandra blinked and sat back. "Dang."

"What?"

"Don't take this the wrong way, but Evil David is *fine*." She stretched out the word "fine" so that it sounded like it had five i's.

I rolled my eyes as I transformed back to myself. "Why is that the only version of me that girls find attractive?" Sandra opened her mouth, but I cut her off. "Don't answer that. The point is, I don't think the demon hunter training is such a good idea anymore. But the Light thing seems to be working. Maybe just focus more on that."

Her face tightened like she was trying not to scowl at me.

"What?" I asked.

She sighed and stood, glaring at the floor. "Nothing."

I hesitated. I wanted to push her to tell me what she was really thinking, but I was due back at the front desk.

"I'm sorry, Sandra, but I gotta go. I'll be back soon, okay? I promise."

She gave me a skeptical smile. "If you say so."

chapter 31
THE AMBUSH

The day of the ambush I stepped into conference room nine shaking with nerves and guilt. These last couple of days I'd almost forgotten what I'd agreed to do. I couldn't believe it had been my idea. What was I thinking?

No, no, no. Confidence, I told myself. *I can do this!*

Focusing on how awesome I felt when I learned how to make Light and Darkness simultaneously, I stepped into the room, my shoulders squared. I had joined the demon hunters. I chose this. Now it was my time to play my part.

I took an empty metal folding chair and waited as my team trickled in, trying not to make eye contact with Raj or Ying Yue. Once Ted, Natalie, and Daisy were all there, Ying Yue called the meeting together.

"Shouldn't we wait for the others?" Ted asked.

"The defenders have been called away on important business," Ying Yue said. "We are going to begin without them."

I avoided everyone's eyes, because I knew exactly where Jake, Frederick, and William were.

Before Ying Yue could say any more, I stood and pulled out the gun I'd made, loaded with angel killer bullets. Without a word, I pointed it at Natalie and shot her. She flew backward against the wall and before she, or anyone else could recover, I lunged toward her and grabbed her by the throat.

Yes, I actually did that. Take a moment to let that sink in.

Why Natalie? Mainly because it had to be someone I could realistically take hostage. Ted had combat experience so I wasn't sure about my chances with him, and Daisy was . . . well, terrifying. I'm not calling Natalie weak, but I was pretty sure she'd be the easiest to take down.

Before anyone could come at me, I wrapped a Light and Dark tie-dyed cloth around Natalie's mouth and disapparated.

Originally Raj and I were going to stage a fight where I'd freak out and hurt someone, but this felt better. It was more shocking without the buildup.

I showed up at the predetermined site, quickly changing into my Evil David disguise with the punk hair and leather jacket. The meeting place was a forest, a place with good cover where angels could be hiding in the trees. On the flip side, I felt like every long shadow was hiding a demon. Jumpy and nervous, I thought of my family and what they'd all be doing right now while I was waiting to meet the evilest demon in history. Likely opening presents with the little ones in their PJs and Christmas music on in the background. It felt wrong to stage something evil on Christmas, but that was mainly why that day was chosen. We figured Malum would like it.

Come find me, Malum, I thought. *I'm here. Come find me.*

An owl hooted somewhere and trees rustled in the breeze. Other than that, it was completely silent. Eerily silent. Even Natalie hadn't made a sound. She just knelt next to me, shaking and wide eyed.

"Hey!" I shouted. My voice echoed, then was swallowed up by the silence. "Mr. Prince of Darkness! I brought you something!"

Flapping sounds startled me as a flock of birds took flight, spooked by my outburst. Natalie started struggling out of my grip, so I shot her again. She slumped and tears fell down her face, disappearing before they could hit the mossy dirt. I squeezed my eyes shut so I wouldn't have to look at her. If I did I would be so consumed with guilt I'd ruin the whole operation.

I forced myself into a sort of cold detachment. Deep down I felt horrible about what I was doing to Natalie—that fear and pain in her eyes cut me like a knife—but I mentally pulled away and remembered why I was doing this. I put my feelings in a box and kicked it out of the way until I had time to examine them later. Was this what it was like to be a soldier or a defender?

No, this was what it was like to be a demon hunter. Because that's what I was, and for the first time, I felt like it. For the first time, I wasn't afraid.

The trees and bushes rustled as all the animals sped off, sensing something coming. A smoky blackness snaked across the ground and expanded, filling the forest floor with dark mist.

"What do you want?" the Darkness purred.

I tried to answer, but nothing came out. The Darkness expanded until the sun was swallowed up by the thick mist of black smoke. Something in the Darkness breathed raggedly like a starving wolf, and I felt it . . . sniffing me. Talons gripped my arms and the sniffing traveled to my hair. A snake tail wrapped around my legs. It was searching me, searching for the fear it craved so dearly.

I squeezed my eyes shut as memories tried to surface. All my old fears, compounded with new fears I'd felt since our first encounter. I could feel them bubbling up inside, demanding to be released. I fought with all I had to keep them in, but it was like trying to hold in a sneeze.

Hands grasped my legs, clinging to me for dear life, and I knew these hands were Natalie. Somehow that gave me strength. She was a tiny flickering flame in this raging darkness, and even in her fear she gave me strength. I remembered why I was here and what I had to do. I could not be afraid. If he sensed my fears, he'd recognize them and figure out I was nothing more than that quivering man boy he'd attacked when he escaped. But I wasn't the same person I was back then. I was a demon hunter and I was going to take him down.

The Darkness left me alone and slithered its way toward Natalie, who was now hyperventilating. I heard her gasp and felt her ripped away from me. It was too dark to see it, but I knew what was happening. Natalie didn't have the knowledge I did. She didn't know this was just a ruse and she didn't know that I would never let this evil demon take her. I wished I could tell her, but her fear was important here. It's what attracted Malum and it was what would keep him here long enough for us to take him. Through the mist, I could almost see a hand wrap around her throat as it lifted her off the ground. Natalie struggled at first, kicking her legs, then the mists parted enough for me to see her eyes glaze over as she froze in terror. I didn't know what Malum was showing her, but the sight of Natalie in that position shook me and I almost lost my nerve. I knew what that felt like. I knew the horror and helplessness. That unending terror like a fall into a bottomless pit.

"Mmm…" Malum murmured. "Your fear is delicious…"

I couldn't stand it anymore. "Hey, that's my hostage!"

Slowly, the Darkness was sucked in toward him.

Within seconds, Malum condensed into the form of a man and dropped Natalie, who curled up into a ball and, despite what I'd done to her, clutched my legs and buried her head.

Malum didn't say a word, but slowly walked up to me and stared at me, expressionless. "You've got my attention. What do you want?"

He looked like your typical white male. Someone so nondescript, it was difficult to even describe him. His hair was so mousy and dull it didn't really have a color. His facial features were so average there was nothing that would set him apart. But his voice was like gravel, and Darkness steamed from his skin as though he had gathered so much he couldn't keep it all contained. I didn't know what was wrong with me—by all accounts I should have been terrified out of my wits—but I wasn't afraid. I'd done as Raj had said and kept a ball of Light burning within me, reminding me that I had someone behind me. Someone who would never let me fall.

"I want to join you," I said, looking into the eyes of my deepest fear.

Malum kicked at Natalie. "What's this?"

"My pet. Or slave. I haven't decided what to do with her yet."

Malum frowned as he considered me. Then he held out his hand. "I've never seen anyone else capture an angel… I could use someone like you."

My heart skipped a beat. Anyone *else?* Did that mean that *he* had captured angels? Or was he just talking about attacking me and Grandma? But he used the word "captured," which implied taking them away. But if he had captured someone, we would know. There's no way one of us could just go missing without anyone noticing. We have to check in and out each time we leave The Resting Place. And Hermes keeps tabs on us constantly.

Shaking the thought away, I took his hand. "I'm with you."

Then I gripped him harder and waited.

Come on . . .

Nothing happened.

General Wolff, what's going on? I demanded, sending my thoughts out telepathically. *That's the signal.*

I'd imagined the defenders descending from above like a team of Valkyries on flying horses, but the forest was silent and still. Had I come to the wrong place?

Malum started to pull away and I tried to decide what I was supposed to do. The plan was that I'd hold him there while the defenders converged. Supposedly if I kept hold of his hand, he couldn't disappear into a mist of darkness. But the defenders weren't coming. If I attacked him, I'd be on my own, but if I did nothing, this whole ruse would be completely pointless.

A voice came into my mind. I recognized it as Jake.

Stall.

What's going on? I asked.

I don't know. Wolff and Moustafa are arguing about what to do.

But I gave the signal!

I don't know what's going on. Just stall.

I glared up at the trees. What the crap were they doing? This was not the plan!

A seed of fear and doubt tried to weasel its way into my heart. I gulped and shoved it down.

"A couple of ground rules," I said as Malum finally yanked out of my grip.

Malum looked amused. "Yes?"

"I'm not your errand boy, all right?" I said. "I'll join you, but I'm not gonna be one of your minions to do your bidding."

"Naturally," Malum purred. "I'll give you a position of power. You can have your own minions."

"And you need to tell me everything upfront," I demanded. "What's the plan?"

Atta boy, Moustafa said in my mind.

I resisted glaring up at the trees. *Information? Is that what you want?*

She didn't answer.

What was going on up there? This wasn't intended to be a covert operation. It was supposed to be an attack. Was that what Moustafa and Wolff were arguing about?

"So?" I said, prompting Malum again. "What's your

endgame?"

"If you don't know that, then why are you joining me?" Malum asked.

Shoot . . . I thought to myself. *That's a good question.*

"I know you want to take over from the Evil One," I said, making crap up that I prayed would keep him talking. "I have my own reasons for revolting, but I don't know yours."

"Because my plan is better!" he hissed. His nondescript face flashed briefly into a red flame as though he struggled to keep the form of a man. "Old Scratch won't deviate from his plan of simply bombarding the mortals. He can't acknowledge my plan is better! He won't take any risks that will end the world sooner than intended because he knows he's going to lose at Armageddon. He believes that deviating from tradition will speed our downfall. But with my plan, he wouldn't have to worry about that! We could have an endless supply of pain and fear!"

"And your plan is?" I folded my arms, trying to mask my nerves with fake swagger.

Malum's gaze flicked to Natalie and a smile slowly crept across his face. "You've already guessed it."

My eyes widened and I stepped in front of Natalie. Did this mean what I thought it meant? Was he planning to—

"*Attack!*"

Angels descended from the heavens. You'd think that would be a comforting sight, but it was all wrong. Why weren't we following the plan? They were supposed to attack while I still had a grip on Malum so he wouldn't disappear into smoke. Before I could reach toward him again, Malum snapped and dozens of demons melted from the shadows, forming into people. Streaks of Light and Darkness shot in all directions as angels and demons converged in battle.

Malum lunged toward Natalie. Before I could even move, Jake, Frederick, and William dropped from the sky, blocking Natalie from Malum's path. My relief was short-lived, because Malum smiled as he floated up to Jake. It was a knowing smile, like he'd won already and was amused that any of us were still fighting. I knew right then that no matter how much stronger Jake was than me, he was still no match for Malum.

I wanted to fly over and help, but I had to do something about my disguise first so I wouldn't blow my cover.

"Good luck!" I called to Malum, and disappeared in a cloud of smoke.

I reappeared several yards away, looking like my regular self. By then Malum was staring into Jake's eyes from only a foot away, his hand slowly inching toward his throat.

For Jake's part, he really tried. He lifted his hands filled with balls of Light ready to throw at Malum with a fiercely determined snarl. But he'd never experienced Malum first-hand and had no idea what he was up against. The Light in his hands flickered and went out. His jaw dropped at whatever terrible memory or fear Malum was showing him. Frederick and William pushed Jake behind them. They were able to hold on to their Light, but that was as much as they could do. Frederick gasped and staggered back and William froze, his arms half-raised to attack.

I couldn't stand the sight of the three of them frozen like angelic toy soldiers, just waiting to be destroyed by the enemy. I pulled out my canister of demon killer bullets and loaded them into my gun.

"Hey, creepy!" I shouted.

Malum looked over at me just as I shot him. He staggered backward, but it soon became apparent that I'd done nothing but make him mad. He lunged at me and pinned me to the ground. His breath smelled of smoke and rot. His eyes were an endless pool of mist. Not inky black, but cloudy with unfathomable depths. In his eyes I could see his age and his power. I could see how puny I was to him. This guy was ancient, and I was nothing but a ten year old angel who died at seventeen.

"I remember you," he purred. "You're the one who let me escape. This is all your fault, isn't it?"

Intellectually, I knew that wasn't true. Based on how my team had reacted to him just now, I knew now that anyone would have frozen. There was nothing I could have done. Even Frederick had been affected! That was more frightening than anything else I'd seen tonight.

Frederick was hundreds of years old. I looked up to him. It was just so wrong to see him terrified out of his wits.

Despite all that, I couldn't shake myself of the guilt and blame. This whole operation had depended on me and it was failing! Malum gently put his hands around my throat and my carefully built wall of faith crumbled.

I saw all the terrible memories and fears he'd shown me before—dying, my family screaming and crying over my body, those feelings of incompletion because I died before my time—but those were only the warm-up acts. I had more recent experiences to give him fuel. I saw Dad sobbing on the floor of his bathroom. I saw David Jr. crying for his dad as his mom drove away. I saw Elena, laughing with her kids one second, then falling apart as she stepped into the other room, releasing all her sadness and fear for her husband away at war. I wasn't there. I wasn't there for any of them. Why hadn't I spent more time with them? What had I done for my family lately? Nothing. I'd been too caught up in myself.

Then there came the fears of things that hadn't happened yet, but in my mind it was like they were happening right now.

I saw Sandra, cursing my name as my plan fell apart. Her wanderers turned into demons and terrorized her day and night. "You used me!" she cried, blaming me for everything that had gone wrong. And she wasn't wrong. I had used her. I'd tried to turn her into a spy for me. I'd done nothing but take and take and take from her. How could I still call myself an angel when I was supposed to be the one protecting *her?*

I saw Sheila looking beautiful at the bar and a terrible realization came to me. I liked her. A lot. I saw visions of me kissing her and laughing. I saw us holding hands, radiating Darkness. I saw us throwing Darkness at stupid angels that were far beneath us. We went around the world, terrorizing poor mortals as a team. I saw myself tempting mortals. I saw Sheila come up behind me, looking gorgeous and I put my hands around her, dipping her into an old-romantic-movie-style kiss. We laughed as the world burned around us.

There was more, much more. Things I won't even write about because they were so terrible. Things so wicked and horrifying I thought I would combust with how filled with fear and shame I was. It was the most horrific horror movie you could never imagine.

I'd given up all hope of escape when Malum was roughly yanked off me. A whip braided with Light and Darkness lashed around Malum's waist, dragging him backward. Pulling the whip from the other end was Raj, looking like the most angry papa bear the world had ever seen. I felt a surge of hope looking into his face contorted with fierce determination. Then, five demons converged on him, and while he put up a good fight, he lost hold of the whip.

EVACUATE NOW! Hermes commanded.

A part of me hesitated. We'd failed to capture Malum. I wanted to go after him, even knowing I'd fail, but Raj took hold of my arm and pulled me back to The Resting Place.

I was struck by the silence. The world went from yelling and screaming to a quiet winter day with a gurgling fountain in the background. Dozens of defenders and demon hunters sat on the ground, breathing deeply, trying to process what had just happened.

"That certainly did not go according to plan," Frederick whispered.

chapter 32
THE BUDDY SYSTEM

I don't generally get angry at anyone but myself. Most of the time, I'm pretty chill. At this moment, however, I was livid, as one often feels after being terrified.

"What the hell was that?" I shouted at no one, surging to my feet.

I scanned the crowd until I found General Wolff, his arm around a crying angel.

"Why didn't you attack when I gave the signal?" I demanded.

"Because I told him not to."

I spun around. "Hermes? But why? I had hold of him! We could have captured him! What were you thinking?"

He blinked, stone-faced, and immediately I was filled with shame and embarrassment. You do *not* talk to Hermes like that.

"I'm sorry, sir," I said, looking down. "I just don't understand."

"Walk with me," he said as he turned away.

I could feel eyes on me as I followed Hermes out of earshot. Why were they staring? Because I yelled at Hermes? Because I'd failed again? Were they hoping to hear Hermes chew me out?

Once we'd separated from the crowd Hermes said quietly, "That plan was always meant to fail. Malum was going to escape in the end no matter what."

I scowled in confusion. "Then why let us go through with it?"

"You understand the hierarchy around here, correct?" he asked. "You know who I get my orders from?"

I nodded.

"Then you know that if you question me, you question him. He has his reasons and that should be enough."

Appropriately abashed, I bit my lip and looked down. "Am I allowed to ask why?"

Hermes put his hand on my shoulder. "Why does God allow anyone to fail? We learn from failure. What did you learn from this?"

I sighed. "Some kind of lesson in persistence or something?"

Hermes raised an eyebrow. "I was thinking more on the lines of information. That is your job, correct? Think, David."

I frowned and thought back. Did I learn something? I'd been so hung up on the fact that we didn't follow the plan. That the General didn't send his defenders to attack when I gave the signal. But . . . well, if the plan was always going to fail, and he'd have called the attack right then, I'd have never had time to stall. And during that time I had discovered some important information about Malum's plan. Stuff I never would have known if things hadn't gone down exactly as they had.

My eyes widened. "Oh my gosh, I need to talk to my team."

Hermes nodded. "That you do."

I sheepishly wandered through the crowd that had mostly dispersed, looking for my task force. Eventually I found Jake, Frederick, and William. Frederick had his hand on Jake's shoulder and William was sitting alone, his head in his hands. They all looked pale and stricken, eyes still a bit glazed as though they were having trouble shaking off what Malum had shown them.

"Hey guys," I said. "You okay?"

Jake threw his arms around me. It was really weird coming from Jake. He's more a bro hug kind of guy, if that, but this was a real one. And it was really tight.

"Are you okay?" I wheezed.

Jake released me and cleared his throat. "I'm sorry, mate."

"For what?"

His words came out in a rush. "I thought you being all

devo when Malum escaped was just you being weak. I thought you were pathetic for freezing and letting him go. I reckoned I could have done better." He shook his head in bewilderment. "I was wrong."

"Oh . . . Uh, it's okay," I said awkwardly. The apology didn't exactly make me feel better because it confirmed that he really did think I'd been a giant baby. At least he'd stood by me anyway.

He grasped my arm. "No, it's not. And you need to know that you were incredible today."

I grimaced and shook my head. "No I wasn't. He overpowered me again. Raj had to save me."

"No, I mean when he first turned up!" Jake said. "You were chatting with him like he was just some bloke off the street and you kept your cover the whole time. That was ace!"

I looked down and shrugged. I didn't feel "ace."

"David."

I cringed, hearing the Russian accent. I didn't want to face Natalie. I knew she'd never forgive me. I'd fed her to the sharks with no warning whatsoever. She'd hate me forever.

Slowly I turned around. "Natalie, I'm so sor—"

She slapped me hard across the face. Normally that wouldn't actually hurt an angel, but she had covered her hand in Darkness, so it actually stung quite a bit.

"I'm sor—"

She interrupted again, but this time with a kiss. My eyes bugged out of my head, and I pushed her face away. "What was that for?"

"You brave little brat! I hate you!"

Then she stormed off muttering in Russian. I looked around at the guys and they just shrugged.

Our meeting in the conference room was awkward. Everyone was quiet. Even Jake and I. We all just sat around looking at each other until Raj said, "So . . ."

"That mission was cactus," Jake blurted.

We all just kind of nodded, though I suspected most of us weren't exactly sure what cactuses had to do with it.

"Let's review what we've accomplished," Ying Yue suggested.

Jake snorted. "We accomplished something?"

"Of course we did," Raj said. "We learn from every mission. Cheer up, kid."

Jake just shrugged and stared morosely at the floor. He looked like . . . Oh gosh, he looked like me! This was not good. I wasn't sure how to process Jake being the self-doubting, depressed one, but I didn't think our duo would do so well with both of us acting that way, so I tried to pick up the slack.

"We learned about Malum's plan," I offered.

"Yes," Raj said, pointing at me. "What did you learn, David?"

"It's pretty bad." I glanced nervously at Natalie who heard the whole thing.

"He plans to do what David did to me," Natalie said, staring down at her hands. "Except for real."

"Capture angels?" Ted asked. "Can he do that?"

"Well, let's see," Jake said. "He was able to incapacitate and overpower Natalie, Me, William, Frederick, and David at the end. None of us had an ounce of fight left in us. So, yeah, I'd reckon he could defo do that."

We all took a moment to let that sink in. Jake, while being uncharacteristically negative, had a point. It would have been really easy for Malum to take any of us wherever he pleased. Frozen in fear like that, you don't even have the presence of mind to disappear.

Daisy looked to be hiding her worry behind a brave scowl. "So, what do we do now?"

"Yeah, David, what do we do?" Jake asked. Was that resentment in his voice?

"Why are you asking me?"

"Lad, you spoke to him face-to-face," Frederick said. "You were the only one of us who was able to look into his eyes and keep your wits about you."

"What is the secret?" William asked.

"Um . . ." I blinked just to make sure this was actually happening. Were Frederick and William actually asking me for advice? They continued to stare at me, so I figured this was actually real and not one of my silly daydreams.

"Well, you just can't be afraid. You have to have faith that it's going to be all right. It's fear that fuels him, so if you sort of tuck your fears away, he can't sense them and he doesn't know how to get to you." They blinked at me so I added, "It helps if you're prepared. You guys were taken by surprise. It's kind of hard not to be scared when you're startled. That's how he got me too. Also, I think it gets worse if you let him touch you."

"What do we do now, knowing Malum's out there ready to take angels captive?" Ted asked.

Raj and Ying Yue looked at each other.

"We'll need to meet with Hermes," Ying Yue said. "But for now we should take precautionary measures so that none of us are taken by surprise again. I suggest we implement a buddy system."

"I'm out," Natalie said, standing.

"What do you mean?" Ying Yue asked.

"I'm done. I'm not doing this anymore."

Guilt surged through me. Out of all of us, Natalie had it the worst today. She was taken against her will, shot, and offered up to the Son of Evil. All the while, never knowing there was a plan behind it all.

Raj's eyebrows knit. "Natalie, you're a valuable member of our team. Let's not do anything rash."

Natalie shook her head. "I'm not being rash. I've been thinking of quitting for a while now. I'm not fit to be a demon hunter."

I rubbed my face with my hands. "Natalie, I really am sor—"

"You did what you had to," she said, not meeting my eyes. "But tell me this . . ." She looked at me and dared me not to lie. "Why did you choose me as your captive?"

I opened my mouth and closed it. How could I answer that truthfully without hurting her feelings?

Natalie nodded and looked away. "That's what I thought. I'm the weakest among us." Then she disappeared, leaving us all stunned.

Raj blinked and shook his head. "Does anyone else wish to leave?" He looked at each of us, trying to keep the disappointment from his face. When no one spoke up he let out a breath. "All right. The rest of you, pair up. I don't want you leaving The Resting Place without a buddy until we get this all sorted out. Now that Malum knows us I'm sure we're greater targets."

"He doesn't know us," Ted said, gesturing toward him and Daisy. They hadn't been invited to the ambush because it was only the defenders and task force leaders who were involved. Neither Ted nor Daisy fit into those categories. Technically I didn't either.

"It doesn't matter," Ying Yue said. "We're pairing up. Should be easy now that we have an even number. David and Jake, Frederick and William, Ted and Daisy. If any of you visits a family member or leaves on a mission, you'll go with your partner. Understood?"

We all nodded except for Jake who just scowled at the ground. The meeting was adjourned and everyone dispersed. Everyone except me and Jake.

"You okay, man?" I asked once everyone was gone.

Jake looked at me sharply. "Don't patronize me."

My head reared back. First of all, that was a big three-syllable word there. Second of all, all I'd done was ask if he was okay. Since when was that patronizing?

"I'm not," I said. "You just look kind of upset and I was seeing if you were okay. That's kind of what friends do."

"I'm fine," he said shortly.

I looked around awkwardly, completely thrown by how he was talking to me. This was not like Jake at all.

"So . . . " I hedged. "You still good to be my partner?"

Jake looked away. "You don't need a partner," he said bitterly. "You resisted him just fine."

"Actually, I didn't. He got me in the end. Raj had to save me."

"Whatever."

We both sat in the most awkward silence I'd ever experienced. I didn't know what to say or do. I'd never felt like I was walking on eggshells around Jake before, but it seemed like whatever I said made him mad. What had I done to him?

Finally I stood. "Look, man, if you have a problem with me—"

"I don't have a problem," he snapped. "Just get on your bike."

I frowned. "I'm sorry?"

"Go away," he translated.

"Look, obviously you have some beef with me or you wouldn't be acting this way. What's the deal? Does it have to do with the mission? Are you mad at me for not saving you sooner? I tried, okay? But I had to switch disguises so I wouldn't blow my cover."

He stood and floated up to me. "See, that's the problem there. You think I needed you to save me."

"Well . . . " I rubbed the back of my neck. "You were kind of frozen, man."

"So you admit it," he growled. "You think you're better than me."

I threw my hands up. "I didn't say that! We both know you're way better at everything else. A fact that you just love to point out to me all the freaking time."

Jake just rolled his eyes. "I'm better at everything *else*? But you admit you think you're better at fighting demons than me? I'm a defender! I'm a captain! I've been training for ten years to fight demons, and suddenly you think you're an expert?"

"No, I'm not an expert, but I do have more experience dealing with Malum. I saw you frozen like I was the first time and you looked like you needed some help. I didn't realize stepping in would be so offensive to you. Maybe I should go yell at Raj for saving my butt too."

Jake laughed bitterly. "So if Malum was able to overtake me, William, and Frederick, what made you so sure you could save us? It's because you think you're better than us! Just because you lucked out and ended up assigned to the demon who was in touch with Malum, a demon who, for some reason, found you attractive even though you have zero game. No, you lucked into all of this, while some people like me have been training for an opportunity like this for years. And then it all goes to the weak one who doesn't even know what he's doing."

I felt like he'd punched me in the gut. He was right, I didn't know what I was doing, but I was doing the best I could! And I hadn't failed entirely. I was able to uncover some of Malum's plan, and I still kept my cover so I could continue to spy on him. Did Jake think he could have done better? Would it have made him feel better if I'd failed miserably? How insecure was he that me doing well actually threatened him?

Anger turned my neck and face red. "What is wrong with you, man? Is your ego so dependent on you being the strong one that the one time I do something right you totally fall apart?"

"Oh, so now this is about my ego? Put a sock in it!" he yelled.

"Oh my gosh, I'm *sorry* for trying to be a good friend! I'm sorry for trying to be there for you when Malum freaked you out! For your information, I don't think I'm better than you, but I do know what it's like when Malum overpowers you. I'm sorry for wanting to spare you from that awful feeling. What a terrible friend I am! I should have just sat by and watched while he took you captive and dragged the three of you down to his army of angel prisoners he intends to build. That's what *real* friends do."

"We're not friends," he spat, disappearing before I could say anything else.

I clenched my fists and growled at the empty room. I knew all this was just him reacting to whatever Malum showed him and how it made him feel. I certainly wasn't myself after I'd been attacked the first time. I was lucky to have a friend like Jake who kept encouraging and supporting me. I never imagined he'd react this way when I tried to return the favor. He was acting like a little kid having a temper tantrum. At least when I was filled with Darkness I only put myself down. Why did Jake have to try and tear me down too?

So much for the buddy system.

chapter 33
SUPERMOM NEEDS A BREAK

"Excuse me . . . Excuse me, mister? Mister!"

I blinked, snapping out of my turbulent thoughts. A little girl was waving a guardian angel report in front of my face, filled from top to bottom with adorable misspelled, first-grade handwriting.

"Oh, uh, I'll take that," I said, taking the report from her. She'd surprisingly done most of it right, but I had to help her fix a few parts she was confused on. When we were done, I pulled out a sheet of stickers. "Want one?"

"Ooh!" She floated up to get a better look. "Why does the seal unicorn have a tiara?"

"That's a narwal, and she's a princess."

She took so long to pick I started staring into space again as my worries pulled me back down the rabbit hole of all I was dealing with at the moment.

"Hello! I said I wanted the one with the dancing pickle."

I blinked and shook my head. "Huh? Oh, good choice.

That one's my favorite."

Why did I have a princess narwal sticker right next to a dancing pickle? Because kids are weird, and so am I. Also, I feel bad for all the kids in The Resting Place and silly stickers make them happy.

"Have a good day!" I told her.

"You too!" The little girl stuck the pickle sticker on her forehead and did air cartwheels all the way to the door.

"You look distracted, dear. What's on your mind?" Grandma Gertie asked.

What's on my mind? The fact that the most powerful demon in the world is not only wreaking havoc on mortals but is now targeting angels. The fact that our last mission was pretty much a failure. The fact that my best friend hates me. The fact that I don't know what to do about any of it.

I just shook my head. "Nothing."

Grandma gave me a shrewd look before taking care of the next angel in line. She wrote something on a clipboard then leaned against the counter facing me. "You know, your Grandpa Todd and I got married when I was sixteen and he was twenty-one. Things were different in those days. World War II was happening and we all thought we were gonna die. Better hurry up and get married now, just in case! To think, if you had gotten married when I had, you would have left behind a widow!"

I made a face and shook my head. "Is that supposed to make me feel better?"

"I'm glad I married your grandfather, but the two of us were wrong. We thought we had to hurry because he was the age where he'd have to register for the draft. And then he was drafted. Neither of us believed we'd ever see each other again if, heaven forbid, he died in combat. Who knows what would have happened, but I do know that both of us would have been fine. We would both move on and I'd have found someone new and he would have too. My point is, death can't stop anyone from finding love. That's what your problem is. You've given up on love because you're dead, but you can't do that. You need to find yourself a girl. That will solve your problems."

I loved hearing Grandma Gertie's stories, but I laughed bitterly at her implication.

"What's so funny?"

The fact that girls have brought me nothing but problems. The fact that out of all the girls in the world, the only ones I'm interested in are either still alive or a demon.

But again, I just shrugged and said, "Nothing."

Just then Jake walked in, saw me behind the desk, and walked right back out. I growled and hit the desk with my fist.

"Okay, I think you need to take a break," Grandma said.

I scowled at the ceiling. "I'm fine."

"You are? Is that why you're punching holes into the counter with your pen?"

I looked down, surprised to find a pen in my hand. I'd been clenching it so hard my knuckles were turning white.

"Oh . . . " I dropped the pen and said, "Sorry."

"Honey, your shift is over in ten minutes. I won't tell anyone if you need to leave a little early. Besides, I've been refiling all the reports you've been taking because you're not even paying attention to where you're putting them."

I sighed and looked down. "Sorry, Grandma."

"Do you want to talk about it, honey?"

"No, not really. But I think I'll take you up on your offer and leave early."

Grandma patted my shoulder. "Go clear your head."

Clearing my head was a bit difficult. Jake and I have goofed around all over The Resting Place, so everywhere I went reminded me of him and the fact that he hated me now. Even if it weren't for that, the looks of everyone that passed me made me edgy. I couldn't tell what those looks meant, but I knew it had something to do with the mission.

I wanted to pretend they were all looking at me in awe, amazed at my performance during the last demon hunter mission. In my mind's eye one of them swooned and asked me for my autograph. Then a reporter came up to me and stuck a microphone in my face. "Tell us, how did you keep your composure in the face of the Prince of Darkness? And what do you intend to do about the friend that betrayed you and dumped you like a pile of rocks? Do you think maybe he's just jealous?"

Back in reality, I passed a couple of girls who weren't whispering quietly enough and almost laughed at how far off base I was.

"Hey, is that that one guy?" one of them asked.

"Nah, the demon hunter guy was way cooler. And hotter."

I ground my teeth, so sick of people liking the fake me better than the real me. I closed my eyes, took a deep breath, and continued floating until I got to the bench Jake and I usually sat at. Too bad it was already occupied.

None other than Jake himself was sitting there, slumped over his knees.

I almost asked him if he was all right, but then I remembered we weren't talking. Jake saw me and he looked like he had just gone through the same exact thought process I had.

"What do you want?" we both snapped.

We blinked, startled that we'd said the same exact thing in the same exact way. Then Jake went back to staring at the ground and I disappeared to go anywhere but The Resting Place.

Screw the buddy system.

I ended up in Elena's house. I really wanted to visit Chelsea and the new baby, but I thought Rocco and

Ginger would be the best medicine for my ugly mood. Which was just perfect because when I got there all I could hear was Rocco wailing in a way that made my ears bleed. Exactly what I needed to cheer me up.

Stop being a pouty baby, I told myself. *You're a guardian angel. You're here for them, not for you.*

I took a deep breath and nodded. This was what being an angel was all about.

I entered the bedroom of the dangerous toddler and found Elena trying to wrangle toys out of his hands so he couldn't throw them. His face was red and splotchy with tears streaming down his face. He looked like he was going to explode.

Elena pressed her lips together, trying to keep composure, but I could tell by the way her jaw was set that she was clenching her teeth .

"Rocco, we do not throw things," she said calmly. "If you're upset, use your words."

Rocco just screamed and went boneless, trying to slide through Elena's grasp. It worked. He weaseled away from her and threw a dinosaur across the room. I hadn't realized Ginger was there until I heard her scream as the dinosaur hit her in the arm. Ginger fell hard on her butt and wailed just as loudly as Rocco.

"ENOUGH!" Elena exploded.

She picked up Ginger and turned to Rocco. "You can stay in here until you're ready to apologize!"

Then she slammed the door and took teary-eyed Ginger to the kitchen and set her down on the counter so she could talk to her face-to-face.

"You know your brother doesn't like it when you take his things," Elena told her.

"I thought it would be funny to dress the T-Rex up as a princess!" Ginger cried.

Elena raised her eyebrows. "Maybe it was funny to you, but was it funny to Rocco?"

"He takes my things all the time! Rocco's a poopy face!"

Elena clenched her teeth. Her patience was running very thin. I couldn't blame her. Rocco was currently pounding on his door screaming and Ginger was crying and I don't know how Elena was holding it together.

"You've got this," I told her. *"You're supermom!"*

Elena took a deep breath and said, "Well, I love Rocco."

"I don't! He threw his dinosaur at me!"

Elena shook her head. "He shouldn't have done that. That was not okay and that's why he's in time out until he's ready to apologize and be nice. But you weren't being nice either, were you? You knew that if you took his dinosaurs it would make him mad and you did it anyway."

"I hate Rocco and his stupid dinosaurs!"

Elena blinked and wiped spit from her face. Her face hardened. "You do not talk to your mother that way. You will talk to me in a calm voice, or you're going to your room too."

Ginger screamed so loud I was surprised none of the glasses in the kitchen burst.

Elena swept Ginger off the counter without a word and set her down in her room. "You can come out when you're ready to be nice!"

Once the door was shut, Elena leaned against the wall and took a deep breath, utterly exhausted. I wondered how long this fiasco had been going on before I arrived.

And of course, as soon as Elena got half-a-second to herself, Rocco peeked through his door, then ran into the family room laughing and yelling, "Ha ha! I got out!"

The little butthead.

Elena rushed after him to put him back in his room, but Rocco kept running away and giggling. Ginger peeked out her door to see what was happening and laughed at Elena, blowing raspberries like a little turd.

I spun around and pointed to Ginger's room. *"Ginny, get back in there right now!"*

Ginger blinked. She slowly backed up and shut the door.

All right, I thought with a smug grin. *Looks like Uncle Dave's a boss.*

Meanwhile Elena was still chasing Rocco around the living room, tears of frustration starting to spill over.

"Mommy's a stinky baby!" Rocco sneered. "Ginger's a

stinky baby! Ha ha ha ha! You can't catch me."

Eventually Elena just gave up and went to her room, shutting the door. She leaned against it and slid to the floor.

"I don't know what I'm doing," she said, wiping tears from her eyes.

My heart went out to her. People talk all the time about how hard it is to be a mom, but I feel like no one really gets it until they experience it first hand. Even as I was witnessing this all go down, I knew I could never fully understand what Elena was going through. It's such a double standard too, because while everyone acknowledges that parenthood is hard, they all act like they have these perfect families and everything is all figured out, posting pictures on Instagram of their perfect lives. But you don't see the behind-the-scenes stuff. The mothers crying on the floor because they're doing the best they can, and yet deep down they know that no matter how hard they try they're going to make mistakes.

Not only that, but Elena was doing this all alone. Her husband was out on deployment, which not only took him away from her, but put him in harm's way. She was constantly worried out of her mind about him, that she'd lose another loved one. A few months ago she lost her mother in a freak accident, and years before that her brother fell to his death. It must have felt like everyone around her was dropping like flies. In that moment, I felt stupid for ever complaining about my dumb problems. At least I didn't feel like I was all alone.

I sat down next to Elena. *"Personally, I think Rocco's being a turd."*

She obviously couldn't hear me, so she didn't respond. *"You're doing the best that you can. That's all anyone can ask for."*

"I just wish I didn't have to do this alone," she said, staring down at her hands. Her bottom lip trembled and she sniffed, trying to hold it all together.

Back when I was alive, Elena used to come to me when she cried. She wouldn't go to Mom, because then Mom would cry and Elena would wind up feeling bad for making Mom sad. Dad, ever the optimist, was never so good at empathizing when someone was upset. He didn't realize that sometimes people don't want you to make them happy, they just want to be heard. And Sam was always busy. I'm not saying I'm any better than any of them because I know I'm not, but it did make me feel special that I was Elena's go-to brother when she was upset. Even if some of her problems made me want to roll my eyes, I was the one she trusted enough to cry to.

When I first died, Elena used to talk to me a lot. She obviously didn't think I could hear her, but she still talked to me. She'd yell at me, whine to me, cry to me. But years passed and eventually she stopped talking to me altogether. Which was fine. People find new people to lean on. The problem was, Charlie was the one she leaned on when I left, and now he was gone too.

The only crappy thing about being dead is that nobody really knows you're there. Sometimes they hear your whispers and they listen, but they just think they're listening to their own thoughts. I wished there was some way I could let her know I was here, but that's not how it works. Leave too many "hints" or "clues" and the person freaks out or assumes they're haunted. Plus, there's this big emphasis on having faith in The Resting Place, which is believing without seeing proof. So all I did was sit there while Elena held in all her tears.

"You can cry, Elena. Just because you're a mom doesn't mean you have to be a rock all the time."

And so she did. While Ginger sat in her room feeling guilty, and Rocco ran around the house without a twinge of regret, Elena let out her own little temper tantrum. At first she just cried into her hands. Then she got up and threw a remote control from the TV stand. The batteries spilled out and Elena kicked them under the night stand. Then she plopped onto the bed and fell over, staring at the wall as her tears wet her pillow.

I knew Ginger was in trouble, but I went to her room and knelt in front of her. *"Hey Ginny. I think your mama needs a hug. Can you go give her one for me?"*

She'd been pouting in the corner with her arms folded, but after I spoke to her, her face smoothed out and she looked toward Elena's room.

"That's right. Mama's sad. She's had a hard day and you and Rocco weren't very nice to her. Go give her a hug."

She frowned and blinked thoughtfully. Then she went and peeked her head out the door. Slowly, probably worried she'd get in trouble for leaving time out, she crept to her mom's room. The door slowly creaked open as she peeked her head in.

She nervously crept into the room and stood in front of Elena. "I'm sorry, Mommy. I didn't mean to make you sad."

Elena wordlessly pulled Ginger onto the bed with her and held her close. "I love you, sweet girl. I'm sorry mommy yelled."

My eyes may have gotten a little misty at the sight, but come on. You'd have to be made of stone to not be moved by sweet little Ginny all perceptive and empathetic.

Little baby feet pattered on the tile running up to Elena's room. Rocco pushed the door open and said, "Mommy! Stranger!"

A stranger? Some guardian angel I was! Had someone just broken into their house?

Elena stiffened and shot to her feet. "Where is he?"

"Out there!" Rocco said.

Immediately Elena pulled her kids close and gave them her cell phone. "Hide in the closet. If mommy doesn't come back, call 9-1-1. You remember how to do that, right

Ginny?"

Ginger nodded, wide eyed.

"Go now!" Elena said.

I wasn't sure this was the best plan. She probably should have been hiding in the closet with them, calling 9-1-1 herself.

"Elena, you go hide, I'll check it out!" I told her.

But Elena didn't listen. Once the kids were hidden safely in the closet she reached under her bed and pulled out a small safe. She dialed in a code and pulled out a gun. Then she took a screwdriver hidden behind the TV, stood on a chair and unscrewed an air vent where she'd hidden the bullets. (They were kept separate as extra child safety precautions.) This all took her a matter of seconds and then her gun was locked and loaded. It was pretty impressive. Charlie hadn't left his wife unable to defend herself.

I apparated into the kitchen to get an idea of who we were dealing with. When I saw the man I gasped. *"Elena, no!"*

Of course she didn't listen. She was in mama bear mode. She crept into the kitchen, gun out in front of her like she really knew how to use it. Then she saw him and her eyes widened. She screamed. Then she switched on the safety, tossed her gun in the sink, and tackled the man. Her arms wrapped around his neck and her legs wrapped around his waist and then the two of them were full-on making out on the counter.

Charlie was home.

I wanted to tell the kids that it was all right and that they didn't have to hide anymore, but I didn't want to contradict their mom's orders. It would set a bad precedent, especially if one day it really was a burglar or murderer. I did feel bad though because they were both silently crying, hugging each other, having no idea that the scary man in the house was actually their dad. Rocco probably would have recognized him if he hadn't run away, but he wasn't used to men just walking through the front door.

Eventually I went back to the kitchen and said, *"Um, guys, your kids are scared to death hiding in a closet."*

Elena pulled away sharply and I will forever be scarred by the disgusting suction-like sound from Elena disengaging her mouth from Charlie's face. No brother should ever be subjected to that.

"The kids!" she said, dropping to the ground and sprinting down the hallway.

I waited in the kitchen with Charlie while Elena went to go calm down her children and update them on the situation.

I smiled, delighted to see the guy. *"Nice to see you, man."*

Charlie grinned and leaned back on the counter. I've always liked Charlie. I know, I know, every big brother is supposed to be convinced that no one is good enough for their sister. But Charlie's great. I like him because even though he's this tough soldier dude, he's a huge nerd. He and I had always gotten along. We used to share books with each other and geek out over every new Marvel movie that came out. We were both pretty bummed when I died because we were just starting to get close.

Eventually Elena came back into the kitchen with her kids in both arms, each of them looking shy and curious.

"You know, this seems like a kind of personal family moment. I think I'm gonna step out," I said to no one in particular.

chapter 34
SHEILA HAS SECRETS

When I got back to The Resting Place, I was glad I'd picked Elena to visit that day. Not just because I got to be there when Charlie came home. It was seeing Ginger and Rocco fighting over stupid crap that made me realize just how dumb Jake and I had been. While I still needed a little time to cool down about the things we'd said, I didn't want to be fighting anymore.

I kept trying to track him down so I could apologize and get it over with, but every time I found him, he'd disappear without a word. Clearly he wasn't ready to talk about it yet. I tried not to be upset by that, but it was really hard not to. What had I even done to him?

By then Hermes had put the entire Resting Place on the buddy system. No one was to leave without a partner until we better understood how Malum was going to target angels. We had no idea what kinds of traps he had in store. Unfortunately, my buddy was being a butthead, and my pride prevented me from telling anyone I didn't have a partner. According to Jake, I didn't need a partner because I'd resisted Malum "just fine." Except, I hadn't. No matter how long I resisted him, he got me in the end. But I guess that didn't matter to Jake.

It did cause an awkward situation when Raj sent me on a mission to check up on Sheila. He told me to take Jake with me and I told him that I would.

That was the only time I'd ever lied to Raj.

Sheila wasn't where I'd left her. I expected to find her at her usual stool at the dingy bar, staring off into the middle distance. At first I was worried, but then I reminded myself that just because this was a popular haunt of hers it didn't mean she never left.

It's pretty easy for angels to track each other. The more familiar you are with someone's spirit the easier it is to track them down. All you have to do is think about them and you'll end up wherever they are. The more you've done it, the more precise you get with the location. I wasn't sure how well that worked with demons. I'd never actually tried to track down a specific demon. Well, I guess that was kind of my job as a demon hunter, but Malum was a special case. He didn't follow the rules. If it was that easy to track him down, the demon hunters wouldn't even exist.

Closing my eyes, I thought of Sheila and willed myself

to show up where she was. I was surprised to find myself in a random suburban neighborhood. The streets were lined with different variations of the same house and yard. It was dark out, but based on the lights on in people's windows it wasn't quite bedtime yet. One lady was rolling out her trash can, and down the street a truck pulled into its garage. It took me about five minutes of floating around until I spotted Sheila. She was glaring hungrily through a window of the house on the corner with the ancient Chevy pickup truck that was probably as old as my father. I crept up behind her to see what she was staring at. Two teenage girls, twins by the look of it, were sitting at a table texting, oblivious to anything but their phones. The table was covered in a lacy tablecloth and set with plates and cups with delicate floral designs along the edges. An elderly woman came in with a cookie sheet of rolls and a tub of butter, while an old man used a scooper to fill the glasses with ice from a bowl. Their grandparents, I assumed. I couldn't hear what they were saying, but it didn't look like the girls were listening.

I wondered what Sheila was going to do. Start an argument between the teens and their grandparents? Convince one of them to sneak out the back door and run off with her boyfriend? There were endless possibilities. It was weird thinking of Sheila in that way. Sometimes I forgot she was a demon. If I was on guardian angel duty and I saw some random demon being a creeper outside someone's house, I'd have blasted them away. But would I be able to do that to Sheila? The fact that I wasn't sure was concerning. She was a demon and therefore she did demon things. She hurt people. And yet . . . I wasn't sure I'd be able to hurt her.

"What are you doing?"

Sheila jumped and slapped me on the arm. "You scared me to death."

I raised an eyebrow. "It's a little late for that."

She glared at me. "You know what I mean."

"Speaking of . . . *Have* you ever died? I'm not sure if you told me if you were a monster or a native. Not that it matters, I'm just curious."

(Quick reminder: monsters are people that died and became demons, natives have been demons since the world began.)

She pursed her lips, tilted her head, and folded her arms. "I don't see how that's any of your business."

Sheesh, when would this girl stop being so secretive and defensive? It was almost like she had reason not to trust me. I mean, I was tricking her and lying to her, but she didn't know that. Did she?

"Sorry." She put her arms around my neck and floated a few inches higher to kiss me, the spirit version of going up on her tip-toes. She did a good job at distracting me, but I did notice that she didn't answer my question.

"Let's take a walk," I said, lacing my fingers through

hers.

We took a stroll around the neighborhood, and it was actually quite peaceful under the stars and street lights. You could hear traffic out on the main roads, but it was just the occasional car or two. The only other sounds were the crickets, the wind, and our own tumbling thoughts. We didn't talk for a while, but it was a comfortable silence.

"So," I said, eventually. "What have you been up to?"

"Nothing terribly interesting," she said. "You?"

"Well, I met my dad," I said.

She smiled. "I know. I was there."

I looked at her sharply. "You were?"

"I was part of the demon army he summoned to deal with those angels."

"Oh . . . " I gulped. If she was there, she might have caught a glimpse of my real self. She still liked me though, so she must not have made the connection.

Sheila looked at me curiously. "How did you do it?"

"Do what?"

"Capture that angel."

I looked at her, searching her eyes for the motivation behind her question. Did she suspect what I was? Was she jealous of what I'd done? Did she want to try it too? Was I being paranoid?

"How did you get on Malum's good side?" I countered.

Sheila pursed her lips and we engaged in a staring contest.

She won. I looked away first.

And then I got clobbered in the face by a ball of Light.

"Hey!" Sheila shouted.

I looked around, confused, and saw a couple of angels floating above us. One of them looked scared, and the other one patted the younger one's shoulder. "Don't worry, I've got this." Then she threw another ball of Light, hitting me in the chest. It didn't hurt, but it was annoying in an infuriating way, like a huge mosquito bite or the sound of a broken fire alarm that won't shut up. I always thought demons scattered because we hurt them, but I was starting to wonder if they left because we annoyed the crap out of them. Either that or this angel just wasn't very powerful.

"What's your problem?" Sheila yelled. "We're not hurting anyone, we're just walking."

The angel threw a ball of Light at Sheila with such force, it threw Sheila back a few yards. This made me angry.

"Screw off!" I yelled, giving them the finger.

I gasped and covered my mouth, because I hadn't actually said "screw off" and I'd never said anything like that before. Neither was flipping the bird in character either. I was deeper into my fake identity than I thought.

Sheila took my hand and swore at them in Spanish.

I blinked and looked over at Sheila. She spoke Spanish? I found this revelation strangely attractive.

"Come on, let's go somewhere else," she hissed. Then she apparated us to a park a few blocks down. We sat on the swings, our hands still entwined as we let the wind blow us back and forth. I tried to get a handle over my anger at those angels. We hadn't even been doing anything. They literally blasted us away for just being there. If this was Sheila's typical experience with angels, I didn't blame her for hating us. I couldn't help but think about how I'd probably done that before. Maybe I was just as pious and self-righteous as she claimed all angels to be.

"Hey, are you for sure joining the Angel Hunters?" she asked.

Angel hunters? Was that what Malum called his followers? Yikes, they really were after us.

"Wasn't that the whole point of all this?" I asked. "I want to follow in his footsteps."

"Why though? Your dad's a creep. No one likes him."

"Then why does he have so many followers?"

Sheila looked away uncomfortably.

"Sheila?" I prompted.

She took a breath. "It's just, once you become one of his followers, you can't really leave. I just wanted to make sure you'd thought this through."

"What do you mean you can't leave?"

Sheila didn't answer.

I got off my swing and stood in front of her. "Sheila?

Has he hurt you?"

Sheila sighed and rolled her eyes. "It's not a big deal."

"If it's not a big deal, why does it sound like you're trying to warn me about something?"

She threw her hands up. "He's a demon, David. The best there is. You expect him to reward us with warm hugs and cookies? He's a tyrant. Is it so surprising he'd be a little harsh to his followers? Look, I'm a big girl, I can take it. I chose this and I'm not exaggerating when I say I'm his most loyal supporter. So don't you act like I'm some poor girl who needs saving. I was just making sure this was what you wanted. Because once you join him there isn't any going back."

"What do you mean?" My heart pounded in my chest. If I joined him as Evil David, would I be stuck as a demon forever? And what did he do to his followers to control them? Was he able to do to demons what he'd done to me? Did he paralyze them with fear until they submitted?

"I'm done talking about this," Sheila said. She got off her swing. "Let's go do something."

I wanted to know more, but I could tell she wasn't going to open up again. She'd turtled up and she wasn't coming back out of her shell until I gave her some space.

"Yeah, okay."

I wasn't feeling very creative, so I just took us back to our beach. Neither of us was in the mood to talk, so we just sat holding hands, watching the moon reflect on the ocean. It would have been peaceful if it weren't the uneasy prickling feeling that something terrible was about to happen.

chapter 35

COVER BLOWN

I sat between Ted and Frederick during our next demon hunter meeting because Jake and I still weren't talking. This confused everybody. As did Jake's behavior being all moody and quiet, just sitting there with his arms crossed like a pouty little kid. I looked down, realized I was sitting the exact same way, and leaned forward on my thighs instead.

"All right," Ying Yue said, with her usual clipboard and pencil. "Down the line, everyone share any new information you've learned. Let's start with Ted and Daisy. How did your last mission go?"

"I blew my cover," Daisy admitted, looking down.

Ying Yue did not succeed in hiding her look of disappointment. "What happened?"

"It wasn't really her fault," Ted said.

Daisy elbowed his arm. "Shut up, Ted. Yeah, it was. My assigned Demon scared me by popping up behind me. So I spun around and punched him with a ball of Light."

If Jake and I were still friends, we would have looked at each other, checking to see if the other one was laughing, because it was a little funny. I'd have loved to see Daisy Light punch someone in the face.

"It was instinctual," Ted said. "She was startled."

"Huh." Raj nodded his head and pursed his lips. Was it possible he was also trying not to laugh?

"That's unfortunate," Ying Yue said, "For now you will simply keep working on Ted's demon, since we are only doing partner missions now anyway." She made a note on her clipboard and looked up at me and Jake. "Do you two have anything new to report?"

Jake and I looked at each other, then awkwardly away. Was he going to out me for not including him even though he was the one who said I didn't need a buddy?

Apparently not. He didn't say a single thing, which kind of ticked me off.

"Yeah," I said. "I learned from my assigned demon—"

"Girlfriend," Jake coughed.

I rolled my eyes and ignored him. "I learned from Sheila that the organization of Malum's followers calls themselves the Angel Hunters. Also, apparently once you join Malum, he has some level of control over you, though I'm not quite sure exactly how. Sheila actually seemed kind of scared of him."

"That's not surprising," Frederick said. "We learned very early on that most demons are frightened of Malum.

This was why they were reluctant to speak of him."

"So why follow him?" Daisy asked. "What does Malum have to offer them that The Evil One doesn't?"

"Maybe they like the idea of capturing and using angels," Jake said. "The Evil One just hates us, but Malum wants to use us."

"They may not all want to follow him either," I said. "He could be threatening and blackmailing demons until they do what he says."

"So, what does all of this mean for us?" Ted asked quietly. He looked weirdly distraught about something but plowed on as though trying to cover it up. "The ambush didn't work. What do we do now?"

"Demon hunters are an intelligence force first and foremost," Raj said. "We'll continue to gather information that will bring us closer to capturing Malum."

Raj dismissed us, and this time, I didn't even try to confront Jake.

I went to visit Sandra instead. I told myself I wanted to check on her and her wanderers, but if I'm being honest, I just needed a friend. Oddly enough, Sandra and I had grown closer since I'd died than we ever had when I was alive.

I caught her at a good time, because she was having lunch and there weren't any students in her class. She had her slip-on Vans propped up on her desk and was leaning back in her rolling chair eating chips.

She waved a chip at me. "If it isn't Garcia. David Garcia."

"Ha ha. Solid spy joke. Really creative." I sat on the edge of her desk. "So, what's up?"

"Nothing much," she said, taking her feet off her desk. "Just eating some lunch. Want some?" She held her bag of potato chips out to me with an innocent smile on her face.

"Rude," I said. "Let's all make fun of the dead guy because he can't eat."

"Honestly, you aren't missing much," she said, rolling up the bag. "These are super stale. I left them open in my car."

"You have a car? I thought that was a dumpster."

Sandra pursed her lips, trying not to laugh. "Shut up."

"Great comeback," I grinned. "You're on a roll today."

"You know what, Garcia?"

I smiled at her waiting for her to tell me what, but she'd run out of comebacks again, so I just laughed at her.

She rolled her eyes. "Whatever."

"That's a lot of papers," I said, gesturing toward the mountains of essays she was grading, all marked up with green pen.

She sighed. "I know. And most of them suck. I asked for three pages. Three of my students decided to go way above and beyond and write ten pages. Then I have papers like this."

She spun around a crumpled piece of *SpongeBob* stationary, and I leaned in to read it, trying to squint around some kind of food stain.

> *During the American Revolution there was this dope dude named Hamilton. He had a frenemy named Aaron Burr (sir). Hammy and Washington were tight! Jefferson thought that was annoying, so he was like, "Let's tell erybody 'bout how he's been hoin' around." Hammy's wife was all, "You skank!" and they split. Then his kid got shot. Then Hammy didn't vote for Aaron Burr (sir), and Burr threw a little baby fit and was all, "What the hell, man! I thought you were my frenemy! Eat my bullet!" And Hamilton died.*
>
> *The end.*

I looked back up at Sandra with a raised eyebrow. "Did this kid just use a Broadway musical to write a paper about the American Revolution?"

Sandra groaned and rubbed her forehead. "Don't even get me started on this kid. Seriously, yesterday—"

We were interrupted by an angel popping into existence in the middle of Sandra's desk. A tall, muscular defender angel that used to be my friend. He took hold of my shoulder in a firm grip and said, "You need to get outta here, mate!"

I knocked his hand off my shoulder. "Oh, so now I'm your *mate*?"

"Aw, are you guys fighting?" Sandra frowned. "I thought you were besties."

Jake ignored her and sighed. "Look, I'm sorry for being an idiot, but now's not the time to talk about it!"

"What are you talking about?"

"I've been following you all arvo, 'cause the buddy system, and when I was out in the hallway just now I thought I saw your demon girlfriend wandering around looking for you."

Sandra raised her eyebrows. "Demon girlfriend?"

"Wait a minute," I said. "You followed me?"

For a second I was kind of touched. As annoyed as he was with me, Jake was still watching my back. I certainly hadn't followed him on his visits.

Jake shook my shoulders. "Are you listening to me? Sheila's in the hallway and if you don't get out of here before she finds you it's gonna blow your cover!"

"Too late."

The three of us turned around slowly.

Sheila floated in front of the door swathed in Darkness so thick it clouded up her eyes, turning them from hazel to smoky black. It was the first time she really looked like a demon to me and I was caught between being frightened by her, being annoyed with her, and thinking back to that line I'd used when I'd called her "beautiful in a terrible way."

"You're an angel," she whispered, deadly calm. "You played me. Used me."

The four of us just stood there in the most painful silence I'd ever experienced. If I was mortal, sweat would be oozing from my forehead and temples and dripping down the sides of my face.

Jake leaned in and whispered. "Just say the word, mate, and I'll blast her. Or I'll get on my bike. Your call."

I patted the air, trying to signal for him to shut up. I gulped and stepped forward. "Sheila, I was going to tell you, but I didn't want to hurt—"

Sheila exploded. Darkness burst out of her in all directions and she started shrieking, acting like all those mindless demons I deal with on a daily basis that I usually just blast away with a ball of Light. But this shrieking devil had a name and feelings, and I couldn't find it in me to hurt her.

Jake stepped in front of me and Sandra, covering the three of us with a force field of Light.

Sheila continued shrieking, and then started knocking things off counters and messing around with electricity. The lights flickered, the pencil sharpener buzzed, the microwave flashed and beeped.

"Sheila!" I shouted, stepping out from Jake's shield. "Calm down! Let me explain."

"EXPLAIN?" She floated up to my face and said,

"Explain what? Why you led me on and lied to me? Do you stupid angels hate us that much? You got sick of blasting us with Light for no good reason and had to come up with more creative ways to torment us?"

"No," I said, grimacing down at my feet. "It was for my task force. I was supposed to get information out of you. But I swear, Sheila, I never meant to hurt you."

She threw her head back and laughed. "Really? And what did you expect to happen? Did you think I would never find out? Or maybe you just assumed that because I'm a demon I don't have feelings."

To be honest, it was the latter. At least at first. But I knew better now.

I took a hesitant step closer to her. "Look, this doesn't have to change anything. I like you Sheila. I like you a lot! I may even like you enough to keep dating you even though I'm an angel and you're a demon."

"Oh, is that right?" Sheila asked with eyes bulging from her head. She floated over to Sandra. "Then who's this chick?"

Sandra looked like she'd just taken a sip of Sprite, expecting it to be water. "This chick happens to be his friend, thank-you-very-much."

Sheila got up in her face. "And yet you're living. Shall we change that condition so you can join your two-timing boyfriend?" She began circling Sandra like a vulture with a calculating look in her eyes, trying to determine the best way to hurt me by hurting her.

What was I supposed to do? I knew my job was to protect Sandra, but I didn't want to hurt Sheila either. I felt like I was being torn apart by these two girls I never intended to fall for. I wasn't sure what my relationship even was with either of them, and yet I cared about them both in different ways. With Sandra, it was comfortable and right. She made me smile and laugh and I loved being in her company. She made my burdens feel lighter. But Sheila was like a roller coaster, with twists and turns. An exciting, dangerous ride that made me feel alive. This forbidden thing with mysterious depth, and a surprisingly kind heart. I knew she'd tried to warn and protect me in the past, which meant she cared for me too. But this was not that Sheila. This Sheila was a demon intent on hurting someone very dear to me.

Sandra, for her part, did not look afraid. She stood her ground, her hands clenched at her sides and said, "He's not my boyfriend. And don't you dare touch me."

Sheila grinned slowly, and I don't know how I knew it, but I saw her intention in her eyes. I froze, wide-eyed, appalled she'd even dare.

"Sheila, get away from her!"

Sheila added a wink to her grin, then disappeared. A second later, Sandra gasped and went rigid as Darkness burst from her, surrounding her with a glowing black aura. Her eyes widened and turned glassy. She slowly, awkwardly, like a girl wearing heels for the first time, stumbled toward me and reached out to me. "David . . ." she purred in a gravelly voice. "You wouldn't hurt me, would you?"

It was so disgusting I wanted to throw up. Possession is the grossest of sins. It is the ultimate violation, taking someone's will away from them. I did not believe Sheila was capable of that. In that moment, I lost all respect I had for her, but the part that hurt the most was that even with her possessing Sandra, I still cared about her. And that made it hurt that much worse, which made me hate her more.

"Get out of her!" I yelled, my face contorted in fury and hurt.

"Or what?" Sandra said in a voice that wasn't hers. A smile crept over her face, disturbing below her glassy, widened eyes. "You'll cast me out like any other demon?"

I clutched my hair and groaned. "Don't do this to me, Sheila! I don't want to hurt either of you, but I will if I have to!"

Sheila held my gaze through Sandra's eyes, and I knew I'd better move fast before she did anything to make Sandra hurt herself. Since learning how to make demon killer bullets, I started keeping a gun on me at all times. I pulled my gun out and pointed it at her.

I gulped, hating what I was doing, then pulled the trigger.

Sheila shot backwards out from Sandra's body and Sandra collapsed to the floor.

Sheila clutched her chest where the bullet had hit her. She looked at me, stunned.

"Sheila . . ." I wanted to say something, but I couldn't bring myself to say I was sorry. What she'd done was unforgivable.

It was too late, anyway. She disappeared before I could say another word.

I groaned and covered my face with my hands. Guilt consumed me. And confusion. What had I done? Was there any way I could have avoided this? Raj and Ying Yue told me to date her! Sheila was going to get hurt no matter what. The difference was, in the beginning I didn't care. She was just some creepy little devil I was trying to interrogate. Now she was a person. It was enough to almost change my perspective on demons in general. But whether or not there were other demons out there like Sheila—who could laugh at dumb jokes and enjoy the beauty of the ocean and stared off into the distance contemplating life—it didn't change the fact that it was Sheila who'd gotten hurt. And I was the bad guy. It was like I was *her* demon.

Cursing myself, I knelt down next to Sandra who'd just groaned and sat up, massaging her temples. "Your girlfriend is a piece of work," she said, her throat scratchy.

I was so relieved to see her okay that I laughed. "Yeah,

she's not exactly my girlfriend. That's why she was mad. I am so sorry that happened to you, Sandra. This was all my fault. Are you okay?"

She nodded, grimaced, and stood.

Jake came up next to me. "Hermes is calling me back to The Resting Place for a defender meeting, but do you need me, mate? Because I can—"

"It's fine. Go to your defender meeting. I'm fine."

Jake looked nervously between me and Sandra and mouthed, "Sorry!" before disappearing.

I locked eyes with Sandra, having no idea what to say.

Before Sandra or I could say a word, a voice came over the intercom. "*The date is January 10th and we are in a full lockdown. I repeat, this is a full lockdown. Immediately implement lockdown safety procedures.*"

chapter 36

BIG MISTAKE

Our eyes flicked from the intercom back to each other.

Sandra immediately stuck her head out in the hallway to check for students, then locked her door and turned off the light. She hustled across the room to lock the other door that adjoined another classroom. Then she went and sat in the corner of the room that was hidden from the window, hugging her arms.

"It's probably just a drill," Sandra whispered.

I nodded. "Yeah, probably."

We sat in awkward silence until I got up the courage to say, "Look, about Sheila—"

"You don't have to explain anything to me, David. I get it. It was for the job. It's not like you actually like her."

I bit my lip and nodded, looking around.

Sandra gasped. "Oh my gosh, you do like her!"

"I don't know!" I said. "Kinda. Maybe. When she's not acting like a psycho. I feel awful about the whole thing, and I don't know what to do about anything. Am I bad for liking a demon? Because the last I checked, angels were all for being nice to people and loving one another."

Sandra gave me a smile that I did not at all appreciate. Remember that smile Jake gave me when I said I wanted to join the demon hunters? The one I said you'd give a kid who just flushed his toy soldier down the toilet? Well he must have taught it to Sandra, because that's how she was looking at me now.

"Oh, David!" she said, smiling and shaking her head. "You *would* be the guy whose worst mistake was falling in love with a demon."

I rolled my eyes. "Ugh. I am not in *love* with her. I did not say love. And don't talk to me like I'm a baby. I'm a big boy!"

We looked at each other, both pressing our lips together, trying not to laugh. Then I snorted just as she squeaked, and we cracked up together, giggling like fools.

There was a sound like a gunshot and the two of us flinched. Sandra's eyes widened and she held her hands to her heart.

"You want me to go check it out and see what's going on?" I asked.

She nodded.

I floated through the door into the now creepily empty hallway. It's weird the things you notice when the halls aren't swarmed with the cacophony of loud laughter and cat calls and kids making out in inconvenient places. The water fountain hummed and dripped. A fly buzzed around a fluorescent light. The air vent coughed as the air conditioning kicked in. I floated around the deserted hallways looking for the source of that noise that I hoped was not a gunshot. I didn't get far before I ran into an angel I'd never met before. She was just standing there, waiting for something.

"Hey," I said, "Do you know what's going on? It's just a drill, right?"

She shook her head solemnly. "There's a shooter. He's in the building. There's a demon possessing him."

My eyebrows rose and pinched together. "Crap. Have we called the defenders? Can't they help subdue the situation?"

"They've already done what they can," she said.

"So what are you doing just standing out here?"

"Not everyone's going to make it. There will be casualties," she said quietly. "I'm here to usher my niece to The Resting Place when it's time."

Guardian angels don't know when mortals are going to die any more than mortals do. But we do get a few minutes warning if a family member is about to croak so we can be there to usher them to the other side. My heart sank as I took in her slightly familiar features. I forced myself to ask the question I dreaded the answer to. "Who's your niece?"

"Sandra Johnson."

"What's going on out there?" Sandra asked when I floated

back through the wall. "What's wrong?"

DAVID, SHE MUSTN'T KNOW, Hermes said in my mind. *WE NEVER TELL MORTALS WHEN THEY'RE GOING TO DIE.*

"Nothing's wrong," I lied.

She scowled at me. "I don't believe you. Tell me what's happening."

I sighed heavily, telling her what little I could. "It's not a drill. There's a shooter somewhere in the building."

She gasped and covered her mouth, looking at me with shining, terrified eyes.

"There's a bunch of angels out there," I said, trying to comfort her. "It's going to be okay."

"If it's so okay, why won't you look at me?"

I didn't answer.

"David Garcia, don't you dare hold back what you know. This is a life or death situation."

CAREFUL, DAVID . . .

"Answer me," Sandra demanded.

"Not everyone's gonna make it," I admitted, grimacing at the floor.

She was quiet for a minute. Then she whispered, "I'm gonna die, aren't I?"

I swore. How did she make that connection so fast? I shouldn't have said anything about anyone dying. I hoped Hermes wouldn't be too mad at me. I mean, she sort of found out on her own.

"Am I right?" she demanded. "Am I going to die?"

I should have lied. I should have found some way to cover it all up. But she was so scared and so trusting. How could I lie to her?

I forced myself to look at her and nodded.

I'd like to say something before I share the next part. Some of you might be tempted to judge Sandra for how she reacted to this news. Call her a coward or a baby, but I defy anyone who claims they'd react any differently. When you're mortal, your overarching instinct is survival. Death is that giant monster everyone must face someday, and no matter what you believe about an afterlife, no one truly knows what's waiting for them. Nor do they look forward to the pain of dying. Anyone would react as she did, and some much worse. Because besides those few that wish to take their own lives, no one wants to die. Knowing you're going to die is terrifying, and even more soul-sucking the longer you live with it.

Sandra's eyes filled with tears and she started hyperventilating, her hands to her head. "No. Not yet. I don't want to die!"

"I know," I said. I wished I could hug her. "No one wants to die. But I promise it will be okay—"

"Shut up!" she hissed. "Don't you dare tell me it's going to be 'okay' after just telling me I'm gonna die!" She sobbed quietly and rocked back and forth, hugging herself. "I'm not ready. What about my students? What about my wanderers? What about my mom? I haven't seen her in months and she has no one else! I can't just leave her alone!"

"You won't be leaving her alone. You'll still be with her all the time."

Her hands clenched into fists, and she slid off the counter to her feet. "Shut up!"

"Shh," I said nervously. "There's a lockdown going on."

"What does it matter if I'm going to die anyway?"

"You're not the only person here," I said calmly and slowly. "I know you're upset, but please keep it down."

She looked at me like she'd strangle me if she could, then she just fell into a chair and sobbed into her hands.

"I'm not ready," she whispered into her hands. She was crying so much, tears were dripping down her elbows onto the floor forming a little puddle. I cursed myself for telling her the truth. What was I thinking?

I knelt down next to her. "I'm sorry. You're right, this sucks. But as much as you hate me for saying this, I promise it *is* better on the other side."

She looked up at me with red, puffy eyes and very wet cheeks, her expression utterly heartbreaking. "I just wish I had more time. I never did all that I wanted to do." She sniffed as tears dripped down her chin. "I was hoping to *do* something with my life."

Oh, why did she have to say that? Why did she have to punch me right in the gut? In my mind I saw myself shouting the exact same thing to Raj. I knew this feeling, and I wouldn't wish it on anyone. Wondering what you would have become had you lived longer. Mourning the family you would never have. It was all amplified when Malum got into my head, but even before that. . . those feelings had to have come from somewhere, deep down. The "what ifs" were maddening.

"Maybe . . ." I started.

"What?" she asked, desperate hope shining in her eyes.

"Maybe we can prevent it from happening."

Sandra tried to grasp my shirt. "Is that possible? I mean, you're an angel. You have powers."

I grimaced again, feeling guilty for the false hope I was feeding her. "Yeah, you're right. I might be able to protect you. But the thing is, if the Big Man says it's time for you to go, there's nothing I can do about it."

"But you'll try?" she pleaded.

I sighed and nodded. "I'll see what I can do."

A voice came over the intercom. "*Teachers and staff. The lockdown is now over. You may continue on with your regularly scheduled activities.*"

Sandra and I looked at each other.

"That's not real," she said automatically. "Protocol is the principal or custodian or a police officer personally unlocks your door to tell you it's over. They remind us over and over at every safety meeting."

"Why not just announce it?" I asked.

"Because somebody could be on the intercom under duress. It's how a shooter can get people to unlock their doors and get complacent again. But once the door is locked, you're not supposed to unlock it for anything—not even a student pounding on the door—until authorized personnel unlocks it and tells you it's safe."

"So the shooter's still out there," I said.

She nodded, her face crumpling again as she remembered what that meant for her.

Next door we heard sounds of students sighing, laughing, and talking loudly the way one does after something crazy happens. They believed the fake announcement. They thought it was all over. Sandra swore and ran to the connecting door to the other classroom. She unlocked her side but couldn't open it because it was still locked on the other side. She pounded on the door until the other teacher opened it. Which was good, because Sandra needed to talk to her, but also bad because based on what Sandra just said, this lady was not following protocol.

"Whoa," she said, taking in Sandra's devastated face. "Sandra, it's okay, it was just a drill. It's over now."

"No, it's not!" Sandra said. "You're not supposed to dismiss students until Principal Newman comes by and says it's safe."

It was too late though. Students were already streaming through the door to their next class, laughing and talking loudly like all was well with the world.

"Dammit!" Sandra shouted. She shoved past the other teacher and sprinted out into the hallway. "Get back in the classroom!" she whisper-yelled after the students. "The lockdown isn't over."

A few teens looked at her nervously, but most ignored her, continuing on their merry way.

Sandra swore. "Let's split up," she told me. "I'll gather those I can and you do your angel Jiminy Cricket thing-y to convince them to come back."

"My angel Jiminy Cricket thing-y?" I knew how dire the circumstances were, but my mouth twitched, wanting to laugh.

She smiled briefly. "You know what I mean." Then she dashed off down the hallway.

"Wait!"

I gaped after her, taken aback by her courage. She was putting those students' lives ahead of her own. She knew what was waiting for her, yet knowing others' lives were on the line, she rushed out to meet it.

I obeyed her final wishes, convincing the teens that ran off to go back to the classroom.

"Listen to your teacher," I said to them. *"It's not safe out here. Don't you notice nobody else is in the hallways?"*

"Guys . . ." A girl said, looking around. "Maybe we should go back."

Most of them hurried back once they noticed all the

other classrooms were still locked.

Another group of teens pounded down the hallway and ran back to class, with Sandra picking up the rear. She had just saved all their lives, and I couldn't have been prouder.

We met up at the door and smiled at each other. Then the door closed with us still on the outside.

Sandra swore. She pounded on the door, but no one would open for her. The other teacher, realizing her giant mistake, was now following protocol. The door does not open once closed. No matter what.

Sandra ran to her own classroom and jiggled the handle, but it was still locked. She frantically fumbled with her lanyard, trying to find the right key, when we heard a sound that froze us in our tracks.

A gun being cocked.

We both turned slowly to face what would be Sandra's certain death. A shaking teen stood there, pointing his gun at us and my eyes widened. Not because of the gun, but because of who was with him. Darkness smoked from every open surface in his face. His ears, his nose, his mouth, his eyes. This boy was possessed, and not by just anyone. I'd become familiar with those dark, fathomless eyes.

Hermes, send the defenders and demon hunters! It's Malum. He's here!

Despair filled my heart. What was I supposed to do? I had learned how to resist Malum's fear-inducing paralysis, but Sandra hadn't and this poor possessed kid hadn't. Even Sandra's aunt froze, staring wide-eyed at the Darkness dripping from this kid's eyes, ears, and mouth, and pooling at his feet. I could feel their fear seeping into me. The walls of faith inside me threatened to crumble.

A small light caught my attention. Sandra's aunt was glowing brighter, preparing to take Sandra away.

Sandra stared at me with terrified, pleading eyes. Then she faced the shooter, and closed her eyes.

I knew I couldn't touch her, but I reached out to hold Sandra's hand, not wanting her to feel alone in her last moments. I gasped and froze as the strangest thing happened. When my hand went through hers, I felt all *her* fears. They filled me up and paralyzed me in place. In that moment, I was not David, I was Sandra, and I was trapped in bitter memories and nagging fears.

My father slammed the door behind him, leaving my mother crying in an inconsolable heap. I tried to help Mom, to even get her to look at me, but she wouldn't move. That night I cooked us dinner, burning myself on the stove that was too tall for me, and continued to cook for us until I was old enough to go to college. Mom cried for a week when I told her I was leaving. I've never gotten over her look of betrayal. I turned down the chance to go to my dream college in order to stay close to Mom, because I couldn't bear for her to feel like I'd leave her like Dad. When I finally did leave, she wouldn't speak to me for months.

I was a child again and a stranger was in the house. An old man. He wouldn't say anything or even look at me. He just stood there, and Mom wouldn't believe me. A little boy showed up in my bedroom as I tried to sleep, crying and moaning so loud I never got rest. The next morning my dead aunt told me I was seeing dead people. They found me wherever I went. Summer camp, school, the basement. Always dead-eyed and mindless, but insistent at the same time, like a baby crying because he doesn't know what's wrong.

Boyfriends came and went, but I never met a single one I trusted enough with my secret. It didn't matter that their dead grandparents, cousins, or siblings followed us to dinner. I couldn't trust them. The only man in my life had left, and they would leave too if I told them the truth. So I left them. Each and every man who showed me interest . . . I sabotaged our chances by breaking up before I could fall in love.

I saw myself growing old alone, never leaving my apartment, never accomplishing anything special. I grew to hate my students, and resented their ungrateful attitudes. I lashed out one day at a girl who'd sassed me and ended up sued and fired. I was nothing but a lonely old woman that used to be a teacher. I was an embarrassment. I was nothing. I'd never done anything right.

The visions turned darker . . . The gun pointed at me discharged and I fell to the floor, bleeding in agony for hours before anyone found me. Mom cried hysterically as I died in her arms, pleading with me not to leave her like Dad. I left her anyway and became another soulless wanderer, haunting poor little girls who didn't know they were seeing ghosts. I became an empty nothing, wishing for death, but knowing it had already come. Death wasn't my release, it was my prison. I was nothing but a ghost, tortured and silent, left to wander the earth alone.

S*NAP OUT OF IT, D*AVID. Hermes said in my mind. T*HESE AREN'T YOUR FEARS. NOW STEP AWAY SO SANDRA'S AUNT CAN TAKE HER.*

I blinked and jerked away from Sandra, my eyes shining. And all I could think was, *I can't let that happen. She deserves better.*

D*AVID, DO NOT INTERFERE. IT IS HER TIME.*

Pre-demon-hunter-David would have waited patiently and excitedly back at The Resting Place until Sandra's guardian angel pulled her through the door. I'd have been thrilled to show her my world, and ecstatic that she could now be a part of it.

But all I could think about was Sandra. This courageous woman who was scared out of her mind, and still ran down the hallway during a real lockdown to save her students. Sandra, who would soon know how I felt when I realized that I'd never done anything with my life and would never get the chance again.

I tried to create Light, but nothing would come. I didn't even feel the pain of trying to force it out. It was like trying to switch the light on when the bulb was out. There was simply nothing left.

Had my priorities been in order, I would have been

freaking out about this. Either I had bad intentions, I was no longer worthy, or I was afraid. Perhaps a combination of all three. If I was in the right mind, I'd be concerned that I'd be kicked out of the demon hunters now. It was in the contract that if we lost the ability to create Light, they'd take us off the task force.

But all I could think about was Sandra and how I'd promised to try to save her.

DAVID, THIS IS YOUR LAST WARNING. DO NOT INTERFERE WITH HER DEATH!

But then the kid pulled the trigger and the rest unfolded in slow motion.

I jumped in front of Sandra just as the bullet went hurtling toward her.

I'm not sure what I expected to happen—it's not like I could stop the bullet—but to my astonishment, it worked. Kind of.

The bullet did not hit her. It hit me.

chapter 37
OUCHIE

Twin screams split the air. One of them Sandra's, and one of them mine.

I dropped to my knees and looked down to see blood soaking my shirt. I couldn't even comprehend what that meant. I didn't have blood. I was dead. And yet, a spirit couldn't possibly feel this level of physical pain. A small part of my brain noted that I was wearing the same clothes I died in. What did this mean?

The kid who'd been possessed collapsed and the gun clattered to the floor.

"What the hell!" Sandra screamed. "How? *How?* You're already dead!"

I couldn't answer. I was too busy writhing in agony. I'd been shot. How was this possible? Honestly, I didn't really care about the answer, all I could think about was how much I wanted it to end. And it had to end. The way I felt, I was pretty sure I was going to die. This would kill me.

Kill me? I'm already dead!

I could barely see Sandra as she knelt before me, terrified out of her wits.

"David, what's going on?" she asked, panic making her voice shrill.

"I don't know!" I said through clenched teeth. Then a moan escaped involuntarily. "It hurts so bad!"

I knew part of it was the fact that I'd been an angel for so long, and pain was unfamiliar to me. At least physical pain. After over ten years—almost eleven now—of painless afterlife, a papercut would have made me cry. But this was no papercut.

"I'm gonna go get help!" Sandra said. She took the boy's gun, hiding it in her jacket and ran through the halls, calling for help.

"Don't go," I whimpered as she sprinted off down the hallway.

A presence surrounded me, and although my eyes were squeezed shut in pain, I knew it was Malum. The presence closed in on me, basking in my pain and fear and I had no defense against it. "Delicious," it purred as tendrils of Darkness caressed my face and body like little beetles scuttling. I wished I was strong enough to flick them away.

"Just leave Sandra alone," I pleaded through gritted teeth.

"The girl?" Malum said. His Darkness expanded, blocking out the fluorescent lights. I heard him walking circles around me on what sounded like hooves. "I was never here for the girl. Did you really think I didn't know who you were, front desk boy? Did you really think you'd fooled me with a leather jacket and a little Darkness?"

I gasped and the pain sharpened. "You knew?"

"Of course I knew. But when you resisted me that day of the pathetic ambush, I decided I didn't want to destroy you. I wanted to use you. You'd make a valuable demon, David Garcia. Join me."

My head was reeling, but I was in too much agony to give much attention to what was happening.

"Demon hunters . . . are on their way," I forced out with a groan. It was a bluff, obviously, but I prayed he'd believe it and leave me alone. I couldn't stand this anymore.

A toothy grin shone through the Darkness with fangs like a beast. "You'll join me. The frightened teacher isn't your only weakness."

Then he was gone.

I lay there for what felt like eternity as this indescribable pain seared through my body in waves. I couldn't remember what had happened or why I was here. I couldn't even remember who I was. All I knew was my pain.

Then something changed. I'd been curled up on my side, every muscle tensed and screaming, clinging to life with all I had. My body didn't relax, necessarily, but I felt it giving up, numbing. My head dropped and I closed my eyes waiting for death to come again.

Please, I prayed. *Please end it now.*

But no one answered. I was alone.

I heard a gasp and forced my eyes open. It was Sheila of all people. Of course it was Sheila . . . I felt like such a fool. She was in on the plan! She'd been playing me just like I'd been playing her. She stood above my head, her expression hard and unreadable. "Well, are you ready?"

"Sheila, no," I pleaded. "I won't go with you. I can't."

"You don't really have a choice," she said harshly. "No one else is coming for you. You messed up and the angels don't want you anymore." She said it with such bitterness I was sure she hated me more than anyone or anything else in the world.

"How long have you known?" I asked, trying with all I had to concentrate. I'm not sure why this was so important to me. I guess I just realized that her interest in me was probably all a lie, which shouldn't have bothered me, especially since I'd been lying to her the whole time too.

She knelt down to better yell in my face. "I didn't find out until I caught you with that stupid teacher."

I didn't say anything, because now I felt even more guilty. She'd actually believed my lies. She hadn't known this was all part of Malum's plan until now.

"Sheila," I moaned, feeling my body numbing, shutting

down, "don't take me."

"Why not? They obviously don't want you up there anymore!" She jumped to her feet, pacing in anger. Her anger was confusing. I expected her to hate me, but I didn't expect the hurt and fear in her eyes. She hated The Resting Place and everything it stood for. She despised angels. And yet, it almost felt like she was against my fall from grace. Like she was personally offended that they wouldn't want me. Why should she care?

I prayed and pleaded for an angel to take me back home, but no one came. Not Mom, not Nana, not Grandma. Why wouldn't anyone come? Where was the mercy? What ever happened to second chances?

I'm sorry! I shouted in my head. *I messed up!*

But there was no forgiveness. I was slipping away, and the only usher here wanted nothing more than to drag me down to hell. There had to be an alternative.

"Sheila, save me . . . " I pleaded weakly, feeling my consciousness slipping.

"Save you?" Sheila looked as though I'd just slapped her. "I'm a demon, David. I don't save. I destroy."

"Please. I can't go there. I won't."

She knelt next to me and leaned in. "I can't help you," she whispered, looking around. "These are my orders. He'll destroy me if I disobey." There were tears in her eyes. Were those tears for me or for her? I was so confused, and yet, the pain was too much to let me analyze it. All I knew was that if I died, I'd either become a wanderer or a demon—so I had to stay alive. The alternatives were unbearable to think about.

"Please, Sheila," I whispered. "I don't care that you're a demon, I know there's good in you."

"What do you expect me to do!" she demanded. "You're dying."

"Heal me . . . " I breathed.

I didn't know how far Sheila's powers extended, but I'd heard stories of people doing dark magic with the appearance of miracles. Usually demons were behind it. Could Sheila use Darkness to save me?

Sheila looked at me with anger and pity and confusion. Then she spat, "I hate you David Garcia. I hate you almost as much as I hate *him*!"

I had no idea who this *him* was, but I was in no position to ask.

She held her hands over me and let her dark powers work within me. Slowly and painfully, my chest spit out the bullet, which clattered to the floor. I felt my body stitching back together and the pain numbed. By the time I was fully healed and conscious, Sheila was gone. I was left alone in a puddle of my own blood, and yet completely healed. When I checked my chest, there wasn't even a scar.

chapter 38

ALL MY FRIENDS ARE DEAD

I tried to get up, but there were several factors that made this really difficult. I had no idea how this had happened, but this was definitely a mortal body. For the first time since I'd died, I felt the pull of gravity, pinning me down and not letting go. Second, I'd just been shot. Sure my wound was gone, but that didn't mean my body was fully healed. Third, I kept slipping on all the blood, making me gag until I finally puked.

"Sheila!" I called, once I'd wiped my mouth. I waited, but there was no answer. I hoped she was okay . . . She'd not only just saved my life, but my very soul. I still struggled to believe she cared about me enough to do that. I shuddered trying to imagine how Malum would punish her. I prayed she'd be all right.

When I finally staggered to my feet, I leaned against the wall and squinted down the hallway. It was so blurry I could barely see a thing. This more than anything convinced me I was mortal—I'd always had terrible eyesight.

I wandered through the hallways on unsteady feet, not knowing where to go or what to do. I tried to transport myself back to The Resting Place, but I couldn't do it. I tried to float away, but nothing happened. Everything had been snatched away from me with no explanation.

"Hey!" I shouted. "What's going on! Please, someone tell me what I'm supposed to do!"

A light appeared in an empty classroom and I followed it. Hermes was there looking down at his folded arms.

"Hermes!" A bubble of light and comfort filled my chest. Hermes would fix this. Hermes would know what to do. "What's happening? Why do I feel like I'm mortal again?"

"Because you broke your contract and are not fit to dwell in The Resting Place."

"I . . . I lost my spot?"

I staggered and fell against the wall.

"Yes. You interfered with the plan, and you disobeyed orders. As you are, you are not worthy of The Resting Place."

His words pierced my heart like a dagger to the chest.

"But it was a trap!" I said. "He planned this all along!"

"A trap that you *chose* to fall for," he said. "You received several warnings, and you ignored them all."

"So . . . I can never come back home?" I whispered, unable to comprehend the words.

Hermes responded much gentler than he had before. "This is a unique case and you've put us in a difficult position. Despite your intentions, there must be consequences to your actions."

My head fell into my hands and I sank to the ground, filled with the despair of a fallen angel.

"But . . ." Hermes continued, "You will still serve as a guardian angel. And the demon hunters still want you on their team."

I lifted my head. "What?"

"Your consequence is not being stripped of your duties. The consequence is that you may no longer benefit from the power that comes with being an angel. You must do your duty now in a mortal body. If you succeed, you may be welcomed back again."

He began to fade, but I jumped to my feet. "Wait! So I'm alive again? What am I supposed to do? Where do I go? My whole family thinks I'm dead! I don't have any money or a place to stay. And what if I die before I've proven myself worthy to come back? And how am I supposed to help them without my powers?"

Hermes reached to put a hand on my shoulder, then realized that he couldn't anymore. "I cannot tell you all the answers. I'm sorry, David. Truly, I am. But you must keep the faith. There is a reason for everything. Don't give up." He started to fade and said, "If it's any consolation, you'll be sorely missed in The Resting Place. This decision has already made many angels very angry. Goodbye. And remember: you're not alone."

"Wait!" I called as I recalled Sheila's angry, terrified, and conflicted face. "What about Sheila? She saved me! Malum is going to punish her! Can we help her?"

Hermes continued to fade, but before he vanished completely, I saw his face darken. I couldn't tell if it was anger or sorrow in his voice as he said, "I am not permitted to say anything on the affairs of demons. It's not in my jurisdiction. I'm sorry."

His body faded away before his voice, which continued to echo in my mind.

Police officers rushed down hallways with EMT's and wounded teens and teachers in gurneys. Meanwhile I sat and stared at the floor. I felt like no one had ever fallen as low as I had. I'd doomed Sheila and I was cast out of heaven. How could I ever make it back?

Before anyone could strap me to a gurney, I left. I didn't know where I was going or where I was supposed to go. I didn't really know how to get anywhere from the school. As an angel, I normally just popped into existence wherever I wanted to be, so I didn't exactly have to pay attention to directions. I walked and walked and walked until I slumped onto a bus stop bench. I was cold and tired and hungry. And I kind of had to pee, which was confusing since I hadn't drunk anything in ten years.

I had this feeling that I should turn back. Find Sandra.

Ask for her help. But I was too ashamed about what had happened to me. I hadn't been dead very long compared to others, but I'd never heard of this happening to any angel before in history. I was the screw up. I didn't deserve The Resting Place.

That feeling that I should go back persisted, until I had to acknowledge the fact that it was probably an angel whisper and I should probably listen. I wondered who it was and wished they'd go away so they wouldn't have to see me like this.

"Whoever's there, please go away," I said dejectedly.

The feeling persisted. They were probably shouting in my ear at this point. I sighed and did as they said, taking that long, lonely walk back to the school.

I sat in Sandra's rocking chair with a blanket around my shoulders and a bowl of soup in my lap. I hadn't touched it yet. It smelled amazing and my stomach growled, but I didn't want to eat it. Eating it would make this final and real, and a part of me wanted to stay in denial for a few more minutes. My bloodstained shirt had been thrown out due to the giant hole in it, so I was wearing some of Sandra's flowery pajamas she'd inherited from her mother, who was about my size. So at least I had some dignity left.

I stared at the TV without really seeing anything— partially because I was zoned out, partially because my mortal eyes sucked. The channels flipped around all by themselves. It freaked me out when Sandra first brought me to her apartment. How chairs would scrape across the floor and lights turned on and off and channels would change on their own. Then I remembered that her apartment was super haunted. Haunted with wanderers I'd once helped train. Now they were just creepy ghosts that made me want to hide under a blanket.

Sandra was talking with someone in the kitchen in hushed tones. I didn't have to hear what she was saying to know she was talking about me and how I was a giant failure. I still had no idea what I was supposed to do, and I couldn't help but doubt that I'd ever figure it out.

"Hey, David," Sandra said hesitantly. I jumped about a foot in the air when she touched my shoulder. My soup flew off my lap and splattered all over the carpet. My actual heart pumped loudly in my chest, which was also quite disturbing.

I got up and walked around, trying to take deep breaths.

Sandra held her hands up cautiously the way one does approaching a startled animal. "Sorry, shouldn't have touched you. I know that freaks you out."

"It's fine," I said, my hand to my heart. "Sorry I ruined your carpet."

"I'll clean it up." She sighed and said, "Look, the reason I came in here is you have a visitor."

I looked around nervously, partially because my old mortal instincts kept telling me to be afraid of ghosts, and partially because I didn't want anyone to see me this way. I plopped down on the couch and hunched my shoulders. "Tell them I'm not up for visitors."

"He can hear you, you know," Sandra said. I hated that she was more in touch with angels than I was.

"Whoever you are," I said, not looking up. "I don't want to talk about it."

"Don't be rude," Sandra whispered, glancing to her left.

I started to protest that I wasn't being rude, but then I realized she wasn't talking to me.

"What are they saying?" I asked, curiosity getting the better of me.

Sandra glared to her left, then admitted, "He just said, 'Nice Pj's, mate.'"

I sighed and almost smiled. "Shut up, Jake."

Sandra rolled her eyes. "And now he's doing a weird dance in front of you and laughing because you can't see him."

I couldn't bring myself to laugh. "Why are you here, man?"

Sandra sat next to me and began translating directly. She even did the accent, which was a nice touch. "I came to see how the most famous demon hunter in history is doing."

"Don't do that, man," I said, shaking my head. "I know I'm a screw up."

"You're not a screw up, drama queen. You're a hero. You saved this chick's life."

"This chick's name is Sandra," I told him.

Sandra nodded sardonically at something Jake said and pantomimed shaking his hand. "Nice to meet you too."

"I guess things are back to normal now, huh?" I said.

She returned to translating. "How's this normal, ya fruit loop? You can't even see me and we've got a mortal medium translating my every word."

"It's normal because you're the strong one again, and I'm the one who hates himself."

It was quiet for a minute, and I figured Jake just didn't know what to say.

"Well, I don't hate you," he said eventually. "I reckon you're my favorite bloke in the world. And I'm sorry I ever made you feel otherwise."

"'Otherwise' has three syllables," I said, my voice breaking.

I couldn't help it, the waterworks just poured out. It started with a lip quiver that led to a sob on Sandra's shoulder. Because I'd just realized that the best friend I'd ever had was dead.

Sandra was really sweet and let me cry on her for a while. It was kind of silly. I should have been happy to be alive. I wasn't even this upset when I'd died. But I couldn't stop thinking about how the people I'd grown closest to over the past eleven years were dead and I wasn't. I didn't know how long it would be until I'd see them again. Jake, Raj, Ying Yue, Nana Maria, Grandma Gertie, even Mom. I'd have to live without them for who knew how long.

Once I stopped crying enough to take a breath and unstick my wet cheek from Sandra's t-shirt sleeve, she said, "She'll be right, mate. I promise."

I jumped. "Jake's still here?"

"Yeah," Sandra admitted. "He's been here the whole time."

I scrubbed the tears and snot from my face. "Not cool, man. I didn't want to cry in front of you."

Sandra smiled a little bit. "If it makes you feel better, Jake is trying to pretend he wasn't crying too." She paused, listening to him, then told him, "You don't need to get defensive. I'm not judging your little bromance."

"What's he saying now?" I asked.

"He says you both need a distraction and wants to challenge you to a kindness race."

I shook my head. "It's not the same. You're an angel. You have an unfair advantage."

"No, you have an unfair advantage," Sandra translated. "The people you help can see and hear you."

"Touché . . . "

Jake had a fair point. As powerful as angels are, there's only so much that they can do. At the end of the day, no one really knows what we've done for them. It's a secret service that asks for no reward. But mortals get to be seen serving. I wasn't interested in the credit, but it sure makes a person feel good when they *know* someone is helping them. There's power in being able to tell someone you care about them. To show them you love them.

No matter what, I was still a guardian angel. I was tempted to feel unworthy of that title, but I pushed that feeling away. Yes, I'd made a mistake, but I wasn't giving up. Some believe that the Big Man has a very specific plan for each of us, and if we stray off his path, we're lost until we find our way back to where we started. But I don't think it's like that. We can't go backwards. We can't change the past. I think God is like Google Maps. If you take a wrong turn, he'll reroute you. You may end up taking the long way around with some potholes and a little off-roading in a car that's only two-wheel drive. You may even have to wait on the side of a road for a good Samaritan to pull over and give you a jump. But the Big Man will lead you back to him one way or another. You've just gotta trust him.

Trust or not, I had a long road ahead of me. I was terrified and depressed and ashamed. But I couldn't give up. And the only way to go was forward.

So I wiped my face, forced a smile, and said, "All right, Jake. You're on."

Acknowledgements

No book is ever made by just one person. If it was, it would suck. So, I would like to give a huge thank you to all the people who have helped me make this book not suck. (Hopefully.)

First, thank you to my fabulous editor, and former coworker, Linda Martell. You are an amazing, intelligent woman who has helped make this book readable. Next, I'd like to thank my amazing friend, Lyndsey Hayes. You are a wonderful writer, and your tough but ridiculously helpful critiques have made me a better writer. Another person who has shared incredible insight is my friend Jared Chapman. I am grateful for your honest opinions, suggestions, and listening ear. As always, thank you to my best friend, Rebecca Stowell, who has always supported me in all I do. You are the queen of honest, yet tactful, feedback. Huge thank you to my fabulous proofreader, Ian Schiefelbein for your incredible support!

Like our dear protagonist, my family is everything to me. It would take too long for me to name all your names and all the ways you've helped, supported, and loved me. Just know that I love you, and this story would literally not exist without you. Making David's family so similar to ours was my way of celebrating who we are. This book is my love letter to you.

About the Author

Kendra Pettit Photography

Anni Sezate is an elementary school teacher from Gilbert, Arizona, and every year she reads her first novel, *Aurella the Witch,* to her students. Though she received her education degree from Arizona State University, she spent a semester living out her acting dreams as a musical theater major. Anni spends most of her time reading, drawing, singing way too loudly to Broadway soundtracks, and Muay Thai kickboxing at the gym. Anni is a proud daughter, sister, aunt, and Ravenclaw.

Keep in touch!

AnniSezate.com
IG: @Anni_Sezate

www.ingramcontent.com/pod-product-compliance
Lightning Source LLC
Chambersburg PA
CBHW021206310726
48971CB00006B/1474